WEIRD TALES FROM THE ISLAND CITY

MATT WINGETT

Life Is Amazing

2023

A Life Is Amazing Paperback

Weird Tales from the Island City
First published 2023 by Life Is Amazing
ISBN: 978-1-913001-06-3
First Edition

WELCOME!

You probably don't know my work, so I should tell you that although I have been writing for years, doing occasional tv, stage writing, advertising copy and stories, in the last decade or so my home town of Portsmouth has become a matter of increasing obsession for me.

One thing I do in many of my books is celebrate the great literature that has come from Portsmouth. Arthur Conan Doyle created Sherlock Holmes here, Charles Dickens was born here, Rudyard Kipling grew up here, while H G Wells, Nevil Shute, Olivia Manning, James Clavell and Neil Gaiman (among many others) are also connected to the city.

Frankly, in the context of these literary luminaries and outright geniuses it feels a bit rich to mention me, but – *yes!* – I too have produced stories, including a novel and various other fiction writings, adding my own small contribution to the city's literary output.

In these pages are several versions of Portsmouth, the old city that stands (mostly) on Portsea Island just north of the Isle of Wight and south of the Hampshire South Downs.

Some stories, such as *The Tourist* and *The Boiler Pool* started their long journey to publication in other settings, but only when I rewrote them in a Portsmouth context did they finally feel convincing. I guess the old maxim *write what you know* is true at least in part. My feel for the place brings my writing to life – I hope!

(This is also true of my novel, *The Snow Witch*, a dark, gritty tale of magical realism set on Portsmouth's icebound streets in an increasingly rare harsh winter.)

Other stories such as *The Night Watchers* and *Old Harry* started as performance pieces on Hallowe'en events in the city.

Some are admittedly silly. *The Case of the Serbian Dwarf Poisoner* and *The Mysterious Case of the Moustachioed Man* tip a nod to Arthur Conan Doyle's life-changing sojourn in the city.

For those looking for a longer read, *Turn The Tides Gently* and *The Song of Miss Tolstoy* are novellas, while *Freda* and *Old Harry* first appeared in printed form in the anthology *Portsmouth Fairy Tales for Grown-Ups*, but never in my collected stories, and similarly *The Night Watchers* and *The Case of the Serbian Dwarf Poisoner* first appeared in *Day of the Dead*.

You'll find that the moods change, but, be they flat-out classic horror, magical realism, comedy, or fable, it's Pompey that ties them together.

I hope you like them. If you do, please look out for my other books. I hope, too that if you're not from Pompey, maybe they'll make you curious about visiting some day.

If you do, look me up. Perhaps I'll take you on a tour.

Anyway, that's it for now. Thanks for your interest!

Matt Wingett
Southsea, 2023

Contents

THE TOURIST

The moment he disembarked the St Malo schooner, *Hylas*, onto the Camber Docks that bright June morning in 1824, Charles de Tilby sought an opportunity to free himself from the life-dulling grip of his pious guardian, Bartholomew Woolman. Picking their ways between the clapboard boat stores, tumbledown workshops, grubby drink dens and groaning whorehouses of Spice Island, his attention constantly shifted from the bearded old Quaker's back as he walked ahead, to routes of departure.

His chance came after they penetrated Portsmouth's defensive walls at the King James Gate and passed the Market Hall in the middle of the High Street in search of lodgings. Further along the arcing line of the road stood more genteel establishments suited to a gentleman of his rank. Thus, while Bartholomew engaged a suite of rooms and ordered a mutton dinner at the Fountain Hotel, Charles slipped down to the stables, took the bridle of a fine-looking, freshly-saddled chestnut stallion and walked him out onto the bustling thoroughfare. After a spring into the saddle and a tap from the crop, he galloped away, scattering ladies on shopping outings, street urchins begging food scraps, shop-boys carrying brown paper parcels and startled bluejackets who shouted blood-curdling oaths after him.

He exploded from the town through the Landport Gate amid shouts from the guards, clattered past the artisan quarters squeezed along the London Road and finally thundered out on to the wide fields of Stamshaw. *What sport!* he thought to himself as he brought the panting horse to a trot, and after loosening his cravat and unbuttoning his fashionable green frock coat took stock of his surroundings.

What sport, indeed! By now, Bartholomew is probably pulling his white beard out – the old fool!

A smile of self-congratulation spread across his twenty-year-old face.

Either that, or he's searching for me in Portsmouth's back alleys... as if I'd tarry in that stinking cesspit for one second longer than ill-fortune should demand!

It was then, as he inhaled a deep lungful of sea air that he looked across the blue calm water to the west, his heart soaring at the sight of the old castle so imposingly situated on the harbour's far side.

It's large, it's grand and it's edifying to the senses – yes – he reasoned – that will suit me very well!

He leant forward to push his sleek chestnut mount to a canter.

In the next two hours of steady riding, he headed through the fortifications known as the Hilsea Lines, crossed Portsbridge on to the mainland and turned west at Cosham village. From here, he passed by the pretty manor of Wimmering and followed the scrappy shoreline past the tiny scatter of dwellings called Paulsgrove. He skirted the north harbour for a while, before heading south through a tidy village that stretched along a single lane by the water – a mix of fine Georgian buildings and smaller, more humble thatched cottages at which Charles sniffed in a superior sort of way.

A little way beyond the last house in the village, the castle overlooked the harbour, rearing up behind a tidal moat on a promontory. He took a good, long look at the edifice, crossed the bridge and made a circuit of its ancient walls. They delineated a great square. Inside a massive mediaeval keep towered moodily. The castle had been abandoned, but only recently, judging by the discarded barrels stacked by the wall and the overgrown ruts where carriages had once rattled in through the gatehouse.

Nearby, a shepherd sat under a tree, who, to Charles's impolite questioning, told him the place had recently housed "Froggies from them Wars with Old Boney". The man was patiently forthcoming in offering a potted history of the Castle, telling Charles what an Antiquary had once told him: "Bits of it is a few 'undred years old – but see them walls? They was builded by them Romans what they say yon fellow Shakespeare done wrote on."

*

In the presence of that old castle, Charles de Tilby idled much of the afternoon away, looking out with dreamy eye over the sun-sparkling water, the wind lifting the heavy yellowed heads of coarse reeds at the water's edge.

He thought of Bartholomew. What an old dullard he was when it came to any question of fun. *He will be at his wit's end, at this very moment!* he thought, and chuckled again.

Charles took the moment to make plans. He decided to leave it a few weeks before he surfaced again. London's card dens and cockpits awaited his largesse, and the young bucks he knew would be glad of his hellraising. In fact, judging from the weight of the bag of sovereigns he had appropriated from Bartholomew's luggage, he might string things out for months.

You know, this really is a coup! Sharp-eyed Bartholemew may have "saved" me from cardsharps in Vienna and dragged me from the fleshpots of Venice – but he lost sight of me here, on home turf in dear old Albion! It is truly comical!

Of course, the old Quaker would have to report to his father, Sir Augustus de Tilby, his son's unaccountable disappearance.

Oh, to be a fly on the wall when that conversation takes place!

He nearly burst out laughing at Bartholomew's discomfiture.

Less comical of course would be Old Man de Tilby's devastation at his son's waywardness. Thus, Charles planned to send him a communication by mail coach in a few weeks' time, informing him he was hale and hearty. It would come as a relief to him, and thus make his father more eager to pay off the debts he would surely incur before he finally trudged his leaden-footed way back to the *paterfamilias* and his damp old mansion in the north of England.

A new part of the plan seized his imagination.

But why stop there? I might send another letter, in six months or so, saying I am kidnapped by notorious felons holding me against my will in a location unknown – and that another prompt financial consideration will surely act to secure my release..!

His heart swelled with excitement.

Of course, these *little deceits* would come to light in the fullness of time, but, he reasoned, he was a young man with a young man's spirit. He was eminently worthy of a father's forgiveness. Besides, he had one major weapon against dear old Papa. The widower Sir Augustus doted on his sole heir, even if the lad was undoubtedly (as the old man had been heard to remark) "well supplied with high spirits – perhaps even to a surfeit. I believe he thinks he is a Radical, but he is rather a symptom of a noble lineage unwilling to compromise."

Bartholomew's opinion differed, however. "Sir, the devil is in the boy and drives him to unending mischief."

Charles smirked. *My old father hoped the Grand Tour would instil the moral effects of beauty in me.* He kicked a stone into the water. *Quite the contrary. It has put lead in my pencil.*

His eighteen-month journey through France, Switzerland, Italy and the Austrian Empire had at first seen him wandering at a loss among Frenchies and their daubs in the Louvre Palace, unimpressed by the barren Matterhorn, yawning at the boring Forum and gazing uncomprehendingly at Old Masters in Florence. But all that had changed when he reached Venice. Or, more accurately, when he finally started to spend some time with its cosmopolitan gentlemen and ladies.

What gentlemen they were! he thought, remembering their knowledgeable ways and their silks and fine clothes, with their stories of fights and duels, and secret trysts contrived with young ladies during masked balls. *And what ladies!* They had cavorted and gambled and debauched with Lord Byron himself, they told him, though there were so many of them it seemed unlikely they could all be speaking truth.

Under their influence (though he didn't really like poetry), he had finally come to a decision that it was good to *seem* to like it. This could be effected by declaring that Classical ruins were *sublime* – a word he had taken to using whenever he could because it revealed his heightened taste, and thus helped him fit in.

Now, surveying the naval hulks on Rotten Row in Portsmouth Harbour and the picturesque toing and froing of sails, he was seized by a whim. As a gesture to his Venetian friends he decided this would make a most apposite place to bathe.

I will do so this very night, by moonlight, he decided, *for full sublimeness.*

Charles thus found lodgings at the Woolpack Inn, an ageing thatched eminence in the village with tumbledown stables at the rear. He was amused to see the young ostler's look of surprise at the quality of the mount he brought in. The boy was clearly about to comment to that effect when Charles shot him an imperious look, causing the lad to bite his lip.

And rightly so! thought Charles. His firm rule was to disillusion the lower classes at the first opportunity that any familiarity between unequal ranks would be countenanced.

Such a rule, however, did not apply to the sweet little maiden of 15 or so who brought him his plate of roast beef that evening. She was pretty enough for purpose, he decided, and he would find a way to get access to her in the next few days. He would show her the ways of Venice, he decided, "its moist canals and back alleys" as one of those Venetian ladies had quipped.

But first, after dinner, he would return to the glory of that romantic Castle, as he had promised himself. When he later wrote his memoirs (as important gentlemen were wont to do) this sort of colour would add greatly to his originality. It was exactly the impetuous behaviour his Venetian friends would admire a fellow for.

The ostler doubled as a general hand about the Inn, and Charles informed him he intended to go back to the Castle with the equipment needed to overnight. He demanded some blankets, a fresh linen shirt and a towel. It was his will, he announced, that he would enjoy a moonlight swim beneath the flint walls of the castle, and sleep there, this fine summer night – "allowing the sublime prospect of this splendid scene to act upon my soul," he added airily.

To his annoyance, the ostler was forthcoming with an opinion that such a course of action might not be the wisest a man could follow.

"Not wise? Not wise?!" Charles exploded. "And who are *you* to advise *me!* I am a gentleman so far above your rank – how could you possibly know what is *wise* for me, and what is not?" Fire burned in his eyes.

The boy shrugged and said nothing, though he appeared to be in some form of internal debate. Finally, a look came over his face that implied he knew something Charles did not, and replied: "Beg pardon, Sir. All I be saying, Sir, with due respect, is the current be strong. The sea all drains out through the 'arbour mouth down in Portsmouth town, and that water be a might treacherous. That's all I means by it, Sir."

Charles grew red with rage: "I ask you again, who are you to criticise my decisions? "

"No-one, Sir. No-one at all," came the reply.

"Exactly. Then, No-one, you'll be no doubt impressed to know you have today met the best swimmer in this whole benighted county! I swam with Byron in the Bosphorus, doncha know?"

This information puzzled the ostler. It was clear to Charles the lie was wasted.

"Ignoramus! Fetch me those blankets and towels, and a means to light a fire!" he shouted and turned on his heel.

But as he turned, he again caught in the boy's expression some sort of superior knowledge – a look which so incensed Charles, that without a second's thought, he turned back and struck him across his coarse, brutish face. Charles's father might think his son considered himself "a Radical" for the company he kept, but Charles would be blasted to hell if such rebellion be allowed to cascade down to the lower classes. In these primitive vessels, high sentiments become ugly indeed, as the revolution in France had shown the world only a few decades before!

He stared the boy in the face with hard, bullying eyes.

"If you imagine I'm going to drown, I assure you, I can swim like a porpoise," he said coldly, before he left.

This might have been a mistake, he reflected as he swaggered out, because the boy's face broke into a broad, mocking grin as soon as the words left his mouth, and after he had departed, he was sure he could hear the impertinent lad's sniggers pursue him through the evening air.

When blankets, towel and shirt duly arrived, Charles ordered that someone carry them to the sea. But by then the inn was thronging with farmhands fresh in from the fields, and when a bearded fiddler struck up a lively tune and the bar erupted into raucous song, service became impossible.

He called to the boy, no reply was forthcoming. A brief search revealed the ostler had slipped away from the Inn, while the serving girl had gone home to her mother's cottage. With no-one available, Charles disgustedly realised he would actually have to carry the blankets himself! Duly, he picked up his burden with one hand, while hefting a lantern the landlord supplied in the other.

No wonder the Romans called the Britons barbarians, he fumed as he stomped down the street to the vastness of the castle.

Soon, under its flint walls, near the ancient seagate, he sat contemplating the harbour. A few lights flamed in distant Portsmouth, while the dark shapes of prison hulks interposed in the half-distance.

There, under the castle's flint walls, he reached into himself and felt for the elevation of the spirit he had read about – the sublime feeling of *terror and magnificence* about which, as far he understood it, the Romantic poets wrote, and which his Venetian friends spoke of incessantly - leaving him feel quite left out.

It's all very pretty, he thought quite blandly, briefly aware of his lack of ability when it came to encapsulating a scene with grandiloquence.

Nevertheless, the night was there to be enjoyed. The sun was an hour and a half below the horizon, and the sky was spread with diamonds. Charles admired the effect with pleasure, and thought about what an interesting figure he must strike in this half-lit world, *if only someone were watching,* he thought, with a pang, before shrugging off the idea and its accompanying sense of foreboding.

How utterly sublime it all is! – he told himself, turning his thoughts to his nocturnal swim. *But first, a fire.*

He arranged his blankets into a comfortable bed and quickly gathered dried wood from the trees and hedges on the shoreline. Then he pushed open the door of the castle's gatehouse and to his delight found inside a pile of tinder used by the shepherds on cold days to muster a little warmth. He took it thoughtlessly, returned to the shore and with the lantern's flame brought a blazing campfire to life. He piled it with two larger logs, sending sparks and flames spiralling upwards, little fleeting suns in the starlight.

Satisfied, he unbuttoned his tailed, high-collared frock coat, undid his cravat and pulled his linen shirt over his head. Then he dragged off his knee-high boots, moleskin breeches and cotton undergarments and stood there, thrilled with the joy of his own nakedness.

Thinking back over the events and people of the day, he resolved that though he would warm himself by the fire tonight, tomorrow night he would warm himself against the hot body of that pretty little maid in The Woolpack. *I'll win her affections,* he announced to himself. *Or I'll get her submission at least,* he added as an afterthought.

With this not entirely amorous consideration, Charles took three steps and dived into the dark watery world before him, noting, as he jumped, the pair of cold eyes formed by the full moon and her silent twin on the breathing waters below.

The mirror surface shattered at his body's impact with a shock of cold. He tasted the salt tang in his mouth and felt the sea's cool embrace.

He looked around as ever-widening arcs of ethereal light scattered across the lapping surface towards the dark silent trees on the adjacent shore of Horsea Island. A dazzling display dappled the uprights of a derelict pier jutting into this part of the bay, lapping around them with soft movements. As he moved through the cool water, the submarine moon fractured into a hundred silver coins. *Sunken treasure,* he thought, and was very pleased with himself. *That's one for the memoirs, you genius!*

It was most ethereal and he told himself he felt a magical joy at what he was seeing and feeling. Churning the water, he watched mesmeric water-moonbeams play about him. Soothing. Calming. And it was strange, because as that water and that sublime scene worked upon him, he began to experience some of the moral effect his old tutor, Bartholomew had tried so hard over the preceding two years to instil in him. The benign effect of Nature, which, as Mr Wordsworth put it:

"...Fostered alike, by beauty and by fear..."

And with that sudden realisation, he began to sink into a kind of timeless daydream...

Floating away. Drifting on the tide...

It was a fantastical moment, which felt, he realised, like an awakening. An awakening that he had not experienced in all that time he had been on tour. He drifted a little more... and then a little more. It was curious, and addictive, and the more he felt of this strange and alien calm, the more he wanted to know of it. *Nature.* It was Nature as he had never experienced Her.

But he had also never experienced this strange oppressiveness in the air and water. He felt an unexpected sensation of lethargy drop through his body.

"What is that feeling?"

His toes brushed the silt.

Time to get out, his foot sank a little deeper into the bay's soft sediment. *Strike for shore.*

But his leg was held fast. Immediately: the bitter shock of salt water poured into his open mouth and nostrils, while the grip crept inexplicably up his leg.

!!Lost co-ordination!! His head went under a second time, and still his leg would not come free. *Panic.* A graceful arc of milky water was illumined by the moonlight as he spat brine and spluttered to the surface.

Calm, he thought. A vision of his body slowly swallowed by silt. *You're a good swimmer – the best at Eton. Take a deep breath and pull, man, pull.*

His gasp echoed from the shadowed walls: "Now!"

A final convulsive effort. The leg rose, weighted by a heavy mass of clinging mud. Dark sediment diffused across the bay, clouding the watery moon.

Twin realisations struck him: *Excellently done – but I'm far from safe yet.* The whole harbour's floor was deep with silt. In swimming back to his entry point, the ebbing tide would deliver him once more into the mud's smothering embrace, while the place where he trod water now would also drain soon. Adrenalin started to flow and he cursed himself for letting this unforeseen complication remind him – *I am mortal!*

As this final thought sent a cold shock through his mind, something stirred in the water nearby. A chill voice bubbled through the dark-stained water: "Swim for the pier, boy."

"Who the devil –?"

A head bobbed in the water at his side. Fleetingly: the impression that no torso was attached. This dispelled by a peculiarly shaped fish jumping briefly from the water: *An arm.*

The man spoke again –

"This has happened to me before, young man. There is a deeper channel which the tide has scooped around the pier. And there is a little set of wooden steps. Swim along to it, then climb up. You'll see, my lad."

Charles stared in mute surprise, his eyes goggling in the moonlight.

The other said: "Come, now," and started a slow crawl towards the rotting woodwork. After a few seconds of wordless confusion, Charles followed.

The mystery bather climbed the pier's slippery uprights with a deliberateness suggesting many long years of unhealthy under-employment that clearly showed he was unused to strenuous activity.

He must be deranged – swimming in this trap!

When he accepted the man's hand to climb up, Charles was surprised at its cold, leathery feel.

"Thank you," he said, wiping his palm of the thick silt deposited there.

They walked in concentrated silence along the slippery pier and around the bay to where his fire still flamed a living challenge to the lunar light. Charles wiped himself down and sat on a blanket, dragging others around his naked body, shivering with shock. Cross-legged, he shook out the water from his hair before the fire and squinted at his saviour.

Disconcerting. Even startling.

In the animated flicker of the fire, his matted hair was slimy: frond-like. His features: unattractive – the nose nearly flat – the mouth distorted. The skin: *strangely dirty.* Overall? *Dishevelled. Filthy.* Tattered clothing hung from his body.

"Blanket?" Charles offered a spare, reluctantly.

"Thank you." The cold voice spoke again, like water in a leather bag.

"May I say, Sir, that I recognise something of the North of England in your voice. Yet you seem to know this place well enough. Have you been here long?"

"Yes, my boy. More than ten years now."

He fixed Charles with a glassy eye, strangely impersonal, almost unseeing as it reflected the flickering firelight. His movements appeared mechanical, unusually uncoordinated as he dried himself.

Shivering, Charles moved closer to the fire. A wave of nausea washed over him. *The man stinks!* he thought. *The same smell which lay heavy in the streets of Portsmouth earlier today – or the reek one smells when one disturbs with a stick the mud in a stagnant pool.*

Charles fought to control a sudden irrational fear of the swimmer. Dismissing the instinct with a shrug, he forced himself to speak through the stench.

"Do you live near to here?"

"Live?" He repeated meaninglessly. "That way."

He gestured across the harbour. Only shadows brooded darkly beyond the expanding mudflats. Then the arm lowered and he was still again. He sat unmoving, like a grotesque automaton. The uneasy pause stirred Charles to try to take control once more:

"I thought – it would be a sublime night to swim, but–"

"Sublime." The word cut him off and was followed by the Professor muttering to himself in a way that was strangely chilling: "A serviceable word. From the French *sublimer* and the Latin *sublimare*. 'To lift up!' Yes, I suppose it *is* sublime... But it can do quite the opposite of lifting up, oh yes..."

Charles felt as if he was a boy again talking with one of his father's stuffy associates from the provincial Philosophical and Debating Society. Forced politeness made his words insincere and meaningless.

"I see... It's... er... yes... enchanting." He was not even sure at which childhood gathering he'd heard one of the old buffers use that particular word.

A strange smile played across the man's face.

"Enchanting." He mimicked. "But you were nearly caught out today, as I was when I first came here. The sea lowered me towards the silt, just like you..." He leaned forward as if to confide. "You mustn't panic when you sink in it." Glassy eyes glared – as if across a great void into a vast distance, or a dimly recollected past. "You mustn't panic. No, you mustn't do that. Not panic. *No! No! No!*"

Charles shifted awkwardly on the grass, cautioning himself: *The man should be in Bethlam hospital. I have heard these lunatics can be dangerous... Nevertheless, I shall engage him awhile in conversation. Such a strange and interesting study might go well in my memoir!*

"And tell me, Sir, what brought you to this sublime spot in the first place?"

Again, the awful blank stare, the features suddenly lifeless, then movement once more. *It really is like talking to an animated machine,* Charles thought. *One winds the spring and one can watch it talk.*

The man's eyes clouded, his voice grew distant – dim recollections were bubbling to the surface. When he spoke again he was hesitant:

"I... am... a university Professor. Have you had the privilege of a good education?"

"*Privilege?!* I have just come back from the Grand Tour, Sir! *Hah!* But I have no intention of embarking on academic studies, if that is what you are asking. I am more interested in the lessons that the University of Life has to offer!"

"...The University of *Life* has to offer!" The Professor echoed excitedly, putting a strange emphasis on the word *Life*, and then trailing into profound silence. Once more the features set hideously. His expression was the fixed stare of madness. Charles was glad the fire was dying. *I shall head back to the Woolpack, I think. But I want him to go before I gather my things. I don't trust him.*

The watery voice spoke again:

"My long studies have taught me many things. When first I came here, I was searching for lost treasure. This was a Roman settlement, you see, and I wondered if antiquities might have been dropped and covered in the intervening years. I was not disappointed. The silt, you see, has a preservative effect on materials thrown in."

Doll-like, he gestured across the bay.

"All manner of victims from centuries gone by lie preserved in there. A farmer's horse drowned in 1697, a Scotch terrier in 1564. Year after year of personal tragedy fills the harbour. And the bodies go back in to the mists of time. This is a place the Ancient Britons held sacred. They initiated ceremonies that demanded the ritual drowning of young people. It was supposed to bring eternal life to the land. So it has gone on since. There are so many people and animals who flailed hopelessly against the Powers of Life and Death – those Powers that dominate all existence."

"Powers?" asked Charles, derisively.

"Powers beyond our control. Unseen hands directing the winds and the tides; deciding the movements of fish through the sea – and how you live your life."

"No," said Charles, prickling, "I get to choose exactly what I do."

"You think you do," the Professor answered, "But what if I hadn't helped you? Without my intervention, you would surely have died."

"I would have found a way out."

"Is that so? Some would call that answer ungrateful. Some would say you owe me your life." The dark air filled with a more intense shadow which exuded from the Professor like a black halo.

"Some would say you're speaking above yourself and do not know your rank," Charles shot back.

The stranger sat motionless for a half second longer than Charles was comfortable. Finally the strange Professor said:

"You have much to learn."

"Do I? And what would *you* have to teach *me*? There's a new spirit sweeping across Europe, you know, my fellow. We don't have to pretend we are beholden to creatures of the imagination – to Gods and Powers, as you call them. I *chose* to go in, and I would have found a way out. I decide *what* I do, and *when* I do it, and there's an end on't."

"Is that how it is?" The Professor laughed to himself. A shadow seemed to pass over the moon, but when Charles looked up, the star-filled sky was cloudless. He refocused his wary attention, on the Professor, whose presence made him uneasy. *Dash it all, I'll get dressed and be gone from here,* he decided, reaching in the half-light for his clothes.

But as he did so, a subtle movement near the man's mouth caught Charles's attention. At first he thought the Professor was licking his lips at his favourite subject, but in the deepening shadow he couldn't be sure. Perhaps the flickering embers were casting those strangely animated shapes... Charles grew fixated by that strange motion.

Oblivious to his thoughts, the man continued, speaking on and on and on.

It felt as if it were no time that he spoke, and at the same moment, it felt like hours. His voice continued in a subtle rhythmic tone, mentioning ever and again the preservative qualities of the silt. He mentioned the date on which a Centurion travelling with the Romano-British Fleet, the *Classis Britannica,* fell into the water in his leather and metal armour and couldn't be saved; how Richard the Second lost a hunting dog and had the serf who'd released it flogged by the water's edge... All manner of detail. How could he possibly make such extravagant claims of such precise knowledge? Yet, Charles had to admit, it *was* a fascinating subject...

The Professor lectured on. For long moments Charles felt a drowsiness sink through him, pressing on his legs and arms like a great stifling weight – as if the years the old man mentioned in his talk had settled on him, or the layers of silt accumulated century after century a few feet from them were closing in. He fought the sensation with increasing difficulty, but still the interludes of dreamy languor increased. He seemed to be falling into a mire made from the Professor's words.

And all the while, as the man spoke, there moved across his ugly face that continuous licking movement. Peering harder, Charles had the impression that physical objects were dropping from his mouth. As if the words he spoke had taken on a solidity and fell from his lips as he uttered them. And they seemed to be advancing toward him.

He shivered.

A trick of this flickering light. Strange how they seem to move, though...

In morbid absorption, Charles let the conversation drift, realising that a single theme underpinned it all, and that the speaker was gradually edging towards it. The more the Professor spoke, the more convinced he became that a reason would surface. The constant talk of history and preservation – *it must lead somewhere.*

Quite suddenly, the revelation came – spat from his lips in those illusory solid lumps:

"...And people have often spoken of the longevity which may be induced by the healing actions of the silt, but I assure you," and here the steel-edged gaze stabbed clean through Charles's soul. "I have found far more."

He nodded his wet, frond-covered head in confirmation of what he was about to say:

"For I have not only found longevity, but immortality."

"Immortality?" Charles uttered it before it could be stifled.

Distantly, only half aware, he felt that something was touching him. A steady, creeping movement, as if slimy, wet creatures were crawling from his feet, up his legs and body.

"Yes! I see you are intrigued. There is a power of goodness in the very mud which gives eternal life. I was like you once – until I was exposed to the mud. As long as I keep it on my skin and in my body I cannot age or wither. The process cannot be reversed – but not being able to stray too far from the harbour is a small price to pay for incorruptibility!"

Charles looked at the man's revolting form and wondered if it was worth preserving. But that creeping sensation had advanced further in the form of a numb, cold tingling, and had reached his mouth. For some strange reason he could not open it to contradict them man, as if something held it shut. The Professor seemed to have bound him to his own will with his words.

"Do you want to know more?"

Now, however, he spoke:

"...Yes!" With shock, Charles realised he hadn't wanted to say that at all. The sensation grew in him that something was on his skin, controlling his movements.

"You would be an eager student?"

"I would," he replied in terror.

"But you must trust me. It is important that you trust me and do as I say." Suddenly the Professor lowered his head and muttered abstractedly to himself: "He is a strong swimmer. And he is stubborn, even now. A rope perhaps?" He raised his ugly head in the dying light. Another shiver ran the full length of Charles's spine.

"For years I have dreamed of having a student. I have so much to share... and you will have so much to learn. You will join me in my research."

"Yes!" Charles responded – his hollow tone mimicking the other's voice, as he felt some soft crawling things now entering his mouth and climbing to the back of his throat. He swallowed involuntarily.

The Professor grinned triumphantly, and glanced back at the glistening mud.

"Quickly," he said. "Take my hand."

Charles couldn't refuse the same cold hand that had hauled him from the water. Immediately he touched it, the warmth drained from his body, while the Professor looked far stronger than when they had first met. With an eager grip he pulled Charles towards the silt.

"Are you ready to learn? Ready, my boy?" The Professor grinned.

Charles nodded, fighting helplessly to shake his head.

They were at the water's edge. Quickly, the Professor bent and thrust a hand deep into the silt.

"It would be better if you are secured. For your own good, you understand?"

Charles nodded again, as he watched the Professor pull a long dank rope from the fetid mud. It crawled with all manner of bristling, many-legged sea-dwellers, glistening in the moonlight.

"Then let me help you."

To his own amazement, Charles saw himself offer his wrists for the Professor to wind the dripping cord around. Then the fibre was trailed around Charles's body and knotted in some ingenious way that left him unable to struggle. "Is that better?" The Professor asked intensely.

Charles eyed the rope and then the mudflats. The moon's reflection was visible in one small puddle on the silt's dark surface, and further off a gash of water oozed down a deeper channel towards distant lights. Thoughts crowded in: An image of the serene bay earlier that night: *As I dived in, the moonbeams scattered like a shoal of ghostly fish...*

With sudden shock he noted activity on the stinking surface of the mud. Like the rope that bound him, it crawled with spindly sea-creatures and sliming slugs and worms – distorted reflections of crabs, or spiders and countless other creatures – all moving with a steady, inhuman animation which reminded him of the Professor's movements. He felt a vague sense of having awakened these things from deep slumber – or that they were controlled by something far distant. – *They are The Dead...*

The Professor's leatherbag voice reiterated the question:

"Is that better?"

Charles wanted to cry out and beg for release. He struggled against a great, immobilising weight, dragging on his limbs. But it was hopeless. In place of the movements he desired, he was aware of his head jerking forward once more in a compliant nod of assent.

"Then I will show you." The Professor said, a foul grin spreading across his bloated white face, the flesh blotched in shadowy patches.

He stepped ahead of Charles, sinking in the slime, and tugged gently on the rope. Puppet-like, Charles edged towards the grasping silt, until he stood at the very point from where he had earlier dived. *Stinking mud.* The bay was steeped in blackness. The stars above were gone. The sky reflected the dark hue of the deadly silt before him. He gasped, trembled and stepped forward again.

Mud oozed between his toes.

No! I don't want this! It can't be happening!

Yet, unable to resist his saviour's tug, Charles took another step forward, The Professor's white face seemed to hang against a background of glistening blackness. *The cold light in his eyes!* A silence. Half rotten creatures watched from the mud as his foot brushed silt: *Stench! Death!* The tar-like surface heaved a soft sigh at the foot's impact. A ripple moved through the assembled beasts. Somewhere a dog howled, as if calling from a distant time.

"My friends," the Professor delivered an incongruous speech to the deathly night, "I should like you to meet the new student we have so long wanted."

A ghastly breath like the wind and a clattering of shells issued from the assembled dead. A jerk on the rope and the fetid mire absorbed Charles up to his knees.

"He is a proud and ungrateful creature, but that will change as he becomes one of us. As he immerses himself in his new studies, there will be much for him to learn. Many names and faces for him to keep close to his heart..." He turned to Charles with a threatening glare. "In a few years we shall examine him. To see how deep he goes." Another tug. The black coldness swallowed Charles further. Before him, the Professor's lower half had already disappeared beneath the silt; and around him the dead pressed closer in the squirming mud. The surrounding beast-corpses grew louder and more excited. *A welcoming party!*

Panting icy breath, a cadaverous Scotch terrier licked Charles's face with a cold, wormy tongue. Misshapen seabeasts approached – more of those crabs on spindly legs somehow fallen under the spell of whatever controlled the harbour.

The mud crept up to his chest. *Fear:* a rising panic a hundred times stronger than the one that had shocked him when his foot first brushed the silt. Through terrified eyes he saw the Professor's head again, now seemingly decapitated by the sludge. Grinning, enticing, drawing the hapless student further into the pool. Then Charles made a desperate struggle in the closing mud, and in surprise the Professor released the rope. It loosened around him as the knot undid of its own accord. Charles felt his will flooding back as he took control of his body.

At last! Some volition again.

"Help! Help! Please! Somebody please help me!"

Charles started to thrash as he screamed and shouted to the darkened night. The air was only distinguishable from the mud in that it gave a minimally slighter resistance to his struggles...

But whilst his desperate cries went unanswered his thrashing served only to draw him deeper. Charles's head became a solitary island. "Swallow," the Professor said before he sank out of sight. "Swallow and be like me. You *will* be linked with the harbour, though you may fight it now. Let its agents cure your mortality..."

"Help! Help!"

He could feel the weight of the dead writhing against him. The same terrible weight he felt when he had earlier pulled his leg free of the silt. Subterranean creatures swarming in a silty underworld. *Dragging. Dragging me down, towards...*

"Hel-"

Splutter. A guttural sound replacing his voice. A trail of wriggling ooze dripping from his mouth as he spat black droplets into the black night before the mud gagged him. His nose stayed briefly unblocked before it, too, was sealed by the silt, so only his eyes and crown of his head were above...

From the bank near the tent, a lantern shone.

"In the name of Jesus Christ – what is going on?"

Charles could see an old man's dim outline on the shore. He raised his hands for help and heard a familiar voice:

"Charles, I'll throw a line. I'll throw a line!"

Then his head slipped under the mud.

*

Silence. Oh God! Oh God! Stifling cold mud. I'm going to die! Oh please, if you really were Bartholomew, then save me. Oh God! I'm going deeper, I can feel myself sliding down. Can't hold it – can't hold my breath. Ahh! Must breathe – don't breathe – must breathe – no – don't breathe.

Oh.... Mouth open. Wriggling mud. Ah! It's flooding in – flooding in – crawling in – inside – !

*

...a long corridor of darkness...nothing real at all...

*

Charles wasn't sure how long this terrible dream went on. Finally he woke to see filtered daylight flooding in through the gatehouse window.

Alive! He basked in warm relief that the night's evils had run from the morning sun. Outside, a light wind ruffled the trees. The gentle lap of harbour water came delicately to his ears.

The wind stirred the branches again. *Last night..? Was any of it real?*

"But no!" Charles spoke out loud. "It can't have been!"

Beyond the gatehouse's confines he heard the *clink* of a pan shifted by an unknown hand. He sat up, alert. *Who –?* As he moved, dried mud pinched his skin. *What?* A flush of disorientation.

With a grimy hand he opened the gatehouse door. His heart pounding – *What to expect – ?* Emerging into stabbing sunlight he shielded his dazzled sight with a dirty, raised arm. *Who – ?*

Kindly blue eyes assessed him from a lined, bearded face.

"Do you want some breakfast?"

"Bartholomew..! How did you find me?"

The old Quaker gave him a long hard look, two emotions warring inside him. He put his hand to his long white beard, his face framed by his neat, blue jacket and black broad-brimmed hat.

"My goodness, you are the most irritating, troublesome young man ever a guardian had the misfortune of trying to herd," said Bartholomew, with a grimace. "And if you hadn't had such a shock last night, I would break the rule of a life time and thrash you with my riding crop!"

He saw the look of shame on Charles's face and his customary benevolence of spirit won out. There would be plenty of time to chastise him later, after all.

"Word came to the Fountain Hotel that a young man of your description had sought lodgings at the Woolpack, here in Portchester," he explained. "That horse you took belongs to Squire Thistlethwayte, who owns this estate and is currently in Portsmouth on business. The stableboy recognised it straight away, and sent word. I set out from Portsmouth the moment the news arrived – and just in the nick of time, it transpired." He shot his eyes to the heavens for a moment in exasperation. "Whatever got into you last night? Did you lose hold of your reason?" He surveyed the boy's face. "I believed for a moment I had lost you forever in there."

He gestured the bay with a sweep of his raised arm. An involuntary shudder needled Charles's body at sight of the familiar movement.

"You were caught in the silt. It was a close thing," Bartholomew added.

He tipped bacon from the pan on to a plate.

"You were raving last night. I didn't want to move you till you regained your wits. I took you into the gatehouse, sat by you the whole night. You were muttering and crying out, in the throes of a deep delirium. Only this morning when a shepherd boy came by did I send for food and cooking gear from the village. I was afraid to wake you lest I distress you further." He eyed the young man, considered what a massive burden he was on the older man's soul and tightened his jaw for a second. Then exhaled before adding kindly: "I wiped off the worst of the mud, but you really need to clean the rest from your body. It has a polluting stench." He sat back. "But my, what a picture you are!" he smiled to himself as much to Charles. Then adopting a practical tone, he added: "Before we go, let's get you fed first. – How's this?"

Charles took the proffered plate with a mechanical movement. A wave of nausea filled him. His head spun in a giddy whirl. He dropped the food and buried his head in his hands.

"I feel sick."

"I've sent for a physician. I wouldn't be surprised if you had a brain fever, the way you've been acting these last few months! It's like the Devil himself got into you while you were in Venice – and I don't speak lightly of such matters," he added gravely, before a new look of concern creased his brow as he thought back over recent events.

"Last night... You were shouting many fantastical things about a night-time swimmer. This can't be right, though. There's been no sign of another person the whole night."

"You saw no one?" Charles stared apprehensively across the water.

"Not a living soul..." Bartholomew suddenly grew serious, as a shadow crossed his face. "It is strange, though. When I said I was coming down to the water's edge in the night, the Landlord told me his stable boy Tom is convinced there's a bewitchment upon it – that unaccountable things go on here. Others fancy they see and hear the strangest things. Did no-one tell you this?"

Charles shook his head, his eyes cast down.

"I suppose *No-one* thought he owed me no explanation," Charles said, avoiding Bartholomew's gaze out of his newly discovered sense of shame. Then he looked up with an intense expression.

"So, I was caught in the mud? Nothing else happened?"

"Except that I hauled you out again."

"Oh, thank you. Thank you, Bartholomew!"

The words were genuine and heartfelt, and they elicited in Bartholomew a powerful emotion.

"You know, all these years of worry and anguish about your wayward nature are almost worth those few words," the old man remarked, his throat tightening a little as he looked closely at Charles. "But, Charles, lad, pray tell me, what else do you think *might* have happened here?"

He asked the question with a deep expression of concern.

The truth was, he sensed something malefic here. It made him deeply uneasy. He had spent the night reciting prayers and reading from his pocket bible by lantern light because of it. His eyes were tired from the strain.

"This place is very strange," Charles said, abstractedly.

Bartholomew eyed Charles thoughtfully, looked down at a pile of something lying in the grass. He thought for few moments to measure his reply. And as he spoke, a wave of nausea wriggled again in Charles's guts at his tutor's words.

"You're right – this place *is* strange," Bartholomew agreed. "I was speaking briefly with an old soldier in The Woolpack who took an interest when he heard you had come this way. An uncommon sort of man – outlandish you might call him... He told me that local superstitions go back a long way. Some say the harbour here houses a malign spirit – others – that it is less malign and more lonely, seeking company whenever it can..." He paused as he noticed the apprehension in Charles's eyes. "Of course, it's all the muddled thinking of folklore."

"I am sure it is."

"But occasionally things coincide with the legends and start the locals talking. The soldier told me that thirteen years ago a man went swimming here. He said he was a History Professor from Oxford, with an interest in Roman artefacts. He never came out."

"...Never...?"

"No. You were lucky. Very lucky."

Charles stood and staggered to the water's edge. The sea was high – the flat inscrutable surface a deep blue iris.

"Well, I am out now," he muttered to himself. "And I am all right."

He took a defiant breath, knelt and plunged his arm in the water. As he watched the lumps of silt disintegrate, a sudden image of a cold hand reaching out to his own flashed through his mind...

He jerked his arm out. His flesh was puffed and white, like a corpse washed up on the strand. He was rocked by dizziness, and staggered to his saviour's side. His clean skin felt like it was burning in the light.

"Get me to a physician!" His voice quaked with fear.

"Have you picked something up from the water?"

"Maybe."

"I'll get the horses. They're down the path." As the Quaker stood, he looked again at the patch of grass by his feet. Turning to go Bartholomew said, half to himself:

"That pile of sea worms and crabs... So many. They must have been dragged up, somehow... Very odd, indeed." Shrugging, he disappeared along a narrow track by the side of the castle wall.

Charles pictured the Professor, seated in that exact spot. He remembered that licking movement he had seen on the his face. Words seeming to become solid and fall from his mouth. Could these rotten creatures really be those writhing forms that had made their ways toward him? Surely, it was impossible?

Yes. Of coure it's impossible!

He chastised himself for thinking crazy thoughts. And even as he did so, the pile of sea worms started to break down before his eyes – as if the sunlight and fresh air had accelerated their decomposition.

This is utterly nonsensical... Charles told himself.

More patches of white flesh, exposed by the flaking mud burned in the light. He straightened and blinked at the hated orb, and felt the desire to shrink from its light.

A tide of nausea rose through him again. He vomited.

Shaking his burning head, he looked with renewed horror at the puddle of his own gastric juices glistening in the grass.

It was writhing with –

No! – those worms and crabs..!

An image rose before his eyes of the moonlight swimmer. His words rang in Charles's ears:

Swallow and be like me. Link your fate with that of the silt. Let its agents cure you of your mortal condition...

The burning sensation on his skin became unbearable.

Instinctively, he stepped back to the the water. He dipped his feet. The silt beneath the surface slipped over his legs –

Ah! Such a relief to feel that healing touch, he thought. *Perhaps I should slip in a little deeper...*

The sound of the horses' hooves along the narrow track awakened him to the stupidity of his actions.

I must be insane – risking the grip of this mud again!

He heard Bartholomew, still out of sight call to him to join him.

"I'm coming!" he shouted back. But to his surprise he didn't take a step.

A movement in the water arrested his attention. A ghastly shape bubbled up from below:

"You cannot leave." The Professor's face briefly poked above the surface. "You are my student."

"No!" Charles answered in fear. "I'm... going back to my father! From now on, I will listen only to him."

An inhuman laugh rose from the dark depths as Charles finally moved to climb out. But his bare skin was stinging, and as soon as he took a step back to land, he burned all over with invisible fire. After a few paralysing seconds, he began to reconsider:

Wait! I mean, I could go in. Just for a while. A period of study, it might do me good, rather than leave right now... Ahh!

His body was again wracked with pain.

I could just slip in a little more – to see what I can learn...

The jingle of harness came nearer and a shout reached his ears as Bartholomew caught sight of him:

"*Charles!* Are you mad? You'll drown. Quickly, take my hand..."

Bartholomew grabbed his arm to pull him back to the shore. Charles once more felt the searing pain that came from moving away from the harbour water.

"Professor!" he called.

The moonlight swimmer reappeared beneath the water. His white bloated face mouthing reassuring words: "Take my hand. It's all right, my boy. Take my hand."

Silty fingers, bloated and deformed broke the surface. Desperately, Charles reached towards the proferred hand, while Bartholomew froze with supernatural horror at the ghoul beneath the water.

"In the name of Jesus Christ...!"

It was not just the Professor who had come to pull the young man back in to the sea. The water teemed with a mass of distorted harbour-dwellers rallying to claim the young man – body and soul...

As these ghoulish creatures came, Charles felt new strength in his body. He was suddenly grateful to them – after all, they had risked the burning heat of the day to free him from his guardian's hold. With renewed strength he fought to free himself.

If I can just reach the Professor's hand...

He stretched out again, inching closer to those vile fingers.

And, finally –

"Yes!" He screamed in delight. He felt the Professor's powerful grip dragging him down. Down into the enchanted waters and sucking silt.

And as he felt Bartholomew relinquish his hold, a final triumphant thought flashed through Charles's mind:

Free at last! How utterly sublime!

THE NIGHT WATCHERS

"Don't let them intimidate you," she says, smiling reassuringly as they enter the new unit at St Mary's Hospital.

"Intimidate me? *Babies? Little babies?*" he chuckles, and sweeps his eyes along the lines of cots pressed against the magnolia walls, noting the curved dome of a newborn's head, another's tiny pink fingers delicately formed from warmth and softness.

They're in a private unit on the hospital grounds, funded by an unknown patron. He is here because of the interview he did. A distraught mother seeking her missing teenage son. He didn't know why, but no-one else was interested in following up.

"*He's probably fine,*" he remembers his police contact saying. "*Just not staying in touch as teens sometimes do...*"

But... he thinks about other whispers he's heard. *She's not the only one who's come to me with strange stories about this place...*

Yes, he has gathered many, many rumours in his role as a local reporter for *The News* up at Lakeside – but never anything solid. This undercover work he's doing now, in this experimental ward, might be the scoop that breaks him into the Nationals...

...Or will it? His heart sinks as he looks around.

This room doesn't look all that experimental, he thinks.

He steps over to the nearest cot, stretching out his hand to a slumbering bundle. "Hello littl'un," he coos. The infant's eyes open and fix upon his face.

Something in the expression immediately halts his hand. He steps to the next cot, then the next. Each child has the same look. *Watchful. Knowing.*

He shoots an anxious look to his employer, an Asian woman in her thirties with neat, bunned hair. "What do I have to do?"

"Ensure they're fed. Very simple," she smiles.

"Why do they..." he stops half way through the sentence, seeing more eyes appear between bars. "Why do they stare like that?"

"They are the once-dead," she says matter-of-factly – raising her hand sharply to silence him as his complexion drains. "No, no, it sounds more dramatic than it is. Each was stillborn. Or, that's how they would have been described before The Process." She raises a flat palm and gestures the room with a triumphant sweep of the arm implying the benediction that is science. "The Process brought them back, you see."

He feels an acid burn in his veins and struggles to breathe a moment. "*And this*, these babies – are the result?"

"Yes."

"Why haven't you gone public? I mean, it's fantastic. Bringing children back who would never have made it without science. It's amazing!"

She waits for a moment, running her eyes up and down him, thoughtfully.

"You're very inquisitive. For a temp." She considers him a moment longer, then explains. "They have very particular needs. So we keep them here."

He looks around. Thirty pairs of eyes are fixed unblinkingly on him. Children of a few weeks to two years. Little flaxen-haired girls and bonny African boys, redheads, pale-skins, soft browns. All silent.

Involuntarily, he shudders.

"Stillborn..." he tries the word, then looks at them with renewed pity."Poor little... loves..."

The sentence dies in the watchful silence. With a flutter of panic, he thinks, *There'll be a whole night of this staring. God!*

She shows him where each baby's bottle is kept. "We haven't been able to wean them yet. It's something to do with The Process. Try it..."

She watches him offer a bottle to a child which takes the teat sullenly and suckles: a pale ginger child – the oldest of them, with skin that nearly glows white, blue veins snaking beneath it, its angry green eyes boring into him. For a moment the child refocuses from him to her, holding her gaze for two silent seconds. It nods slightly. Satisfied, she nods back and turns to leave.

"You'll be perfect," she says, switching on the lamp at a little table in the middle of the room and killing the main light.

"You shouldn't get any trouble. Don't fall asleep yourself." Before she leaves, she points to a bookcase with rows of books. "Should you need entertainment."

Alone, he lays the blue-veined child in its cot, and tries the next child. It squirms away from the bottle, silently screwing its face. The next is the same, and the next. He goes to the door for help, and finds no handle on the inside. He bangs and shouts for a few minutes. No reply. No signal on the phone, either. With growing discomfort, he turns to see, in the half-darkness, thirty pairs of eyes weighing him.

He shakes his head and notes how heavy his breathing is. He yawns. At the bookcase, grabs a handful of books and sits in the well of lamplight.

One book takes his eye. *The Baby Manual.* He opens it for a clue as to what he should do about feeding them.

Inside the front cover is a note written in pencil. It says:

"One becomes many."

He leafs through looking for clues as to what it means. There is underlining on *feeding baby,* on *playing with baby,* on *how baby responds to strangers.* There are more cryptic marginal notes in a cramped hand, saying things like:

"An abandoned house is a home," and "change baby."

Another says in big desperate letters:

"STAY AWAKE!!!"

The room feels airless now and there is more glittering in the darkness, like cat's eyes on a road all directed at him.

What are they watching for?

*

He wakes into a dream. In the night's half-darkness, the red-haired baby is standing in front of him, its green eyes just above the height of the desk.

"Hello," it says, with an adult voice, neither male nor female.

He smiles. It's like a tv advert he saw of a child speaking little wisdoms to its dad.

"Hello," he answers, experiencing an hallucinatory sensation of himself, disembodied – floating. "Why are you out of bed?"

The child grins, a malicious light in its eyes. Through parted lips, the lamplight reveals sharp white teeth. "Haven't you guessed?"

"What's to guess?" he smiles, bemused, his gaze held by the child's.

Its grin grows wider, revealing deep red gums glistening wetly. He feels dimly that there is something he should stop, but his body feels so heavy.

"It's a test," The pale child answers."I left you clues!"

"Clues?" he repeats, an alarm sounding in his brain.

"We like to give you a chance," the child says. It climbs on to the desk and jabs the pages of *The Baby Manual* with a short finger, then pushes its face close to his. "It's in here if you care to work it out."

I need to wake up, the thought gnaws at him as he considers the child. It is rolling its eyes with disappointment.

"I shall have to tell you," it finally says. "Let me explain. When you have been seeking a place to stay for years, travelling through darkness, and you find a warm, empty space, vacated, kept habitable and inviting long after the original inhabitant has left, how can you pass by?"

It pauses a moment before it continues.

"Then you arrive, and find a world of soft warm, moist people; surely, you invite your friends to join you?" it adds. "That is The Process and how it works on the stillborn. These scientists and doctors – they kept an empty home open for me. So I moved in."

Wake yourself up. Come on! – the reporter thinks stridently

"After that, when the doctors think they have scored a success, brought a child back from the dead, they make more empty homes," the child says. "So, of course, your friends join you."

"This is what happened?" he asks."With The Process? When they thought they were saving the lives of babies?"

The child nods.

"Yes, we have strayed into this world before. Surely, you have heard legends of Changelings – and demons? But we've never come like this, thanks to your medical advances and experiments – thanks to your doctors who monitor us and want to keep us safe but have no idea of what we are. Except for the one who brought you in here. She knows what we can do. Because she came here before, in the old-fashioned way, before science made it so easy."

"What do you mean? – What you can *do?* – Science made it easy?" the reporter asks.

The child leers cruelly, licking its lips with a thin, red tongue before it speaks.

"When we are all together like this, so many of us in one place, we find that inviting new friends to this world can be controlled. We no longer wait for vacant homes in the stillborn bodies inside mothers' wombs. No. Instead we take possession of others' homes, when we find them unprotected. Alone."

Somewhere in his clouded dream, he senses hands, tiny soft hands tearing at his clothing. Thirty mouths attaching to his body. White teeth digging in. There is a body somewhere. *His* body. Vulnerable.

He looks around him, at last acutely aware. He is a spirit, he realises. A slender silver cord runs from his spirit forehead to his body which has been dragged away to a dark corner of the room. He peers more closely. His body is covered with writhing children, sucking life from him. He looks in horror at the husk of himself, shrivelled, a shrunken homunculus with a tail, now the size of a baby.

He gasps.

Somewhere, hovering nearby, disembodied, a dark shape moves closer, quivering it seems, in anticipation of its new home.

The child before him laughs again.

"We are evicting you," it says. "Your body has a new tenant."

And with a sweep of its hand, the child breaks the silver cord.

*

The next day, the Asian woman with her bunned hair steps in with a temp.

"Don't let them intimidate you," she says, half smiling.

Thirty one pairs of eyes are watching.

OLD HARRY AND THE KING OF THE SEA PEOPLE

Old Harry was a drinker, that's for sure. From early in the hungover morning till late in the legless night, booze gripped him as tight as he gripped his bottle.

In the venerable institution called The Coal Exchange at Portsmouth Point, where once the young Nelson (alongside other heroes innumerable) had stumbled out to give its walls a watering, he sat each day and watched the big ships.

The sea. *Lifeblood of the Empire* he called it as the afternoon light seeped through the window and the booze hoisted a limp pennant of nostalgia in his soul. "God Save the King."

"What's that, you old soak?" Angus, the ginger-haired landlord called affably across the bar at the Salt, who had just that moment ranged an expectant pay parade of big copper pennies and tiny silver sixpences on the table.

All to no avail, as it turned out. With a glance at the clock, Angus lifted the hinged bar and announced to the tobacco-and-sweat-smelling saloon: "Time, gentlemen, please. Drink up, now!"

Old Harry flinched and glared at his coins. *Five bells! Damn it! I lost track! Three and a half hours till evening opening.*

Most days when he stumbled three sheets to the wind into the diesel-sweet sea air, he nipped a worn hip flask from his pocket for a plug of Nelson's Blood, smacked his lips and laughed at bamboozling the beak and all his idiot licensing laws. On this particular day, however, his rum ration was dry.

"Bugger," he said and marched back to the pub for a quick off sale – *on the Q.T.,* so to speak.

But no. Angus, always a stickler for King's Regulations, signalled *no* through the frosted glass door.

"Oh come on," Old Harry cajoled, pushing the handle as the Landlord slid the bolt home.

"Half two," Angus called cheerily through the door. "Go on. On your way, Harry. I've got to go out."

Harry kicked the frame and came about, to face the unpleasant truth that today reality might just slip a torpedo through the submarine net. That meant facing the wife sober with the swelling shiner he'd dispensed last night, and meeting his grown-up kids straight, something he hadn't done for three years. *Pub closing time. It's not civilised. This is 1951, after all!*

A Destroyer, two tugs in attendance, black smoke pluming from her stack, served to remind him of his Navy years.

"God I miss those days," he said, to a vision of native girls waving from the wharf as he made port somewhere exotic, his wallet bulging. "That's what life's about. Loose women and drink – both at a fair rate of exchange."

He wheeled to glare at The Coal Exchange and to his pleasure, saw red-headed Angus bump through the front door encumbered with a bicycle and a flat cap. With a quick push and swing of the leg, Angus launched himself up Broad Street.

Now, Old Harry had been through that door so many times he knew it better than his own. He also knew that Smudge Smith had strained the lock while he and two doxies swung on it while offering to the world a boisterous rendition of *All The Nice Girls Love A Sailor, And I've Got Two Right Here* just the night previous.

He listened closely to the breeze with the growing conviction that he could hear his name upon it.

"Come to us, come to us, Harry!" A chorus of siren voices called him. *Yes!* The bottles inside were crooning his name.

After a quick push and a kick at the bottom of the door, a drunken survey of the saloon bar confirmed every soak's dream: alone in a boozer!

Licking his lips and rubbing his hands he grinned gleefully at the spiritual delights before him. He placed his trembling hand on the hinged counter, his personal gateway to oblivion, then...

"Good afternoon," said a sing-song Scottish voice from nowhere.

Old Harry spun on his heel to see, seated by the window a small, powerfully-built fellow who might have been a boy had it not been for the thick red mutton chops framing his delicate face. He appraised Old Harry with girlish eyes beneath his Tam o' Shanter.

"Who the Devil are you?" Old Harry blurted.

"A visitor," the other replied. "Doon from the Highland and Islands. Dull at hame. – Bonny, nae doobt. But droochit. Glabber everywhere!"

"What?" Harry said, his face contorted in confusion.

"Glabber. Mud, you call it."

"Oh."

Harry lifted the counter and stepped behind the bar, staring all the while at the newcomer.

"Pour me a dram!" the Little Man called.

"That's the ticket!" Old Harry called back with relief, slapping his palms together. "A man after my own heart."

"Couldn't do it, mysel'," the other explained. "Iron strip on the bar. Allergic to iron. All my folk are."

"Well, I'm here, now, little fellah," Harry answered absently as he surveyed the lines of bottles, serried like sailors on parade. "Don't you worry 'bout no allergies."

Inspired by the Little Man, he brought his sights to bear on the single malts: Laphraoig, Talisker, Dalmore, Glenfarclas, Macallan. Liquid gold glittering behind glass. He ran his finger along the bottles with childish delight as his tongue licked his lower lip.

"Here's the rule," said the midget, annoyed at the interloper's poor manners. "Seniority. I drink first. It's just polite. Do that, then good luck to ye."

The words washed past Old Harry as he lifted down the '42 Macallan, poured himself a hefty slug, then tucked the bottle under his arm.

"Bring it here!" Yelled the Little Man with growing impatience. As an afterthought he added: "Bring yoursel' a glass, too!"

Harry put the bottle, his brimming glass and the Little Man's empty tumbler on the table.

"Very good," said the other, grabbing Harry's full measure.

"Hey!"

The Little Man raised an arresting palm. "Smoke before we drink."

Harry glared and dispensed a hefty slug into the second tumbler then lifted it to his lips. The Little Man shot him a black look.

"Seniority, remember? Not impressed with Sassenach manners. No, no. There's far more respect for royalty in Scotland."

Old Harry slammed the glass down and roared with laughter. "Royalty?" he said, slapping his leg heartily. "And you said you hadn't touched a drop!"

Something in the Little Man's expression made his laughter choke in his throat. He watched with puzzled eyes as the other stuffed his pipe with leaf, struck a match indignantly and filled the room with sweet-smelling smoke.

"What do you mean, then, royalty?" the Englishman asked, sceptically.

"Exactly that. Ancient royalty. From a line that lives in the secret places of the North. On desolate shores. Where rocky bays roar. My people come ashore to meet in fairy rings in the woods and speak of old times together." He lifted a bushy red eyebrow and said pointedly. "Where the bee sucks, there lurk I. We bring fortune to your sort. Good and bad. We favour some. Others... we curse."

"Hahahaha! Curse? Curse!" Old Harry roared. "Where's your bundle of heather, eh, Gypsy Joe?" He wheezed at his own joke.

"Not a gypsy. Not Joe. Crógach, King of the Seonaidh – the Sea People."

"King of the Seven Dwarves, more like! Where's Snow White, then, Grumpy?" He howled again, mighty pleased with his own line in humour.

Crógach's eyes narrowed and his body shook. He gazed furiously upon the Englishman, who just before sinking his first glass of golden fluid toasted him with a mocking – "Splice the mainbrace, Sneezy!"

The Little Man fumed as Old Harry poured another and knocked that one back, too, this time with "Down the hatch, Dopey!"

He poured another and said, "Absent friends, eh, Bashf –"

The Little Man, seeing where this was going, cut him off:

"Don't say I didn't warn ye."

Then with an ironic "Slainte Mha!" he knocked back his own glass, glowering all the while.

"Remember, I drink first and good luck to ye. Works roundwise, too. Ye drink first – and bad luck to ye!"

Harry sneered and wafted his hand, as if the Little Man had just made a very bad smell. "That's one dwarf who's not Happy!"

"Right! That's it! I'll grant ye three wishes..." the Little Man said, a threatening edge in his voice. He snatched the bottle from the old sailor and emptied the last of it into his glass and muttered under his breath, "Ye'll see."

Old Harry glowered for a second, then laughing, tottered to the bar and brought over the Glenfarclas.

"Three wishes," the Little Man insisted.

"That's easy, Doc," Old Harry slurred. "There's only three things I want in life. The first is to be back aboard ship!" His eyes defocused in a dream of imperial glory for 20 seconds. Then he muttered – "Oh, now look who's Sleepy" and started to nod and snore a little.

The Little Man poked him angrily in the ribs with a bony finger. "What else?"

"What else what?" Old Harry twitched back to wakefulness.

"Second wish."

"Always to have a whisky bottle nearby!" He lifted the Glenfarclas to the light and kissed it.

"Your third?"

"My third. Hahaha. I know. That's easy! Never to leave this pub ever again!"

And with those words, just as if a press gang had blackjacked him, he dropped into unconsciousness.

*

When he woke, he was lying on a wooden floor. In the walls were neat ornate windows. A desk nearby had a chart and sextant on it and some ship's biscuits on a plate. A picture on the wall showed a Little Man in a wooded clearing sitting on a toadstool. *Strangely familiar, that figure in a Tam O'Shanter,* Old Harry thought after he'd groaned back to full consciousness.

He was in a ship's cabin. Indeed, there above his pounding head was the hammock he'd just fallen out of.

Dragging himself off the floor, he looked out at the weird foggy air and saw land in the far distance. Pushing the window open and poking his head out, he realised he was aboard an old tall ship, its wooden walls painted in black and tan. How he'd got here he had no idea, but he was reassured to see, through the strangely distorting air, they were just sailing into – yes – Portsmouth Harbour.

A shadow filled the sky. The ship rocked so violently he was forced to grip the window frame to prevent being hurtled across the cabin. Then the whole structure lurched on its side!

"All hands to the pumps," he shouted instinctively to an imagined crew. "Prepare to broach!"

A massive orb moved along the outside of the ship, white with a black circle inside a blue one and shot with reds. It disappeared. Then with a jolt and slide the ship righted and came to rest.

Old Harry scurried above decks to assess the damage.

*

"I should have fixed that lock!" Angus said the moment he walked in. Two empty glasses on the table bore witness to the crime. "Ach! Thieves, breaking in and drinking my best whisky!"

Whoever they were, he decided, they weren't so bad. In fact, he was more puzzled than angry – because they'd left him a gift.

"Now that *is* queer," he thought, as he hefted it and turned it on its side to examine the extraordinary workmanship, bringing his eye close up. "Beautiful! I'll keep it safe, up here," he thought, and placed it on a high shelf over the bar.

It was a whisky bottle, and far more than that, too. For in that whisky bottle was the most uncannily wrought model of a tall ship he'd ever seen, the sails billowing as if it were racing across the ocean, white capped waves overtopping the bowsprit while seagulls wheeled above. The model was painted startlingly realistically and fashioned with minute precision, even down to the brightwork. A thing of almost magical wonder.

"I wonder where Old Harry is?" he thought, placing the old boy's customary pint of Brickwoods with a whisky chaser on the bar, ready for him to breeze in.

Then his thoughts roamed to consider his new lodger: a fellow Scot on holiday looking for a berth for a night or two.

"Nice to hear a voice from home," he told himself. "And glad to help him out. Queer little fellow, though, now I think of him."

In that moment of silence, as if from afar off, Angus thought he could hear a high-pitched voice, frantically calling –

"Angus! Angus! Help me. I'm up here!"

He looked up briefly. That did *sound* like Old Harry, but surely that high pitch must be a fly buzzing about? His ears were playing tricks on him!

At that moment his diminutive mutton-chopped compatriot strode into the bar with a regal bearing. Angus smiled and greeted his guest with a –

"What'll it be?"

"Whisky, always whisky," said the other with his peculiar curt way of talking. Then, with a wry look as he waited for the drink to arrive, the little man nodded up at the bottle on the high shelf.

"That new?"

"It is. Someone left it here. I think in payment for a tot or two."

The little man took the glass of liquid, sniffed it, then sipped and savoured for a moment, a deep look of satisfaction on his face.

"Well. It looks like a rare object," the smaller man observed.

"It does indeed. Even I can see the workmanship is something special."

"Then a fair settling of accounts," he observed, casting a vicious eye upward.

Then, to Angus's surprise, the little man started laughing wildly at his own words, a merry look in his eyes.

Above, in that tiny ship-in-a-bottle, Old Harry's desperate shouts were drowned by laughter echoing all around.

FREDA

"She's sad, Mark," she says to the man she is soon to marry. "I can tell she is."

Impulsively, she lifts the wooden marionette from the table and eagerly turns it over in her hands, its silk dress shimmering in the sunlight. "Shall we take her home?"

The man beside her bends closer to examine the carved figure; fine face, delicate features – so out of place among these paste tables heaped with domestic bric-a-brac. What a pretty little thing!

"We could keep her in the bedroom," he grins, devilishly. "She'll add a bit of oriental spice." He leans close and whispers in her ear – "As if we need any!"

Spontaneously, she hooks the back of his neck with her palm and kisses him passionately, ignoring the hagglers and bargain hunters jostling by in the cool spring air. Then she turns to the old bearded man hunched behind the table, who meets her questioning expression with a nod and raised eyebrows.

"How much do you want for her?"

"How much..?" he echoes, considering a moment. "A pound?" he answers, almost with a question.

"Is she Indonesian, or something?" the young man asks, intrigued.

"Something like that," the other says with a shrug.

"What's her name?" asks the woman, eagerly.

The trader looks dubious for a moment, then says:

"Freda."

"Freda – doesn't sound very exotic," she answers, screwing her face and lowering the doll a little in disappointment.

"Well, you asked," he shrugs again.

Mark says: "Do you have the other hand in the box somewhere? She's got one missing, see?"

The trader shakes his head and looks away. "Sorry, no."

Mark looks at the doll a moment more, and decides he can't resist.

"We'll take her," he says, thrusting a pound coin towards the old man. "Here," he adds, so insistently that he takes even himself by surprise.

*

Sitting her by the little palm in the bedroom, Mark says: "There you are Freda. How's that for you?"

His partner, Jo, claps her hands playfully at the entity gazing enigmatically from the palm fronds.

"She looks like she's waiting to ambush us!" she pronounces delighted. "She's wonderful, isn't she?"

The young man's eyes sweep the doll up and down for a moment, alighting on the string attached to its one hand.

"Watch this."

A tug and the puppet jumps to life, her playful wave bizarrely contradicting the severity of her face.

"Oh, that's weird," Jo giggles with a thrill. "Look at the way she moves – so natural. You know, *she really is weird!*"

As she speaks, the puppet's balance shifts and the head snaps round to stare at her.

"Oh, don't!" Jo laughs at Mark. "You could almost think I'd offended her!"

His tongue pressed against his lower lip, Mark examines the doll's face, the curving line of the body finely carved and painted, dressed in antique orange silks.

"Exquisitely done – her face... so beautiful," he says, feeling as if he somehow knows her. "And the wood. So unusual. Is it sandalwood?"

He lifts the marionette and holds her close to his face, sniffing the wood's heady scent and closing his eyes for a moment.

In his mind's eye a scene manifests from nowhere – *level dust-yellow exotic lands; a jagged, snow-capped horizon; a warm sun to bask and luxuriate in.* He opens his eyes, startled by the richness of the image. After a moment's thought, he closes them again and sniffs the elusive scent once more. Now he sees – *the flash of a girl dancing, her eyes fixed upon the watcher as she moves with fluid movements, gesturing him to come to her. Her eyes, bright and shining, her lips a beautiful red* – The image dissolves and he opens his eyes once more, looking around astonished. *It's so real!* He thinks he hears the girl calling to him, like an elusive memory from childhood.

Closing his eyes again, he starts his third deep draw of air into his lungs. Now Jo says with a puzzled stare: "Stop it, you weirdo!"

He freezes for a half second, like a rabbit paralysed by a poacher's lamp. He exhales through his mouth, letting his lips vibrate together.

"She's great," he says, shrugging off the compulsion he still feels. "I wonder where her other hand is?"

A shadow flutters across Jo's heart.

"Leave her," she orders, in a sharp tone she has never used with him before. "A grown man playing with dolls! Come on, let's get some lunch. We've got plans to make. In case you've forgotten, you did ask for my hand in marriage – and I accepted. Remember?"

Reluctantly, he sets the doll down by the plant pot.

As he leaves, he looks back to appreciate her one more time: sullen, silent, exotic; contemplating her new foothold from the shelter of the palm fronds.

To him, her enigmatic face is the world.

*

After lunch and a plan-filled walk along the sea-scented shore, they step into the house from air that is cool with the approach of evening, and she makes her way upstairs to seek the warm hug of a jumper.

Stepping in to the half-lit bedroom, she gives a stifled scream and recoils, arms bent in front of her, palms outward as if to fight away danger.

"Shit!" she squeals. "How did that get there?"

An interloper is lying on her bed. One arm by its side, the other behind its head, staring at the ceiling as if deep in thought. A nervous shock pulses through Jo's body and ends in a flush of sweat from her palms.

She turns to the sound of a footstep behind her and looks concernedly at Mark. He says airily: "Everything okay?"

"What the bloody hell? You left her by the palm! I saw you," she says, looking back over her shoulder.

"Didn't you move her?"

"No, I didn't bloody move her."

"Well, somebody did..."

For a moment she contracts in on herself in a spasm of fear.

"Mark, I don't like it!"

He can't hold it any longer. His face broadens into a mischievous smile that spreads with vicious delight. "It was a joke," he laughs. "I came back up – remember – when I said I'd forgotten my keys? I moved her then."

"Well why the bloody hell did you do that?"

"I don't know. It just popped into my mind," he shrugs. "I suppose I thought it would give you a scare. I mean, you're so funny with your flights of fancy and fairytale worlds!"

"Fairytale worlds? How dare you!" She repeats melodramatically, withdrawing to her little dressing table in annoyance.

She glares at Mark a little longer for full dramatic effect, then admits with a contraction of her shoulder.

"You did give me a scare, though!"

Her face cracks into a smile. Then, with a lightning movement she reaches down and swings a pillow full in his face. She giggles as his surprised expression converts to one of mischief and he grabs a retaliatory pillow. Two more blows and counterblows and he launches himself at her, panting and kissing as they tumble onto the mattress.

"I hope this doesn't set a template for our wedding day," he laughs, pinning her to the bed, his weight on her midriff.

"Which bit?" she asks with a wry grin, before pulling him in for another passionate kiss.

As they make giggling, joyous love, the doll lies beside them, its painted face turned to watch.

*

Later that night, Jo wakes. She is staring at the half-darkness of her bedroom; the Ikea wardrobe in beech effect, the double radiator on the wall that needs a lick of paint, the toy puppy she has owned from childhood with big soppy eyes.

Then she looks at Mark.

She notices in the soft glow of headlights from a car hissing by outside that his eyes are half-open, rolled up inside his head so only the whites show, his breath coming in quiet ghosts, little unseen movements stirring the air with their passing. Beside him she sees Freda on his bedside table. Her body is slumped forward, giving the uncanny impression of leaning in to confide. In her unfocussed state Jo imagines the sweeping headlight beam animating the doll's wooden face. In this strange feral hour of the night when life doesn't obey the daylight rules, she fancies the doll senses her presence and turns its head ever so slightly. Jo stiffens on the bed in shock and the vibration sends the doll tumbling off the table with a wooden clatter, the fall forcing a yelp from Jo's lips.

Mark turns in the dark air and opens his eyes in a trance.

"I was in a dream," he says. "You woke me from a beautiful dream."

He turns and pulls the duvet around his neck, putting his back to her as she lies on the bed, inexplicably trembling.

When morning comes, the fantasies of the dark creep into the recesses of night-forgetfulness and Jo wakes with nothing more than a sense of unease.

Later that morning she insists Mark takes the puppet downstairs.

*

The bright light of the spring days stretch increasingly long fingers toward summer, and the preparations for the wedding go on apace. Guest list, dress, stationery – the hustle and bustle of a couple in love planning for the future. A magical feeling that fleets the days carelessly – as if all the world is filled with gold and laughter. The special day draws nearer still.

There are times when Jo's mind runs ahead to meet the future. After the wedding, there will be the honeymoon, the settling in (even though they settled in with each other two years before), the kids. She watches their kids in her imagination, crawling, growing, tottering to their feet, the safe mundanity of the school run in the car. *We have so much to look forward to,* she thinks.

Freda is not completely forgotten, though. There are times when Mark seems tired by the whole business of arranging the wedding. At times he withdraws to the living room to sit and read in the big comfy armchair by the fireplace.

She catches him sometimes in there looking drawn, his head off to one side in a drowse.

When she approaches him at these times for opinions about a venue, a particular shade of tablecloth or a favour to adorn their guests' tables, he exhales heavily before labouring an answer – as if something is on his mind he won't tell her about. She wonders if all this preparation can really be dragging on his soul so badly.

*

Over a latte in one of the little coffee shops in Southsea she says to a friend, "Yes, we're *engaged,* but he's just not *engaging* with the wedding."

"He needs shaking. Get his interest. Sex him up," her friend advises in a convincing tone, pretending she knows as much as the agony aunts whose pages her advice comes from.

Jo responds by spending a day at the Gunwharf shopping centre. She picks a tight, short dress, suspenders and stockings – enjoying the frisson of the apparatus of clips and hooks, feeling how it frames her sex, how it invites exploration. After a manicure and makeover, she arrives home, decked in new clothing, glitter and perfume, determined to bring back the sparkle to their lives.

She finds him in the hallway, bowing to the cup of tea in his hand while supping at its rim. He looks distant – about to close himself in the front room again.

"Put that down," she says with a voice of command she didn't know she had. "Come with me."

She leads him by the hand to the bedroom where he responds to her sexual energy with his own; she plants hot kisses on him and their lips seek the soft places of the other.

It's an evening of long, sensual passion in which they become intently focused on pleasure, a mutual moment of giving. Just like the old days.

Afterwards, she falls asleep in his arms; he huddles close, spent and drowsing in post-coital warmth and Jo thinks: *All is right with the world.*

*

She wakes in the small hours to find he has gone.

She stands and looks around her, feeling a mixture of annoyance and bewilderment, before stepping from the room.

Downstairs, she finds an accusatory crack of light below the living room door and quietly pushes it open. He is asleep in there, with the doll next to his head, propped on the low table beside the armchair. It's almost funny, because it looks as if somehow the doll has climbed up there and fallen asleep with its head next to his.

*

But it isn't funny. Something inside her contracts with a cold dread, and she returns to the bedroom with a sickly sinking feeling in her stomach. She sits on the bed for ten minutes, inexplicably afraid before switching off the light and letting night creep back into the room.

She wakes the next morning to the sight of Mark lying next to her. Her anger and fear have burned away in her hallmark way – sudden moods and passions petering out like forest paths. All she has left is a dull resentment, but for what she is not sure exactly.

She heads down to the front room again. What was that crazy feeling she had the night before? Did she somehow imagine she had seen her man being unfaithful? *Unfaithful.* Yes that was the emotion!

She is standing by the door in the morning's cold light when the reality of the situation strikes her. He was sitting with a doll. *A doll!* A stupid little puppet that she herself spotted. Really, she needs to take charge of herself. *Unfaithful?!*

She pushes the door open and enters the room.

Before her is the doll on the table with its painted kohl eyes. She steps forward, sensing tension in the air. It's as if the doll is assessing her, watching, emanating waves of malevolence towards her. She is frozen to the spot as the doll's painted eyes blindly take her in. It is going to do something terrible, something really awful, and her whole body tenses with foreboding.

She waits like this for an interminable few seconds, wondering what will happen next. Then she jumps with a sharp jolt and gasp. A car door slams outside. A couple are laughing.

The moment is gone. She is not looking at a malevolent entity. Of course not. It's just a doll. A little doll she found at a car boot sale.

Her shoulders slump forward and she lets out a breath. *What have I been so afraid of?*

Hesitantly at first she lifts the figure with a kind of forced careless indifference. She weighs it in her hand, feeling the lifeless wood. A childish grin crosses her face mixing with chagrin at her own stupidity.

Afraid? Of this? I'm being ridiculous!

With a flick, she throws the puppet in the air, giving it a spin as it launches. It flies up and tumbles down, clattering and flailing as it goes, its arms flying out as if trying to claw the air with its one hand.

She catches it and hefts it again, its face whirring angrily by, a rush of silks flapping in the air.

Why should I be afraid of this toy? she thinks, catching the doll again, and with a giddy sense of malice spinning it up into the air once more, its arms flexing out with a chaotic *clack-clack-clack.*

She is exhilarated by the power she holds over this thing she imagined to have power over her.

When it comes down, she catches it awkwardly – a violent twist of the marionette nicking the little finger on her left hand as it lands.

"Oww! Bitch!" Jo hisses as she puts a little bubble of red to her mouth and sucks. "Where did that come from?"

Her little finger stings and she looks at the doll with fresh eyes. Overcome with a desire for petty revenge, she considers dropping the figurine into the fireplace and being done with it. *But it would be far too much bother to light a fire,* she thinks. No, she will just tuck her away. In the shed in the back garden. *That'll show Mark* – a revenge for that first day when he put her on the bed and freaked her out. *He'll never find her.* She'll tell him she walked out on him!

With mischievous glee, she takes the doll into the shed. Here, she finds a little ice-cream container into which she roughly throws the doll before clipping the lid down with firm fingers. She hides it under the toolbox – a heavy old thing of pressed steel loaded with heavy-duty tools – a lump hammer, a monkey wrench and spanner set.

When it is done, she half runs back to the house with an exultant spring in her step.

*

Half an hour later she takes Mark a cup of tea.

He is in a drowse as she carries it to him. The room is still in darkness and she steps carefully over the tumble of clothes thrown on the floor the previous night. He sits up abruptly, pushing the cup away and spilling it on the bed.

"Something's wrong," he says fiercely. "There's something wrong."

She watches him rush from the room; hears his bare feet thumping on the stairs. After a few seconds an enraged shout bellows from the front room.

He appears back at the doorway, face contorted with rage. She shrinks from him as he roughly takes hold of her shoulders and shouts in her face.

"Where is she? Where is she?!"

Jo freezes. A hole seems to open up beneath her. The solidity of their relationship, their love – everything is falling into the chasm below.

He continues to shout and shake her and she starts to cry. Her emotions whirl inside her – a crowd of spiteful children laughing and smashing the things she loves.

"The shed," she blurts. "In the shed."

He runs from the room and the back door bangs open. Not sure what else to do, she follows him down, treading quietly in a bubble of shock that makes her notice the tiniest sounds in the house, the smallest play of light.

The everydayness of their home strikes her. Little motes of dust dancing in the summer light, the streaks on the rear window left by the previous night's rain, the milk carton with the lid off that she hasn't put back in the fridge (so unlike her). She sees it all in a detached dream, stepping out on to the concrete path from the kitchen door and hearing, at the little garden's far end, crashes coming from the shed. Above it all, her husband-to-be's voice.

"Where are you? Where are you?"

Then his own voice, higher-pitched: "Here. Under the tool box. Here."

The accent he is putting on has the half-formed consonants of the Far East.

"Ah, here you are. Under here."

"I'm safe now. Thank you. Thank you."

A high-pitched sobbing sound comes from the shed.

"I was so afraid, Mark. So afraid!"

Jo has heard enough. She turns on her heel, goes back into the house and gathers a few possessions in the bedroom, pushing – bizarrely – her favourite pair of stiletto shoes and a jumper into a cloth bag. She does it quickly, her breathing a chain of short gasps, tears pushing behind her eyes, the only thought in her mind: *he's losing it. God knows what he'll do.*

She hears him go into the living room and she rushes to dress and find her car keys. She pulls on her flat shoes, picks up her handbag and steps quietly down the stairs, aware that she must pass the living room doorway to get to the front door. *Slowly. Quietly. Don't disturb the nutter.*

It is silent in the house as she steps down. She visualises waves of fury emanating through the door ahead of her. There is a resentful silence more unnerving than his weird display of anger.

At the bottom of the stairs she steps across the living room towards the door and snatches at the handle. It doesn't move.

Still locked from last night. Oh, how stupid!

She scrabbles through her handbag for her key as the living room door quickly opens.

"Jo? Where are you going?"

His face is a mask of gentle composure.

"I need to pick up some breakfast, Mark," she says, clutching her bag tight to her chest as she finally extracts her door key, pushes it in the lock and turns it with a frightened energy.

He looks at her levelly. "And you're taking your stilettos shopping with you?" he says, looking at the heels poking from the shopping bag. He pats the door shut as she tries to open it, then rests his hand on it. "People might call that a little strange."

She takes a breath and considers him for a moment. She is afraid of him, she realises. This calm determination on his face is something she has not seen before. Like he's another man.

She looks over his shoulder. Behind him, the doll is on the table by the armchair, where she found it this morning. God how she hates it now. *That look on its face - it seems to be gloating,* she thinks, wondering how its face can now look so different from the gentle pretty painted one she saw at a car boot sale on a spring day. She shoots him a look of alarm.

"Mark, is she going to fall?" she asks, urgency in her voice. He turns quickly, dismay on his face, arms out ready to catch her – and sees the doll has not moved.

He turns back, an accusation on his face –

But his wife-to-be has slipped out of the door onto the streets of Southsea.

*

Half way up the street, the pressure in her head becomes unbearable. Her face flushes red. She has a tingling in her arm, spreading up from her hand. She raises it to her eyes. With shock she sees it swollen and pulsing with an angry redness. *That tiny little cut! That bubble of blood!* An explosion of nausea pulses through her body in one great quake. She tries to stand, gripped with deep shivers. She rocks on her feet for a second, her head filled with the loud beat of her heart. She doubles up as a spasm seizes her. Gastric acid fills her mouth and nose as vomit gushes from her. In another instant, she has collapsed on the street, the whole of reality disappearing in an onrush of kerbstones and paving slabs.

She feels a hand on her shoulder. Mark says:

"It's okay. We've got you."

*

Mark comes into focus for a moment, standing above her.

"Can you hear me? Yes? Stay with us."

She nods and closes her eyes. Silence takes her.

*

There is a sound in the darkness now. A low hum, it seems, but as she becomes more aware, the hum shatters into its component parts: consonants and shifting vowels. *Words.* Someone is speaking over and over, but she can't understand any of it. The sound continues on, droning through the night. She calls out –

"The radio. Switch off the radio."

The motionless face of a doll floats above her.

A dream, she realises, closing her eyes.

The rhythmic speech drones on in a monotone.

"Please! Turn off the radio."

She opens her eyes again and sees Mark, cold and detached, standing in a white-walled room. She vomits.

Darkness takes her a while. Then a nurse hovers at the end of her bed, a ghost in the darkness.

The nurse transforms into a human-sized doll with wooden-hinged limbs that float as it walks. The figure moves towards her through the night, reaching out a stump to her and rubbing the side of her face affectionately. She feels it and goes cold.

Mark appears beside the doll.

"Are you ready?"

The woman's voice: "Now is the time."

"Very good. Very good."

Jo's eyes close and delirium takes her.

*

After a long, exhausting sleep, she finally wakes to see Mark standing above her.

He is looking at her with interested eyes, reading her face intently, a beam of sunlight striking across the upper half of his face, hiding the rest of his expression in shadow.

"And here you are," he says flatly. "Back with us. Welcome."

Recognition rushes in on her. They are in her front room in Southsea. Instinctively she looks around her.

"The doll. Where is the doll?" she says to him.

He considers her with a straight face.

"You don't need to worry about the doll any more," he says, reassuringly, sitting back on a low chair beside the sofa. "It's all been sorted out. Everything has been tidied up and arranged."

"Arranged?" she asks. "What does that mean? What's been arranged?"

He is about to answer when there is a knock at the door. He looks up with bright welcoming eyes.

"Come in, come in!" he says, excitedly.

The door swings open and a woman walks in, her face hidden from Jo by a silk scarf over her head. She is slight, light of step, dressed in a shimmering orange and black silk dress.

The woman glides to the fireplace and stands by it, the scarf still masking her face. Jo watches her intently, dumbly fascinated as the woman looks around the room, appraising it proprietorially.

Finally, she turns her attention to Jo and pulls off her scarf.

Those fine features! Those kohl-painted eyes, the enigmatic look!

Jo tries to mouth something, but her body does not respond. Tears prickle behind her eyes.

The other woman turns back to the fireplace and looks along the mantle shelf. With a smile she lifts a little jewellery box. Turning toward the bright sunlight, she opens it and holds it up. A sparkling ring glitters in the light; a smile of delight spreads across her face.

Jo feels a flush of anger as she recognises it. *My engagement ring.* She lets out a low weak moan as she sees the other slip it onto her hand.

"A perfect fit!" the woman says with luxurious pleasure as her silks shimmer in the light. "As if it were made for me!"

Jo's eyes go wide in horror. *That hand!*

There is the lurid line of a scar where it has been grafted on to her arm.

The woman looks to Mark. She reaches out to him and clasps the back of his neck, pulling him in for a passionate kiss. When it is done, she looks down at the figure of Jo on the sofa and says to him, "We have a date set, huh, Baba?"

"Yes, my love. It's all going ahead," he answers. "It's been so good, having our little wedding planner do the work for us. I will miss her for that."

The woman in silks looks down at the doll on the sofa. A little marionette of a modern Western woman, exquisitely crafted, its lifeless, painted face set in an expression of frozen horror. One hand is attached to a string. The other, the left hand, is missing.

The woman lifts the painted doll, eyeing it with cold hard eyes before turning to Mark with a carefree air.

"You know, I think it's time we got rid of this. Ugly little thing."

"Do you think we need to... really?" he asks, a hint of guilt briefly crowding his face.

"Well of course we do," she answers sharply. "In case you've forgotten, it was *my* hand you asked for in marriage. Remember?"

THE MYSTERY OF THE MUSTACHIOED MAN

"The fact is, it's gone," said Westwood, dropping the pile of musty old books on his overloaded desk with a dusty thump, puzzlement all over his face. "Disappeared."

"I'm not surprised you can't find it," Grover sniffed, surveying the room through his little round Lennon glasses. "Look at this place!"

Westwood had to concede the point. The bookshop was one giant jumble of volumes. From the tiny 32mos to the full calf folios he affectionately referred to as *tombstones*, stacks of books rose at amazing angles, like crazy tottering architecture. The truth is, his first US edition of Raymond Chandler's *The Long Goodbye* seemed to be appropriately titled. He really might never see it again at this rate.

"You spend too much time thinking about football, and not enough on business..." Grover added.

He fell silent, realising he'd crossed the line. Westwood was not your average rare bookdealer. Few bookdealers stand over six feet tall and are covered from head to foot with tattoos proclaiming a lifelong obsession with Portsmouth Football Club. A man with "Pompey Till I Die" pointillised in two inch tall letters across his chest does not take kindly to being criticised for monomania. This was the strange and remarkable nature of this two-headed beast: he was both a gentleman bookdealer and a wildman of the terraces.

"You can't spend *too much time* on footie," Westwood responded with restrained passion as he eyed his Pompey paraphernalia on the wall, and the football in the big glass case above the door signed by the whole team after their 2008 FA Cup win. Then his eyes alighted on the piles of volumes closing in around his desk. "But you're right about one thing. It could be anywhere. It's weird, though, the way they disappear..."

Westwood felt a supernatural shiver go through him. He didn't mention the strange dreams he'd been having. Nor the nagging feeling he had that a mysterious entity was watching him. For the last few days a mustachioed gentleman in shorts had been materialising just on the edge of his vision and loitering in the vicinity of a box of Sherlock Holmes collectables that had recently manifested in the shop. But whenever he looked straight at the figure, it was gone. Now he shuddered and muttered a single word under his breath:

"Ghosts."

Grover, his betweeded and long-suffering employee, turned his goat-like head and trotted from the room with the bustle of a man getting on with things, while Westwood turned his attention to the prize item that had come from that box: *The Adventures of Sherlock Holmes, 1892, pub by George Newnes, London, Octavo, first edition first state, in fine light blue cloth with black ink design depicting the offices of The Strand Magazine, gilt edged with very minor rubbing to head and heel of spine.* He rehearsed the catalogue entry to himself as he opened the sharp-cornered binding – and his breathing faltered for a heartbeat... *Yes, it was genuine!* There, on the half title page, was a lovely clean signature of Arthur Conan Doyle himself. Westwood inhaled with deep delight and imagined a mystical connection through the years. One of the beauties of bookdealing was just this: feeling close to historical figures who'd long ago slipped in past Saint Peter, the great goalie in the sky. He felt pleased to know that even after all these years, he still had the romance inside him.

It's a treasure, he thought. *A real treasure!*

He eyed the clock. Time was pushing on toward tonight's match. A mid-week FA Cup tie with Pompey at home to Villa, Pompey fielding a new line-up after relegation difficulties, looking to prove they were still on form. *A few bevvies, tonight,* he thought, *and then maybe a few more. Need to get my warpaint on.*

Half an hour later, Westwood was leaving in his three-foot-tall blue and white stovepipe hat, blue wig and stripey pants, drum under one arm, face painted to match his clothes. "Play up Pompey, Pompey play up!" he shouted to the genteel streets of Petersfield, a tin of Stella in his other hand. *Well!* The Hampshire market town didn't quite know what to do with Westwood. *Books and football! Who'd ever heard of such a thing!* Westwood was a modern Renaissance man.

*

Back in the shop the following day, another book had vanished. Before its dematerialisation, it had been a first edition in dustwrapper ("some loss to extremities") of Agatha Christie's *The Secret Adversary*.

- *Her second book! Pretty rare in a wrapper!* Grover stood stiffly beside him as Westwood buried his head in his hands and groaned, partially out of disbelief, and partially due to the steam-hammer battering his head. It had been a famous victory. 2-1, the winning goal cannoned in on the full-time whistle. How they had celebrated! And how he was suffering!

"I'm sure it'll turn up," said Grover.

"No," Westwood growled impatiently. "I left it here, on the desk. I definitely left it here!"

"Let me help you look for it," Grover offered with an air of slight impatience. "And whatever you do, don't lose *that!*" He chided, pointing a bony finger at the signed Conan Doyle Westwood had just lifted down from a shelf.

There's no doubt that if a book wants to hide, its best camouflage is its own kind. Somehow, as Grover and Westwood searched together, Westwood lost track of where he had already looked. What's more, there was something not entirely constructive in the way Grover moved piles of books from one place to another. At one point in the proceedings Westwood was sure he had looked through the same stack three times. After two and a half hours, the book still hadn't surfaced. Westwood's headache was bursting his eyeballs, and he realised he needed some respite from the baton charge going on in his head. But before he went to find it, he eyed the desk where his precious signed Conan Doyle had been sitting.

"Now where's *that* gone?" he bellowed, in near terror.

"What?" Grover turned to him with wide disbelieving eyes. "Surely not the..."

"*My treasure!* Where's it gone?"

Westwood goggled paranoia at the books around him. He suddenly felt afraid of them. Were they circling for the kill?

"Something funny's going on here," he pronounced. "I think we're haunted..."

Grover gazed levelly. "Haunted?" he echoed with a curled lip. "You're not serious."

Crease-browed, his right index finger scratching his temple, Westwood replied: "No. You're right. But whatever it is, I'm calling the Old Bill."

He wobbled on his feet for a moment, then gave a quiet grunt as he contemplated an afternoon of forms and questions: "But beforehand, I've got to have a think. Look after the shop," he ordered, before trudging off to the cool quiet of the packing room and stretching his aching six-foot-long frame on the packing table, switching off the lights and succumbing to the throb behind his eyes.

"Midweek ties," he groaned self-pityingly. There was nothing for it: next time there was a midweeker he would close the shop or get someone to cover next day. There was no way he would miss a match, despite the more snooty end of genteel Petersfield *tutting* at his passion.

Lying in the dark among the wrapping paper and parcel tape, Westwood nodded off and began to dream. In the dream, a benign gentleman from another era ran across a football pitch towards him. He was mustachioed, had a shock of red hair, and gave a *hail-fellow-well-met* smile before speaking in a Scottish accent that seemed to echo down a well of time. "Westwood, catch! Catch him!" And he hurled a heavy old brown leather football in his direction that thumped into his guts with a jarring crunch.

He woke up with a start to realise he'd rolled off the packing table and was lying on the floor. His headache was gone. Then he heard a *thump*, a shout, and a heavy scuffle from the shop.

Bleary-eyed, he trotted past Topography and Children's, out to his desk, to discover Grover sprawled half-conscious, clutching the handle of a battered leather case, catches now sprung, contents spilled on the floor. Westwood noted *The Secret Adversary, The Long Goodbye, The Adventures of Sherlock Holmes* and a dozen other crime classics, strewn around him. Grover was groaning.

"You didn't have to hit me, you know," he sat up, rubbing the back of his head. "I've always loved books as much as you love fooball," he whined. "I thought I'd just – er – *borrow* these a while – no harm done. But you throwing *that* at me – that's assault, that is! Ooh!" he moaned, and pointed to the offensive weapon.

"I never threw nothing," Westwood rejoindered, following Grover's finger and seeing his precious signed football snuggled against a bookshelf on the far side of the room. Someone had taken it from its glass case and thrown it at Grover as he'd tried to make his getaway. Thrown it with such strength it had half knocked him out.

"Well who did, then?" Grover purpled, indignantly.

Westwood scanned the room and seemed, again, to sense someone watching him, somewhere in the vicinity of that box of Holmes paraphernalia. He walked over to it, and fished out a framed sepia photograph of Sir Arthur Conan Doyle crouching on a football pitch. A caption read:

As a young man, Conan Doyle lived in Southsea. Beside his work as a doctor and a writer, he also played as goalkeeper for Portsmouth Association Football Club.

Westwood recognised the face and the ancient sports kit instantly. *The mustachioed footballer* from his dream! Could it really be that their shared passion for the Beautiful Game had united them across the gulf of time, of space – of death itself! Was it *really* possible?

Westwood imagined the cool voice of a Victorian sleuth speaking in his ear: "When you have eliminated the impossible, whatever remains, however improbable, must be the truth..."

He returned the photograph to the box, and turned to Grover.

"I know who threw it..." repeated Westwood, feeling sudden gratitude to the spirit of Sir Arthur Conan Doyle.

"Who, then?"

Westwood tapped the side of his nose in a knowing way.

"It's elementary, dear Grover... Elementary!"

THE CASE OF THE SERBIAN DWARF POISONER

"Observe the way in which the victim is holding the napkin, Jenkins," said The Legend, drawing on his meerschaum as they stood over a corpse that lay sprawled in a grime-filled alley half-lit by the lambent glow of gaslight. "What does it tell you?"

Sergeant Jenkins turned his dull brown eyes toward his senior officer, his internal blankness seeping out across his face.

"That he wanted to wipe his mouth, Sir?" said the other, sighing. He was painfully aware of being in the presence of Portsmouth Constabulary's finest. A man of infinite imagination, who knew exactly how to piece together the evidence to create what he valued most: The Incriminating Narrative.

The Legend smiled superciliously as he peered at the napkin.

"Really Jenkins, have you learned nothing from your time with me?" he asked in that superior way, adding insult to injury by poking him rhythmically in the chest with his pipe-stalk in time with his words. "Here we stand at the start of the 20th Century, and still your mind remains unreceptive to the sensitivities of my Narrative Method."

The skin around Sergeant Jenkins's eyes turned puce as he considered those final words uneasily.

The Narrative Method,

With it, The Legend claimed to have solved the most baffling crimes. For example, The Case of the Disappearing Dockyard Donkey.

That had been last year. The creature in question had just been loaded with the paymaster's strongbox, prior to disbursement to the crew of newly docked *HMS Connaught*, when it had disappeared without trace.

The Legend had demonstrated, through the construction of an elaborate narrative, that its disappearance had been initiated by a gentleman with a hare lip, angered at his rejection by society. This hare-lipped gentleman had arranged a meeting with a one-legged red-haired Russian, the pair concocting a plan that had somehow involved the Donkey's abduction and theft of the funds held in the strongbox. In fact, The Legend had insisted, the loss of the strongbox was a diversion. Their true interest had been in the donkey...

"Or something," Sergeant Jenkins thought, his brow creasing to a distressed furrow as he tried to remember the tortuous narrative The Legend had devised to explain the Dockyard Donkey's Disappearance.

The case had caused a sensation in the *Portsmouth Times,* and The Legend had taken great pleasure in declaring to its editor his famous dictum:

"The Narrative Method is that by which the investigator weaves strands of gossamer to produce a web in which the villain is captured more surely than any spider apprehends its fly."

The hare-lipped Donkey thief and Russian monopod had spirited the creature away at night by hot air balloon, The Legend had explained. Enquiries through his secret network of urchins/helpers showed the co-conspirators to be living beyond the British Empire's jurisdiction, somewhere in Northern France. The Donkey's whereabouts and the nefarious uses it had been put to remained a mystery.

The case had filled many a column-inch and many an advertiser had advertised because of it. Indeed the Paymaster had become something of a minor celebrity as the victim of such a bizarre crime. So, when a few weeks later, Sergeant Jenkins spotted the submerged undersides of four hooves pointed at the sky, and beneath that the bloated corpse of a donkey, right near to where the Disappearing Donkey had vanished, it was declared by all parties concerned that this donkey was not *the* Donkey, but another donkey – in fact, an Appeared one.

Investigation had shown that *this* donkey had most likely fallen off the wharf in the night. The fact that there was no strongbox in sight was further evidence of it being "a completely different and unrelated donkey", as the Paymaster pointed out with a somewhat panicked look.

"Upon a barrowload of bibles, I've never seen *that* donkey before in my life," the Paymaster declared with the fervour of one perhaps apprehensive at losing not only his credibility but his Liberty. "I never tied the strongbox on *that* donkey's back, not never," he added, which raised all sorts of further questions.

In the ensuing moment in which suspicion took wing and neatly alighted on the Paymaster's shoulder like the heavy hand of the law, The Legend had stepped in, looking down at the inverted creature in the murky depths.

"This definitely isn't *the* Donkey. *Obviously*," The Legend pronounced, his superior tone quelling all dissent, and giving the Paymaster a reassuring nod. "Observe the shape of the hooves..." he began, at which point Sergeant Jenkins went into something of a daydream.

So, with the solving of one mystery – that of the Disappearing Donkey – another was born. Not that The Legend was remotely interested in it. The Appeared Donkey's manifestation remained an unsolved mystery. The very afternoon of its discovery, The Legend refused to investigate. After leaving the Paymaster's premises and putting down a deposit on a new house in the smarter end of town, he told Jenkins:

"*Disappearances,* these are matters for the force, Jenkins. But what is one to do with *appearances?*"

"Keep them up, Sir?" Jenkins had replied with rare wit, only to receive a glare of disapproval from The Legend, who nonetheless later that day used the very same line with the Lord Mayor, to much hilarity.

Now, standing in the alleyway over the body, Sergeant Jenkins huffed as he remembered the Donkey case. With a sinking feeling, he realised he was going to be forced to have another crack at the Narrative Method, which he always seemed to get wrong.

He suspected this was because his own father had been a man of little imagination.

"You've read one book, you've read them all," the Old Man had once told him.

Taking him at his word, Jenkins had decided to read them all; Charles Dickens's *Hard Times* being the one he chose. Gradgrind, that humourless individual who knew the danger of imagination was the character he most identified with.

Asked his opinion of Dickens's book by The Legend, Jenkins had replied: "Mercifully short, Sir." At the same time, he was pleased he had mastered all of English Literature in such a brief span.

As he was bid, Jenkins stepped up to the body and studied closely the napkin it still clutched. There was a crumb upon it, and a little smear of grease, along with the faint smell of stale beer.

He looked along the street. The body was not three hundred yards from The Mystery – a public house of dubious reputation. There was a deep dent in the top of the man's skull where someone had stoved in his brains.

In a flash, he saw a sequence of images moving in his mind like a play. Was this the elusive Narrative Method The Legend so oft quoted? He decided to unfold his story to The Legend and see what he thought.

"Well, the way I see it, Sir... um... bear with me," he straightened and cleared his throat. "H-hm. The unidentified man having had a beer and perhaps..." He knelt again and sniffed at the man's greasy fingers. "Perhaps a lamb chop smothered in gravy, wandered out here in the night, where he was set upon by an assailant or assailants unknown, using –" he leapt across the path to a pile of discarded newspapers in a corner of the alley and drawing a pen from out of his pocket, inserted it into the neck of a heavy stoneware bottle protruding from the pile. He lifted it victoriously. On one side it was spattered with a crusted, sticky substance darkening to black, but still showing its original colour – blood red. "Yes – using this empty blood-smeared ginger beer bottle as a weapon, Sir!" Jenkins announced, with genuine pride. "Now, Sir, how's that?".

"Excellent. Excellent, Jenkins," he said with a flat, ironic tone, then followed his words with a slow hand clap. Jenkins stiffened. Were the slappings of those bony palms not enough to go on, the tone of voice told him what was coming next. It was the tone that preceded the one word he found the most infuriating whenever it issued from The Legend's lips. That word was –

"*However* – there are one or two things you appear to have overlooked."

"Sir?" said the Sergeant, a sinking feeling taking hold of him again. "Really Sir?"

"Indeed. You will recall, Jenkins, that I asked you to inspect the napkin still clasped in the dead man's hands. You will notice by the way it is folded that it was prepared for the table by a left-handed person. I wrote a monogram on the folding of napkins by left-handed people, and this fold conforms exactly to the Belgrade Variation. Furthermore, the angle at which pressure was applied to the napkin and the nature of the fold reveals a person of diminutive stature."

"Diminutive stature, Sir?"

"Correct, Jenkins. Now observe the twisted lip this man has developed. A sure sign of snake venom. The man who poisoned the unfortunate victim used a venom drawn from the fangs of the krait, perhaps the world's most deadly of snakes, revealing that the murderer has spent years in the subcontinent of India. In sum, we are seeking a left-handed travelling

Serbian dwarf well versed in the art of poisoning. I believe that if you search the local hostelries –" he broke off for a moment, perplexed by Jenkins's behaviour. "By the way, what are you doing with that bottle?"

Jenkins was carefully wrapping the stoneware bottle in a sheet of waxed paper he had drawn from his pocket.

"Keeping it as a reminder, Sir," he replied. "Of your brilliance, Sir."

"Ah, very good," replied The Legend. "Because I can assure you, it has nothing to do with this case," he added, blithely ignoring the dent in the corpse's cranium.

"By the way, you don't think that asking the police to find a well-travelled Serbian dwarf with a pet snake might be a bit of a tall order, Sir? If you will excuse the pun?"

The Legend was about to answer when, to Jenkins's surprise, a short man in a wide-sleeved shirt and baggy trousers distinctly reminiscent of the style worn in Eastern Europe emerged from a boarding house nearby. In his hand he held a small wooden cage from which a hissing sound proceeded.

"Seize him Jenkins!"

Called to act, Jenkins never let the Constabulary down. He leapt towards the Serbian with truncheon drawn, only to find that The Legend had done exactly the same. A struggle ensued, in which Jenkins and The Legend sought to disentangle themselves from each other. In the mean time, the sawn-off Serb made his getaway, through the dark and noisome streets of Old Portsmouth.

Jenkins was still ready to fly after the fugitive, but The Legend dulled his keenness with an angry look, poking him violently in the ribs with his pipe stalk.

"It's no good Sergeant, Serbian dwarves are renowned for their fleetness of foot! By this time he'll be halfway to Timbuktu. – And damn it, my pipe has broken!" – he added as the stalk cracked under the repeated impact with the Sergeant's ribcage.

"Very good, Sir."

The Legend threw the pipe on the ground and glared imperiously at Jenkins.

"All that remains is for you to contact the newspapers to describe how I have solved yet another case –"

"– And how yet another villain has got away, Sir," Jenkins said with narrowed eyes, a shade of puce once again around them.

"Well, we can't get them every time." The Legend answered.

"Just once would be gratifying," Jenkins muttered under his breath as he stooped to lift something from the ground.

*

Several weeks later, in response to a knock at his door, The Legend called "Enter," in his imperious way. He was not surprised to see Sergeant Jenkins standing in the doorway, as he had done countless times before. He was holding a sheet of paper.

"Sir, I wonder if you would take a look at this."

Two large images filled with lines and whorls could be seen on the sheet.

"What is this?" The Legend asked, impatiently.

"New information, Sir," Jenkins replied. "Regarding the Case of the Left Handed Serbian Dwarf Poisoner. Not that he poisoned dwarves, you understand, Sir."

"Well, what are these?"

"Fingerprints, Sir," replied Jenkins with a flat, respectful voice. In reply to The Legend's questioning look, he explained: "Impressions left by the hands on the objects they touch, Sir. A new method of identification used to track down criminals. Have you not heard of it?"

"I have not."

"I thought not, Sir. What with you concentrating so much on the Narrative Method. Fingerprints are proving most effective in tracking down villains. Because you see, Sir, everybody's fingerprint is unique."

The Legend's eyes bulged as his Sergeant went on: "So, for example, Sir, were one to test for fingerprints an object one knows a person has held, and compare those fingerprints with a piece of evidence an unknown felon has held, one could safely deduce that if those prints were the same, then the people who held both objects were in point of fact one and the same person, too."

"Very interesting, Jenkins, but –"

Jenkins cut him off with an impatient, raised hand.

"It appears, Sir, that the person who held the ginger beer bottle we found at the scene, which a pathologist has confirmed fits exactly into the depression in the skull of our deceased man, was the same person who held the pipe you so petulantly – not wishing to be rude to you, Sir – threw on the floor at the murder scene. Do you remember, Sir? That was after poking me in the ribs with it, Sir. Quite a lot," he gazed in an offended way at The Legend for a half second. "In fact, Sir, it would seem that you and the murderous bottle-wielder share an identity," he continued as The Legend's eyes grew wide in realisation and his jaw dropped. "*Your identity, Sir, that is,*" Sergeant Jenkins added, in explanation.

"Enquiries reveal that a small foreign herpetologist witnessed you smashing the poor drunken victim over the head in a fit of rage. And further enquiries reveal that the victim is none other than the cousin of the Dockyard's Paymaster and that he, neighbours inform me, claimed to have some information about you and the missing strongbox in the Disappearing Donkey case."

"Jenkins, that case was closed long ago –" The Legend began, but Sergeant Jenkins raised his voice a little and ploughed on undeterred:

"I haven't quite finished yet, Sir. You see, in the light of his own cousin being murdered after he tried to blackmail your good self for your involvement in covering up the strongbox theft, the Paymaster has confessed that you shared the loot from that little job, Sir. There were no men with twisted lips involved. No Russians, nor donkey-lifting hot air balloons to northern France.

"Nonsense. You saw the Serb run – a sure sign of guilt –" The Legend countered, but Sergeant Jenkins cut him off.

"True. But I found and spoke with him. In fact, he is our key witness. It turns out he ran for it when he saw you because he realised you were a police officer and would try, as criminal parlance has it, Sir, to *fit him up*. That is why he scarpered, Sir. A sign of guilt, Sir? Definitely. But not his."

Sergeant Jenkins paused for a moment and drew himself to his full though inconsiderable height, as The Legend stood frozen behind his leather-covered desk.

"I am beginning to realise after years under your brilliant tuition, Sir, that murder does not usually happen because of a great narrative, as writers in Penny Dreadfuls will have us believe. No, Sir, quite the opposite. In most cases, murder is devoid of imagination. That's why I am going to call my new approach to crime, Sir, The Gradgrind Method. In deference to you Sir, and your wonderful stories."

"Oh, and by the way, Sir. You are under arrest," added the Sergeant with a degree of satisfaction. "For theft and for murder... Sir."

THE BOILER POOL

- You're coming tonight, John! Do you have any idea how much that tux cost?-

She is glaring at him from the mirror, with a look that won't be denied. He opens his mouth to argue back, but at that moment another face appears, a fleeting vision, superimposed over hers in the glass. A wave of heat rushes through his body and he drops his tumbler on the tiles with a thud. Spirit of whisky strong in his nose.

- Not you! - he mutters.

He looks down at the shattered pieces, then apprehensively back to the mirror. He exhales when he realises the vision has gone, feeling slightly sick in his stomach. She is glaring half an accusation and half a question, her right eyebrow up, her make-up brush poised over her right cheek.

- What the f -

He kneels to gather the fragments, lifting them clumsily into a cupped hand, then rises and turns to catch his breath in the next room.

- I - I'm sorry -

Her eyes needle his retreating back.

- I should think so - she calls after him, then shrugs, repowders her brush, tilts her head left and forward, and refocuses on her face in the mirror.

In the living room he tips the shards in a wastebasket. They jangle as they fall.

- My nerves, he thinks.

He places a foam barrel between his lips and cups a flame in a flick – *that should do it.* He presses his forehead against the pane and views the city shimmering on the glass's far side behind a film of greasy rain. He tells himself:

- Down there they're greening the beer -

Between steel valleys, shamrocks edged on white foam, trad music played by fourth generation immigrants, tricolours at every corner –

- Saint Patrick's Day! -

A circle of panic clouds the glass and evaporates.

- Someone else's celebration in someone else's country. It's all bullshit. I'm English - none of this - bogtrotting Mick bollocks. English. -

Reflected in the window on his left, he distractedly watches a tv clip of NASA astronauts hanging weightlessly in a weightless room. Another mist circle ghosts away in the conditioned air.

- A glitzy dinner. Bankers or something. I mean - why not go? -

Then, as he imagines the smiles and the questions, and the looks of puzzlement from these people he has nothing in common with:

- God. How did I get here? -

In answer, the presence he saw in the mirror presses closer. It is right here, in his head. Growing in power. Strong enough to reveal itself –

- What! -

In the window's reflection a figure moves behind his shoulder. He sees her clearly. A grim-faced woman with a hard mouth and disillusioned eyes. He freezes as she speaks:

- John. -

Home. She calls to him from –

- No! -

A panic lifts through his body and he tries to focus on something – anything – solid. He pictures the woman in the next room – considers the minute powder strokes of the brush against her skin and imagines her breathing huddle asleep in the morning light. But reality is altering its register and the room wavers like his resolve. Her perfume is overwhelmed by a smell – a tang he recognises –

- The sea. The sea..! -

He tenses as if to call to the woman in the room next door – but an old habit checks his action and he reaches for the bottle. Whiskey will save him – stifle the panic – send the old witch to sleep. But before he lips the neck, the room has gone.

*

He is alone in the place where the boiler pool ripples on the sandbanks. He eyes the clarity of the water where red seaweed – the hair of the drowned – torches the brine, growing from the rusting cranium of the dumped ship's boiler. A tiny sea where bigger morsels eat lesser morsels.

He squats at its edge, looking down, tracing with his eyes the scoop the tides have formed around the metal, feeling his foot sink a little more in the sand. He prods with a gull's feather the muzzle of a marooned eel waiting for the tide. It lunges with murder in its jaws, and he recoils with excited joy.

The pool is his pool and his alone. None can come here without his say-so. Its rippling edges mark the boundaries of his private kingdom.

A cloud passes over the sun. He looks ahead, shivers and looks down again. His mother's eyes are glaring at him from beneath the surface of the water. He feels a shock, and drops the feather. From her face he knows he has been found out –

– John! You little git! –

He flushes red with fear and anger. *She should not be here!* The pool is his moat. Standing to face her, he knows she will not understand how she is barred – is oblivious to the secret laws passed against trespassers. He knows suddenly that she is inescapable.

She towers over him, pushing her hard finger at him in time with her speech.

– You will never do that to your father again. Never. –

The bruise ripening near her left eye tells him all he needs to know of her latest conversation with – Dad.

– I will, too! –

– Don't answer back! –

Her hand lashes his face. There is a shared moment of perfect statuary. In the line of the cut in his mouth's soft interior, John tastes his escape. He spits blood at her – and starts running –

– John! Come back. John. Please! –

Along the shoreline near the Ferryboat Inn he seeks sanctuary. There is a little hut, here, nestling by the car park, and an old motorhome that was parked there when the rocks were first made. The pain in his mouth transforms into defiance.

But he falters a moment. His solitude frightens him, and he frets beneath the oppressive summer heat on the jetty's hot gangway, secretly wishing for a friend, and swinging on the railing, feeling the metal quiver beneath him as he hooks his hands over it and, bends his legs, swinging his body down and up again, not knowing what to do with the energy inside.

He looks across the harbour and senses invisible ushers quelling every voice in the world. Something is rushing to fill the void. *Tat-at-at.* John turns to face him. There he is. The Old Man. *- Of course - Tony -* he won't let John down. He knocks his pipe again three times and, with the world's attention, finally speaks –

- Not a cloud, eh, John - the Old Man mutters with a casual sigh. The boy scans the eyeblue horizon above the lowlands of the island city across the water, and the hills to the north. It is enough for John that it is true. His defiance melts again into what it was before – a will to love and never be let down.

John tells the Old Man of the argument with his mother and how he'll have to go to the priest for forgiveness. The Old Man listens attentively, nodding thoughtfully.

- That's the way you Micks organise it, is it, lad? - he says *- Your mum's dad being Irish? That's a long way back, though don't you reckon? For your mum to be loadin' her dad's stuff on you? -*

In the silence that follows, John thinks how many times before he's slipped away to be with Tony. From Tony sipping on whiskey he first heard the names of the heroes Dick Turpin and Biggles and King Arffur. But now, with this break from his mum, these tales seem more important than before. They are his past newly revealed – his history. He needs them because they tell him he came from somewhere other than his mother's skirts.

Tony sits back, sucking on his empty pipe, then says –

- It's not so bad, John. I'll tell you what I'll do. I'll tell you a tale. Now, this is the true history of England -

John smiles at the onset of a new tale. He drinks the air with heady pleasure and closes his eyes. What will happen? Will Robin Hood shoot an arrow into a seagull right above that very jetty? Will the Old Bill turn up and nick old Robin for stuffing up the wildlife? Or perhaps a forest of masts sent by a French King will sprout in the Solent – awaiting destruction from Henry the Eighth, who would cut all their heads off, as if those Frenchies were his wives or something.

Often Tony places himself into his adventures. New tales spring up. They take time. *Our roving hero* interrupting his flow with long pauses in which he lips Bell's Whiskey and gazes into the bottle.

- Ah, my poor memory. -

At those times, the neck is consulted further, while John waits for the spirit to rise. Last man off the Titanic, first man in India, Tony's bottle is an unending fountain. Nearly.

When it runs dry he goes silent, gazing hostility at the burnished sea as the water drains out of the harbour. Today, despite his promise, a tale is not forthcoming. It is a bad day. Real ghosts of his own are pushing in. An anniversary has brought them all back. The Malay Crisis. A Royal Marine in the jungles of Burma. Dayaks who eat human flesh. The images are there, before his eyes.

After the too-long pause following his announcement, Tony instead pronounces on what the boy has told him:

- *You may have done wrong, or you may not. But why confess to that old magpie? You're sorry for what you did, incha? -*

Tony grows angry, his red face tingeing the roots of his white beard, while John bows his head, as if in prayer.

Tony presses again, and taps John's arm below his shoulder:

- *Incha? -*

- *Yes -* John blushes at the confidence and raises his arm to push the hand away.

- *Well there it is. You don't have to tell him. I have - what d'ya ma-call it? Absolved you, that's it -*

- *Thank you -* he wonders - were anyone to find out - how many extra Hail Marys this qualifies him for?

- *Priests don't know nothing -*

Tony is right. Despite being told many times he has one, John has never seen a soul - nor does he feel his own to be in danger.

- *What do they mean - 'I will make you a fisher of men'? Think about that! What do I do with a fish when he's caught, eh John? Lay him on a slab and cut out his guts! -*

John thinks of a mass of shining life twisting against nylon, of eyes frozen in ice. - *Laid on a slab? -* he repeats with a thrill. He looks out to sea with new horror.

Tony stares once more into his bottle. The air grows hotter and stiller, as if the whole day is held beneath a magnifying glass. Finally, he speaks again:

- *This is my Word -* he raises the bottle and as it arcs in the light it transforms into a crucible of gold. Both John and Tony look at it in wonder. Then Tony places it jealously in the cool shadow of a mooring stone, and searches once more for a story to tell. But the Word has gone from him. The smell of the jungle is too close today. He turns to John, shrunken, a man able only to crew a ship in a bottle.

- *Leave me a while, will you boy? -*

John feels the sinking in his guts. Is Tony going to let him down, too? But no – the Old Man sees his face drop and says:

– *Come back tomorrow – whenever you like.* –

At a loss, the boy makes his way along the beach towards the tumbledown terrace on the common. His family lives in a flat there – faded Victorian splendour of a seaside town. The fact is, Tony *has* let him down. It's all right, him saying what he was saying about the Church and all that. But he doesn't have any stories for him today. So maybe, maybe there is something good to be had from the Magpie. He will go and see, he decides, changing his course. Because he is feeling alone today, more than he ever has before.

*

– *Forgive me Father for I have sinned* – he rehearses as he approaches the mirthless Anglo-Catholic red-brick pile up Manor Road, past the holiday home showroom on the right and the little faceless housing estate on the left. After the formulaic response – his explanation:

– *I stole my father's Sports Mail and cast today's fixtures on the water* –

He sees again pink sheets at the bottom of the pool, scanned by uncomprehending crabs. Then he hears the echoing silence of the cool church and the priest's low voice sounding through the curves of the Confessional grill.

– *And why did you do this thing?* –

The voice reassuringly calming and kind.

– *To float paper boats* –

He blinks at the sombre confines of his box. A coffin reminding him to bare his bones even before his death. The Father's judgement pours gently through the grill and acts on him like honey. And John thinks he will drown in the glory of God's mercy (which endureth forever):

– *My son, you are forgiven. For though you took the paper without your father's consent, gambling is nonetheless frowned upon by the Holy Roman Church. In this matter I believe you were an instrument of the Lord* –

In the cool air of the belltower's shadow John emerges from this daydream of the confession to come. Dawdling with hands in pockets, he scuffs his shoes against the knees of an angel. Yes, the red-eyed priest must be faced.

He wets his fingers in the stoup by the door, where he imagines ghostly fish must slide, and creeps beneath the uncomprehending gazes of plaster saints into the church's dark womb.

Before a white statue of an agonised Christ, Father O'Brien is leaning over another figure, their heads held low and close together. Silent. The two are silent. The shape of the head, the shoulders, he recognises and he is frozen for a moment as he watches the two of them.

– I can't take much more of it – the woman says. *– It's all getting too much. –*

The father, putting his hands on her shoulder, bends closer than he needs to. But John doesn't understand that. All he knows is that their heads are close for a while longer, and somehow, his face hovers near her neck. She holds her head there, her eyes closed, raising it and dropping it again, slowly, with a gentle, holy ecstasy.

– I can't even stand the sight of my own son, he looks so much like him – she says.

Then she turns as she senses someone watching, and her eyes light on him for a second. At his haloed head shining in the stained glass light, her dreamy eyes suddenly grow wide.

The priest senses the tension and turns in fear of discovery, his eyes adjusting slowly to the haloed apparition.

– John! – she says.

The priest's focus returns from an imagined future to the real present. His face reddens.

– You! You! – he sputters, rage and shame fired involuntarily from him at the sight of this woman's child *– when he was so close –*

John feels a tumult of bewilderment. The saints frown as he runs past them pushes against the heavy door, and heads out, out into the light of the real day –

He has done something wrong. He doesn't know what it is, but he has done something, somehow. He will never confess again. Tony. Tony was right.

By the time his mother is at the door calling him back, John is far out of earshot. He has nowhere to go, and finds himself skulking angrily in the fields behind West Lane, looking across at the duskbound lights of Portsmouth on the far side of the harbour. Then, night begins to fall properly. Gold lights shine out through the windows against a darkening blue night, and he makes his way slowly home.

When he arrives at the plastic tidiness of his mother's tired kitchen, her fat neighbour from the ground floor, Sylvie Budden, inspects him through thick lenses as if he is an insect.

– He always was a bit wild – She says, in response to news of his angry declaration that he will not go to church again *– He gets that from his father*

- she adds, landing her good friend no reproach, but inwardly wondering why his mother isn't putting her foot down as she always has done in the past. She seems to have shifted in the last few hours – a new pattern – a cycle of simply complaining helplessly about the boy. Like she does about his dad.

- *And can you believe his latest trick? – Not wanting to go fishing down the beach with his father! It's an all-nighter, and John was going to go down there. Now, all at once, he refuses. He'll feel his belt tomorrow, I promise you – when –when – Jim gets in –*

His mother speaks with undisguised relief. John feels an unbridgeable chasm opening between them. She is no longer acting to protect him with her soft body. She is calculating how – after spending his fury on the boy – Dad's drinker's paws will be all worn out for her. John hates her.

Sylvie casts pitying eyes on the tiddler shrinking before her.

- *Is this right, John? Is this true what your mother tells me? –*

- *Yes, but –*

An alien intelligence moves behind her glasses – an intelligence John feels it is impossible to communicate with. What can he tell her? He can't tell her anything because she would never understand. He doesn't understand himself.

He gulps the viscous air, and sways under her suffocating gaze. He senses machinery turning in her mind like a factory, and from somewhere a curly-haired girl is produced, as if Sylvie Budden has manufactured her afresh.

- *And how are you going to provide for young Sally here, if you aren't a good boy? –* she tries to cajole from kindness – for his own sake. She knows they are friends. Like a brother and a sister, she sometimes says. John digs his heels in. He won't be landed – no – not without a struggle...

*

...The image melts and releases the man from his boyhood awhile. Three hundred metres above Manhattan's streets, the rememberer stubs a dogend in a silverplated ashtray and nods fresh understanding of the boy's resolve. It was only one thing – independence – he craved. He had raised that standard in opposition to all invading forces like King Henry had done at Southsea Castle. He would enlist the help of any forces willing to resist. Tony had shown him a way of succeeding: through invention. He recalls his never-ending series of constructions on this American shore – life after life. But he remembers from the time he was in LA years back how even skyscrapers can topple in a moment – how solid earth can liquefy when subterranean forces are freed. Now – again – he feels his life unravelling around him, ripping like fishing nets snagged on rocks. The rival shoals of panic and relief spilling back into the sea.

    – *To be free we must be ruthless* – he mutters, as the mnemonic spirit descends once more. – *We have to cut our lines* –

*

This time the spirit coming to him is not his old mum as before, and knowing this, John does not fight it as it moves over the face of the waters. Up, up it rises above the iron jetty from where it finally escaped. It hovers over the boy who – at fifteen years old – is so nearly a man. Old Tony has gasped his last story, the hunted man finally captured by insurgents in the tropical night –

*

Night closes in on Tony's funeral day with a long grating rumble of thunder, as if something heavy is sliding in place overhead. The night is dark, and the rain rattles in pools on the summer-baked roads. Standing in the downpour, John mutters half to himself as he raises his hand to wipe his eye –

    – *Here's to you, Tony! Can't believe you're gone* –

Tony's bottle is his at last. It will give John his freedom, as it gave Tony his. He shivers on the jetty – dazed – confused by the rising whiskey nausea. He remembers how the sky had seemed a blue bowl on uncounted summer afternoons. He remembers how, when he had sat next to Old Tony it seemed he'd grasped the infinite – glimpsed something beyond the dull lives of ordinary men – a *real* infinite beyond the knowledge of priests. But suddenly, while sitting in the silence of the industrially efficient crematorium, he realised the mystery was closed. How to reopen it?

    Tony had lived and died in the old motorhome by the sea. Into it, John had stolen in the night and taken the crucible. Even as he did so, the clouds boiled above the jetty like a failed chemistry experiment in a giant classroom. He waited – if he waited and watched – perhaps they might part to reveal Old Tony's truths –

    But no. Half a bottle later he is just woozy and sick. Without thought and only misery like dull metal in his body he treads his way along the shore toward Sally's place, clutching the bottle of *Bell's* like a baby. A knock on her window he doesn't know why. Perhaps – perhaps – it is – assurance he wants –

    But when she answers and he looks into her face, he sees the images he hates rise before him. He, a night angler standing fishing just where his father always fishes throwing his line in the water while the moon's cold eye pins him to the earth. He imagines himself soaring on gull's wings, smashing the glass bowl of the horizon and letting whatever might be beyond come flooding in –

Sally is at the window, hunched against the night.

– *What is it, John?* – she asks, with a gentle voice.

Her soft smile – the smile of his mother in the sunlight when he was young. He tenses. He *mustn't* believe... Love, love is a weakness. He *mustn't* trust her. Only Tony could be relied on – *and now even he...!* – He smashes the bottle against the wall with a yell of grief. He wants revenge for this death – another betrayal.

– *John* –

He looks at her, realising how small she is compared to him. How, if he wished, he could swallow her in one gulp, like the eels he has seen caught in the boiler pool swallowing passing fry. The urge is strong – to take her face in his hands – to kiss her, and in that kiss, to end the thousand natural rhythms of a living breathing body. To exact some retribution on a fickle existence. A fatal power courses through his hands – a Judas kiss – the desire to crush her windpipe, snap her neck with a single twist like he's seen in films –

– *I want to, I want to* –

She leans forward to him, seeing him reach out to her –

– *Yes?* –

– *I want to* – he touches her neck with a shaking hand.

She leans to him willingly. His fingers caress the soft flesh of her throat. She sighs with an excited breath –

– *John* –

His fingers find their strength. His palm presses her skin as his fingers contract. She struggles, but not enough to break free. He imagines: *She wants this – trusts me – wants my touch.* She is choking a little as he pulls her face towards him and presses his own on hers. He panics in sympathy as he feels the panic rise in her – feels her fight to breathe grow increasingly desperate. She drives her weakening fists uselessly against his shoulders. He dimly senses her knuckles bruise themselves on his skull in ever-lessening impacts. He kisses her, breathless with excitement at the power he has found –

–

– !

– *What was that – smash?* –

Dad Budden is moving toward the window. John lets her go. Her teenage legs buckle slightly, and straighten. She puts a confused hand over her neck to conceal from her father the bruise darkening there. He is at the window, squinting into the dark –

– *Are you all right, boy?* –

Sally partially turns to her father and hoarsely says – *We're fine, dad* –

Dad looks at him.

– *It's raining. Do you want to come in, John?* –

– *No, no thankyou Mister Budden* –

The old man cautions with his eyes.

– *Take it easy, son* –

– *Yes Mister Budden* –

Mr Budden is gone. Sally blinks her innocence.

– *John, what was that – kiss – I don't underst –? –*

He feels sick. The energy goes from him. He supposes it was the Bell's.

– *Just forget it* –

– *John* –

Not for the last time he turns from her. He starts to run, to escape that maddening call – or escape his need for it. But a need is a need and will always rise again. And here, on this American shore, there were bound to be other drunken nights.

Other women: did they escape so lightly? Unbidden, a blurry memory rises before him – a trailer park in Missouri. An image of a killer standing over a twitching body by a compact gas stove – a gash with a spirit bottle – a pool of blood – fumbling in the night with matches and the gas line – the evidence burning. Suddenly the memory lifts itself into his consciousness and he seems to recognise – someone – is it himself – is it? – Or is it just the reflection of a bad movie in the window?

*

– *John! Will you put that Tuxedo on?* –

Her voice bursts the bubble. The silt settles again – but the pattern is eternally preserved beneath the smothering sediment.

– *Yes, my eye's apple* – he mutters, mimicking a line in a film he saw once.

Manhattan. The latest city, the latest woman in a never-ending line of reinvention. How long has he run? Nausea and fatigue electrify his body and he sweats at the sound of that sweet voice he told himself a few months back he loved. The soft trap of her body.

– *The Ambassador will be there. We've got to wow him. And can you believe it – a bishop from England? Your homeland, John!* –

John's eyes widen – shocked white pearls.

– A priest? –

– A bishop, John. High power stuff. Why – he'd probably hear you confess! –

He wheels on her in anger – *I'm English. Don't you kikes get it? We don't do confession. Left-footer crap. Anyway, what have I got to confess? –*

He moves towards her – his hands tense – he eyes her neck and she pulls back instinctively –

– Excuse me!? Did you just call me a 'kike'?! Sometimes I can't tell with you English what's deliberate, what's ironic – and what's just – you know – two languages. But don't you ever call me that again! Never –

He freezes as he sees the anger in her face flash out at him, grounding him again.

She takes hold of herself as she sees his response. The power play, it excites her. *And he is kinda cute.* She can't help herself, stops and smiles. *He's handsome. That's why it's so easy to forgive him. Even if he is looking worn at the edges.*

– Anyway, John, we'll wow them all –

He stops and takes a breath.

– Wow –

– What's with you? –

She walks behind him and kisses him on the nape of the neck, like she did that first time in a bar in Manhattan a year ago – after he'd drunkenly said to her – *the grass growing beneath my feet makes them itch* – and then he'd laughed and said – *Jude, can you wipe the mark from my brow? –*

She looks at him. Appraising once more those good looks. He paws the ground – a deep unease beneath her gaze – good stock studied by a rancher. She presses him again:

– What is it? –

– Nothing –

– You sick? –

– and tired –

– You've drunk too much, already! – She squares her shoulders in mock anger as she catches the strength of the scent.

– It's Saint Patrick's Day, innit? What d'you 'spect? The whole world gets pissed on Paddy's day, dunnit? –

– And you'll look a clown at the dinner –

– I won't look a clown –

– Do you promise? –

– I promise. Let me get a shower, will you? –

- Hey - don't -

He pushes through her to the warm cell of the bathroom, pulls off his $500 pants and his $250 shirt. A final glimpse of the glittering city as he closes the door - quietly - gripping the handle with fierce strength, with a hand not tamed by duty, nor strong enough to love.

The lights burn bright in the penthouse suite and the shower hisses like the sea. Below him, he knows little pools of humanity are crowding in cafes and bars. All manner of humans; some washed ashore; some stranded - some waiting for a wave to free them -

- I promise to change. A fresh start - he whispers an empty promise to the water raining down. The charm seems to work. For now, the past is washed away. He asks:

- Did I ever lie? Did I - did I kill? -

He can't answer. The images prompting these questions arrive and depart of their own volition, seemingly having nothing to do with him. He is grateful at this makeshift absolution. The present, too, is losing coherence. He inhales and spits a long arc. A growing sense of emptiness spreading through his body. Now he grinds his teeth and runs an alcoholic's tongue around his mouth's hot interior. Apparitions rise. - *Who's this? -* He peers at the indistinct shapes on the far side of the steamy glass. But he knows the ghosts too well - the old man and the boy. How they beckon! He speaks to them:

- What? What d'y'want? -

The young boy speaks:

- Remember the boiler pool? When I was king? -

- Yes. Yes - of all the things - yes I do remember - I do! -

The boy steps forward, pressing his child's nose against the glass:

- It's still there -

A moment's hesitation - *It is? Where? -*

The boy's laughter fills the air like the rush of the sea. He points to an imagined distance.

- Out there -

The Old Man speaks:

- Come with us -

He's tempted by the relief they offer. A freedom from this latest variation on the same old blueprint - heaped from the bright wooden bricks of his past. He is ready to swipe it all down. The old pattern of endless reinvention. But still a doubt flits round him:

- Isn't it impossible. I mean - she always finds me. Isn't that how it was at the pool? -

- Don't I always find you, too? -

- But - wasn't she - alive before you? -

The Old Man smiles.

- Now John - think - what was alive before me? What was there in the beginning, before me? -

He remembers his Sunday School lessons.

- Null and void -

The doubt vanishes. A decision descends like a drunken white dove offering hope. New life floods him. He stares at the showerhead. A swirl of water fills the room, lifting him on its current -

- Yes! -

He feels it happening. The rising need for release, to swim with the tide, away from the shallows of this false boiler pool, away from the yellow cabs threading their ways below like minnows, away from the submarine light of the streets, away from the congregated crowds in Greenwich Village. Is it possible to reclaim that - that crown he once wore? Yes! When he was king.

He knows now. He knows that if he doesn't go, he'll have Jude's corpse on his hands. He runs his trembling palms down his dripping face and exhales - prepares for the evening's pretence - the smiles and the easy charm he's mastered over the years.

- And tomorrow? -

By the time she wakes to Manhattan's early afternoon, he will be five hours on the road.

"...TURN THE TIDES GENTLY..."

The hallucinations start in silence. They always do.

First, carriages moving beneath starlight, then the sound of wheels clattering along cobbles. Next, the pungent smell of horses: dung on floor, the acrid reek of piss.

After this first stage, people appear in the night-city's streets: uniformed old soldiers not old any more, a police officer on the corner in cape and high helmet. On the Common, Royal Marines sleeping in tented rows before embarkation start awake at a long-dead trumpet-call drowned by the present's waking birds.

He heads through the shifting Pompey night, along island streets toward the shoreline. In the air hangs coal smoke from a fire lit by a maid; the smell of frothing carbolic, copper-warmed for morning chores; voices from sleepy servant-children stretching awake in the pre-dawn.

When he steps onto the shingle, deep silence breaks out. Stillness for a few seconds, then the reappearance of the modern world: shimmering across the Solent, a ferry all lit up, stacked decks, like a wedding cake, sparkling and iced.

- I have visions, he tells himself, relieved at their passing. *- They seem so real - realer than the world I really live in. -*

He looks at his hands, hoping they might help him grasp this world more tightly.

- Doctor Cassell tells me to ignore them. But... I always get another one. -
Sure enough, a new vision.

- A woman. There's a woman in the sea! - with long, lank hair - there, in the moonlight! -

Her face, breasts, stomach, back, reflect moonbeams – then she is gone, sunk beneath the moon's silver path.

He glares accusation at his trembling hands, bites his lower lip, shakes his head, rubs his eyes, looks again.

– Nothing there, of course. –

Nothing...

Except an ever-widening circle spreading outwards, reaching toward him. He holds his breath, knuckles his eyes and checks once more.

A glance across the sea satisfies him. *Just water.*

But then she surfaces again.

Her head is up now, out of the sea. She tips back. He supposes this is what a woman drowning must look like: arms raised, helpless. He sees her for a second or so more, then down she goes again.

– It's just another vision. – He tells himself. *– But, what if it's not? A clubber, maybe, a little high; she took a playful dive in the water, and here she is – drowning in front of my eyes! Is she real? –*

After maybe two minutes she surfaces a third time.

– She is! –

He shouts – cutting the night with a voice thin and shrill, as if he's shouting in a padded room.

"It's okay. Don't worry! I'll help..."

Startled, she stops stock still in the water, fixes him with a curious gaze. Her movements are like those of a woman interrupted by a stranger walking into her boudoir while she combs her hair. Their eyes meet, and realising the situation she throws her arms up with an ironic expression, then sinks, the sea closing over her head.

He steps into the water. The cold shock sinking through his trainers makes his neck hairs stand in reflex, and he remembers he cannot swim. She surfaces again, spitting an arc of brine. Shocked back to reason he scuffs up the beach to the life-ring in its plastic box by the ice-cream kiosk.

– Drowning. I can't have her drowning. –

He grabs it, *champ-champ-champs* down the shingle and with a grunt hurls it to her.

It's a bad throw: over-eager, panicky. He curses as it collides with her. Her body flattens on the water and she grips the ring in a daze. In this way he pulls her in – hooking her from the sea.

Wading in to land her, he says:

"It's okay. It's okay!" He reaches down, only half able to see her through the moonlight surface, hooks her under her arms and pulls her up. But something isn't right. She struggles. A violent crazy thrashing in the water that makes him gasp at her power.

"Don't panic, I've got you," he says – but he really hasn't.

- Slippery as a fish -

They lock into a battle of wills, her thrashing scatters moonlight, while the air fills with noise. Other voices. An unknown language hissing around him. He looks up. Heads in the water, shouting, glaring.

He stops, frozen in surprise. She seizes her moment – slips from his arms, splashes back to the deep.

And then, something he can't explain.

He is sure, utterly convinced, as she dives into deeper water, the crossed fins of a tail rise high in the air behind her.

He stands, staring at the scatter of widening circles where the heads he saw have disappeared. Then he sits down on the water's edge, cold and afraid, not sure what to do.

*

At the hostel, on Albany Road, the nurses are serving breakfast to the residents.

In the corner sits Joe, a lean, wiry old man who can play the guitar as if he has sunshine in his fingers – and play the piano as if the Devil himself gave him the magic.

Only when Joe plays does the calm come. Serenity creeps across his features and for a short breath his inner warfare stops. His life is a see-saw of interventions, teetering between medication and music.

Near him is Bob, baring his teeth to sniff the air. Sometimes – urged on by a voice inside – he barks like a dog. At such times he curses himself for his stupidity – but, unable to resist the voice inside, barks again when he finishes cursing.

Across the room, sitting alone in a padded chair is a giant. Gordon: big, happy, placid – never saying anything to anyone. Withdrawn, pulled in on himself – always ready to smile when the moment comes.

The young man from the beach ignores all his friends today, stepping in wet shoes and dripping trousers to one of the nurses.

"Cath... I think, I er.. think I need some help," he says, and spills out everything in a jumble of words.

A few hours later, Doctor Cassell considers him across his office desk.

- Shame - he thinks. *- He was doing so well. -*

When Doctor Cassell speaks, his face is clear and reassuring, his voice always steady and sympathetic – though Dave notices his eyes flicker sometimes.

Dave likes Doctor Cassell, and because he doesn't want to upset him, he doesn't tell him about the Butler standing behind him. Dave has worked out that this is not the sort of thing Doctor Cassell likes him to say. When he does, Dave thinks he makes Doctor Cassell angry, because he prescribes him pills that stop him thinking properly. It takes him weeks to get his thoughts together after that. During these periods of vagueness in which he doesn't feel present, Doctor Cassell writes a satisfied note in his file: *psychotic episode subsided.*

Doctor Cassell is speaking now, Dave realises, as he draws his attention back to the present from the Butler pouring the tea. That is how it is. The Butler behind Doctor Cassell pours tea from a silver pot into four china cups, and then takes them on a silver teatray out of the room to the place where the Master is waiting. It is a loop that has been playing that way for years. Dave has learned to live with it, unremarked.

"We thought you were getting better, Dave," Doctor Cassell says, a tone of mild regret in his voice. He is writing a note that says *Relapse*, and working out which drug to prescribe. "Tell me, is this all you've seen?"

Dave could tell him about the old sailors in stripy shirts, or the Royal Marines in red coats he sees beneath the walls of the Round Tower, practising their drill in a tight formation of fighting men's bodies, with muskets on their shoulders. But he knows not to.

"Is this all I have seen?" Dave repeats the question in his head with a kind of indignation.

Doesn't the Doctor get it? This is different from his *normal* visions that he received all that therapy for, and which he has learned to let the Doctor think have gone away. He mentioned this one because its subject was something that *never could have been.* That's why it is *weird.* Clearly the Doctor has no idea about the rules. He just thinks the visions are all the same. Dave suspects that explaining this to him will make things worse, and he goes quiet for a while.

"No, I haven't seen anything else," he eventually says, pauses a moment, calculating how to dissolve those pills away. "And this, well, I *knew* it wasn't right. I think..." he considers carefully, wondering how weak a dose of anti-psychotics he can get away with. "I think it was a dream. I fell asleep on the beach, and I think it was a dream."

Doctor Cassell looks up at him and smiles as if Dave is an errant child. "That is very... perceptive of you, Dave," he says with a tone of encouragement. "You're making progress. So, you can recognise the difference between what's real and what's imagined? I am pleased with you, Dave."

He prescribes a mild sleeping pill, envisioning the case study Dave will make: a testimony to his techniques. He follows up with a final question:

"So, let's be clear, are you saying it *wasn't* real?"

Dave shrugs and puts his head down. "It was in my mind," he says, non-committally. Doctor Cassell half relaxes. He will ask the nurses to keep an eye on this one, he decides. To make sure he doesn't come to any harm.

*

Alone in his room, Dave lights a piece of self-medication, and considers the vision again. What can it mean, this enigma that appeared in the waves? How could it be so real that he held it in his arms, that his shirt was wet, and that he can still feel the pull in his muscles from straining?

- It must mean something, right? -

When he smokes a joint, he feels more lucid. He can see more clearly and understand what's going on.

During such times he gets important messages from things out there. One time the man on the radio let slip that cats could travel in time. Since then he has watched them closely: the way they disappear into nothingness, and then come back again, smelling of other eras – one with a hint of ancient Roman herbs on its fur, another smelling of the old town of Portsmouth before the Clean Air Act: heavy with the musk of coal fires and the carbolic smell picked up from the playful rubs of the 9-year-old scullery maid who lived at that very house 120 years before.

There are the other cats who smell of something clean and bright and electric and futuristic. *– They belong to all times, cats. That's why they were worshipped in ancient Egypt, and are still alive on the streets of Cairo today. Some of them are the self-same ones. –* He likes them for that. *– They understand about time. –*

He is listening to Jimi Hendrix on the ageing CD player, a cheap little box he picked up years ago at Argos with money his mum gave him for his birthday as a boy: *1983... (A Merman I Should Turn To Be)*. Jimi is speaking to him, he realises. He is telling him something important. Not letting it slip like the man on the radio – but telling him straight out.

In his moment of clarity, Dave learns from Jimi Hendrix what makes this morning so special. There are three things:

1. Before this morning, none of the creatures of my inner eye took the blindest bit of notice of me. But she – she looked straight at me. She struggled against me, too. That is a major change.

2. Every other creature I have seen was real. Real in the past – but real.

But she, she came from out of a children's picture book. That's what makes her unique. And interesting.

3. And then there's the fact that she is from the water. From the sea. She might have news for me, from Jack.

"I must see her again," he says out loud, and quickly opens the window to let the smell of weed escape.

*

The following morning, 2am: the *scrunch scrunch* of shingle, feeling its collapsing resistance under his feet.

He smells the rich presence of the sea as he walks past the night fishermen who are working by lantern light in their striped shirts and felt hats. They are pulling a boat ashore there, beaching it properly with horses that skitter on the shingle, whinny and snort in moon-and-lantern-light. As he heads toward the water, they fade away, down to nothing – down to the empty air they showed through for a while.

– It's like I see the world through polarised glass, and it picks out things at different angles – he thinks.

All the world is silent. Trails of lamplight stretch like little yellow-brick-roads across the black water from the Isle of Wight to where he stands on the beach.

He waits for hours, but she doesn't show. Looking out at the black surface reflecting the twinkling shimmer of the Island in the distance he shrugs, says:

"Nothing there."

He thinks about the sea: how he loves it, how he hates it. For the first time in a while, he thinks of his mother, grieving in a home somewhere. Then he thinks again of the sea: that unreadable sheet that hides so much beneath, which links all the shores of the world. A shared resource that no-one realises is the power that unites human beings, all of us, together on the land.

– Even on this little island of Portsea, you are never really alone, because the sea can carry your secrets and loves, and whisper it into the ears of sleeping Chinese on the far side of the world. If only you have the ear and the mind to listen to what the sea is telling you, you can hear the secrets of the Chinese, too. –

As the sun begins to rise, he gives up, and makes his way past the early morning dog-walkers with their half-filled plastic bags like a deli gone wrong, back to the hostel, his halfway house. But halfway to what?

It is six by the time he gets back. He expects everyone to be asleep, but Doctor Cassell is waiting for him on the porch, for a moment looking like the Victorian preacher Dave saw down the road a few days before – severity in a frock coat, with pinched face and frowns. He wonders if he should tell him of the similarity? But no, he won't. He has a feeling something really bad will happen if he does.

"Where have you been?" Doctor Cassell asks, suspicion on his face. He was called here in the night because Barking Bob had one of his fits. Tears, and shouting and clasping his head to try to shut out the voices. He had not been taking his medication as he should, and Doctor Cassell needed the help of two nurses to hold him long enough to give him a quietening jab.

After that, he noticed Dave hadn't closed his bedroom door, so he looked in – only to see he wasn't there. Curious, concerned, he looked around, and found Dave's old tin of tobacco with its little lump of brown resin inside.

Waiting in the porch, Doctor Cassell is a little angry with Dave. He searches his face, to make sure he isn't hiding anything else when he asks:

"Did you see your mermaid?"

"No," Dave answers, shrugging a little. "I didn't see her."

Doctor Cassell relaxes a little. "I found this in your room, Dave," he says, holding up the tin. "You know we don't allow smoking of any sort in the house. We can't have this."

"It helps me think," Dave defends.

"No it doesn't, Dave. It's bad for you. There is a lot of research on this. Cannabis causes psychosis in some people. Answer me this: when did you experience your hallucinations? Were you smoking this? I bet you were. And so, you've been seeing mer – think you've been seeing things," he says, his voice dismissive.

–

–

Anger: Dave feels it grow inside him, spinning up in his body and out through his legs and arms. It makes him see the hypocrisy of Doctor Cassell, who thinks he can see inside other people's heads and then accuses *them* of hallucinating. He's had enough of this. Of the constraint, of treading carefully in the Doctor's version of the world that Dave can't see. It all needs to come out, and he can't stop it as it crawls up to his throat: The Truth.

"I didn't see her," he says. "I didn't see her because she wasn't there."

His anger rises inside like a wave and he struggles to force it back down. But it's too late, and he spills it all out.

He shouts about his visions – the people in the night and the day who are there all the time, who no-one else knows about. He can describe in detail the neighbour who lived on that street a hundred years before, he can tell him the name of ships going out of the harbour mouth on a sunny day in the 17th Century. He can tell him how the town walls used to surround Old Portsmouth, with elms growing on top. He can detail the delivery of timber on barges, how they were dropped in the water near The Hard to supply the shipyards. He can give the names of the wives of seamen lost when the *Mary Rose* sank. And he can tell him the exact words the King shouted when he wept on the shore, speaking a language so unlike the language we speak now. He has seen it. He has seen it all.

His eyes flame as he shouts his frustration at people thinking he's crazy.

"Why can't you see how it is? Don't you understand? I *have* to talk with her! She might have a clue to all this – how all this turned out this way. When I was a kid I was okay. Why did I just drop out when I was 16? Why did I tell you all about the things I saw back then? I could have kept them to myself and you would have all thought I was just a quiet kid with an imagination. But I didn't. I let it all out: the stuff that everyone else keeps in. I stopped being normal back then – but only because I stopped playing your game, and now... I don't know how to start again."

Doctor Cassell stands with his hands interlinked in front of him over his stomach.

"Now, Dave, it's okay... you're okay..."

"I'm not okay. I want answers. I want answers to the things I see that make you think I'm mad!" He puts his hand to his face and starts to cry, speaking half to himself. "I was lost, that's all. Just lost, and you all thought I was psychotic, or paranoid or schizophrenic – or whatever you think it is. But you don't know what's supposed to be wrong with me, and the words you use all mean the same thing: mad. I'm done with it."

And as soon as the anger rises, it recedes, leaving on the bare shore Dave's soul, washed up, helpless.

Doctor Cassell softens his tone, eyeing his patient's state with renewed pity.

"Come in, Dave," he says quietly. "We need to talk."

He shows Dave into his office. The Butler is there again, excitedly pouring tea into four teacups. Dave knows he made a mistake letting it all out, just like it was a mistake when he was a teenager. He senses something is going to change in his life, and maybe not in a good way. He says nothing about the Butler and buttons his lip down. But the Doctor, the Doctor has plenty to say.

As Doctor Cassell talks, it seems to Dave that he really likes rules. He has so many of them. And he likes other people to follow them.

These are Doctor Cassell's rules, that he wants Dave to follow:

1. There will be no more smoking in his room. (*It's dangerous, Dave.*)

2. There will be no more of that stash business. (*No, Dave. None of it at all.*)

3. He is to stay in at nights. (*That means no wandering, Dave.*)

4. He will take new medications for a while, because they will make him better. (*You'll see, Dave.*)

5. He will forget about mermaids. (*Really, you will forget about them, Dave. You'll change, you'll see.*)

*

Actually Doctor Cassell is right. After he has been taking the pills for a few days, Dave's world begins to change. It is as if the colour leaks out of it, and runs away down the drain. His legs feel so heavy they are difficult to lift, and he feels constant pressure inside his head, as if a mains pipe has been stoppered and water inside stops moving.

His limbs grow even heavier, until he finds himself shuffling when he walks. When he steps out of the house, the people he used to see in all their different clothes from all those different times have gone. There is a handful of people in modern clothes, down-at-heel, hands pushed in their pockets. He can't explain it to anyone, but he feels like he has lost an extra sense. If he had lost his sense of touch, other people might understand it, but how does he explain he has lost his sense of time? He no longer understands how all time happens in the same place all at once. Now, all the times apart from now have disappeared.

After a few weeks, he doesn't have to work hard to follow Doctor Cassell's rules. He starts to realise that really he did not see the woman in the water. He stays indoors, learns to be afraid of the sea, looking out of the window with anxiety as the spring turns to summer, hiding when people walk by.

When he takes the pills, sometimes his hands shake. It is as if his body is telling him not to take them, he comments to Doctor Cassell. But Doctor Cassell, who is not his body, tells him that he should take them because they are good for him. And after a while longer of taking them, he forgets why he is taking them and forgets that his body is trying to tell him not to.

He notices another big change happen when the cats stop disappearing. He can watch them for a whole day, and they don't disappear – not even for one second. But what is strange is that he can still smell their electric future and their coal-filled past. That is something that doesn't go away, despite the pills.

But he decides to keep that to himself.

*

Six months after their first talk, Doctor Cassell asks Dave about the whole business of mermaids. Dave is confused. He doesn't know what this man is talking about. In fact, he can't even remember the man's name. Doctor Cassell is satisfied. He reduces the anti-psychotics and leaves Dave to himself.

Dave enters a new phase of being when the pills are reduced. He is a kind of innocent fool as he walks out from the big Victorian hostel into the Autumn streets. The sunshine comes down through leaves turning gold and littering the pavement, and he turns his face up to the branches and smiles. Doctor Cassell watches him sometimes from the window of his office, and concludes he seems happy enough, shuffling through the streets of Southsea, picking up the dog-ends thrown down by passers-by, getting as drunk as hell, once a week, when his benefit money comes. Doctor Cassell decides to stop the treatment completely. It has worked.

*

A week before Christmas, a serious-looking man arrives at the hostel to tell Dave that he must come with him, to visit his mum. He explains that he is Dave's second cousin, and that his mum is very ill and that he should come and see her –

"Before," as he puts it, "it is too late."

Dave has not seen his mum for four years and doesn't know what to think about this. He doesn't know what will be too late. He totters on his feet when he sees her lying in a ward at Saint Mary's hospital, a white tube up her nose.

The serious-looking man steadies him. A nurse with red hair looks at him suspiciously, comes over, asking the man if Dave is drunk. The man shakes his head and explains something about care in the community. Dave looks at his mother coldly. Unlike the way they show sick people on the tv, there isn't a continuous green blip bubbling away by the side of her bed. That would be silly. It would keep the old lady awake, when all she wants to do is sleep.

On the bed, she paler than her sheets.

He thinks he remembers for a moment playing with his brother, while she looked on in a cramped garden somewhere in Fratton. Her hair was dark then. But he can't remember things so easily since he took those pills. It's as if the past has been switched off.

Her eyes are closed, and her breathing is slow and laboured, which is no surprise considering she has that thing in her face, getting in the way of the air. She looks so frail, and the serious-looking man he doesn't know says to him:

"They say it won't be long now."

He thinks he knows what that means, but can't be sure, and stretches forward to take her hand in his, feeling the smooth skin that is so cold and has the texture of uncooked pastry. He squeezes it a little, and imagines her fingers turning to putty and collapsing under his grip, squeezing out between his knuckles.

She stirs at the touch and opens her eyes... They hover in a haze of unfocus for a few moments before fixing on him and opening wide. "Jack?" She says, with a confused voice. "Jack? They said you drowned. They said you drowned."

"Not Jack ma... Dave," he says, and then her eyes cloud over and she remembers a voice from somewhere a long way back:

"Dave, my little Davey. You used to paint so much. Your little hands in the colours, all in technicolor. Do you still paint, Davey?"

He stares at her and feels the tears pushing with hot insistence to the front of his eyes, a headache drawn from a well of pain building behind them. He opens his mouth twice, but says nothing. Instead, he croaks, like a lonely old frog in a marsh somewhere.

His mother suddenly casts a hostile glance at him: "One dead, one mad, what use is that? I wish it was you instead of Jack!"

And then she turns her frail head and rolls her eyes. He has heard that wish before. Her voice rings in his ears long after she has fallen asleep. They shake his world. He feels as if the mains pipe in his head is unstoppering, as if the colour is running back in.

By the time he gets out of the hospital, he can see carriages again. Great rumbling, tall broughams and phaetons and dog carts on the busy road outside. The sound of hooves loud in his ears, the smell of the dung mingled on the road with sweat and coal smoke soon follow. A horse-drawn hearse pulls into the cemetery across the road, mourners in top hats, a boy walking by the carriage sobbing professional tears.

The visions fade like slides or gels, one overlay on another, as if the whole of time from the beginning to the end is a telescope, and somehow he snapped it shut all in one deft movement, and can see both ends, all at once.

The serious man takes him in his car back in the direction of the hostel. He doesn't say much.

"She thinks it was my fault," Dave says as they drive. "Was she right?"

But the silent second cousin shrugs, and if he does answer, Dave can't hear him for the sight of an elephant walking down the street – crowds gathered at the roadside, the excitement of seeing them come to town. Little urchins in cloth caps stare from between the legs of police officers on the roadside, and the lions smell of the future, too: warm and electric. They all can do it, all the cats, it seems.

– *It's a circus. A circus!* – He grins to himself. His visions are fully back!

At three o'clock that morning, Dave finds himself in the hostel's kitchen. Though it is winter, there is the unexpected smell of Indian summer in the air – the relaxed warmth of clean sheets and promise. Flower scents in the night, the quiet breath of a cooler wind blowing on the neck. – *What time is that? What year?* –

Jimi Hendrix has been talking to him again. Reminding him of the mermaid, and the time he saw her before. It has all come back, and he knows that he just needs to see her again. There is a chance, a pretty good chance that she will be able to tell him what happened that night. That night when the police knocked on the door and he was just a teenager. When the boat went down with Jack in it. His brother. His older brother, who he'd played with in the sunshine in a little garden in Fratton. Jack, who had gone through school before him, so different from him. So much more made for the task that Dave didn't want to do.

Out on the street, under the light shed from Narnian lamp-posts, he sees the cats eyeing him from beneath the bushes on Merton Road. The bushes are flat stage-props, made of flat dark material out of which the sodium lamps have drained the colour. The pungent smell of drains comes to his nose. The Victorian sewage system lurking beneath the road, a creature in the depths.

There is no-one around tonight. The road itself is a country path with a few houses dotted along it, while the converted townhouses of the modern day are gone. The houses that replaced the one the Blitz flattened Villas, modern yellow-brick affairs – none of these have been built. The trees close in over his head, and they sing to Dave with the voice of Jimi Hendrix as he makes his way on and on. Through the city, he follows the lines of the road through the fields, goes past modern houses which are not yet real – all projections on glass. Sometimes when the light hits them he can see them from one era, sometimes from another.

He is heading to the Camber Docks – the place where Jack headed out on the water.

As he walks, a remembrance comes of speaking with his brother:

"I can't go out tonight, Jack, I can't go out fishing. I've got this cold, you know. A cold."

Jack looks at him with a look that says he isn't fooled at Dave's desire to buck family tradition. "You hate it, don't you Dibbs?" he asks. "It's not what you're about. Don't worry about it. I want the money, I'll go."

He can see it now: the *MV Acheron* bobbing out to sea from the Camber Dock entrance, a red light moving in the darkness, the slow diesel *guttle guttle* sounding over the water and staying at the same volume even as the boat moves away, his brother stowing the ropes and checking the gear. For a moment, his brother looks up from the stern, a shadow moving on the mirror-shifting water, and Dave feels for a moment that – *Yes! Our eyes really do meet – across the years, across the chasm of life and death. –*

He stands at Portsmouth Point now, watching the boat fade. It's midweek and no-one's around. Not a soul. There are Christmas lights on the Still and West pub. They twinkle in the sea. He freezes, looking down at the breakwaters – piles of heavy boulders built up around Point to prevent the Solent from gnawing the land. He is mesmerised by the rhythmic effect of the sea, the harbour all around him. Then it seems, as he looks up at the moon, that all sound has stopped, and the reflected light is a pathway for him to cross.

He climbs over the railings by the sea and steps on to the rocks. A pathway, across the harbour to Gosport, and then beyond. It's an escape. He hunches down and weeps by the sea, a wave of confusion over him again. His mother going, his father gone, his brother gone – soon all that will be left will be Doctor Cassell and the serious second cousin. A tear drops from his face into the water.

He doesn't belong here. Is it possible the world is trying to wipe its memory of him?

He realises he is being watched. A pair of eyes both kind and utterly alien, stare at him from the water. – *She's there! Right there!* – A little below the surface, hair billowing around her head like seaweed – all lit up by the moon in the water. Pale, and beautiful and kind.

A van pulls up on the road behind him, and a blue light flashes on and off repeatedly. He hears a door slam, and footsteps coming towards him.

She carries on looking at him, not speaking to him, and she puts her finger over her lips to quiet him. Those lips do not move at all, but he senses a meaning coming from her eyes – something that conveys a word, or a thought. "Come back tomorrow," the thought says. "You will have an answer."

She considers him a while longer, until the dark figure casts its reflection on the water, next to his. And when he looks again at the spot where she was, she has gone.

The police officer speaks with him in a kindly voice, asking his name and what he is about – asking if he is thinking of doing anything stupid.

Dave answers with a kind of indignation in his voice that he just came down here to see his brother, who is dead. The policeman asks Dave where he lives and when he tells him about the hostel, the policeman carries on speaking in a kindly voice and offers him a lift home. Sensing that he would be stupid to argue, Dave nods quietly and gets into the back of the van. In the front, the officer who was inside waiting for him says with distaste:

"Nutters. We're not a charity."

But the kind one says: "Give it a rest. He's harmless enough."

*

The next morning Doctor Cassell looks agitatedly across the desk at Dave as they both sit in his office. The Butler is behind him again, as he always is, pouring the tea from a silver teapot for the Master, a look of excited pleasure on his face. Dave notices a painting on the wall where there is, even now, in the modern day, a tiny witness mark – a darker area of paint, where it once hung.

"There used to be a painting there," says Dave, pointing up behind the Doctor's head. "It showed a family. A husband, his wife, a brother and sister. It is as if they are mourning. One of them is dead."

Then he bites his tongue. Doctor Cassell is giving him a look again, surveying him with disappointed eyes for just a few seconds.

After a while, the Doctor says: "And here you are again, back in the seat. Like we're stuck in time," he adds the second sentence half under his breath, with a tinge of remorse. "We need to put you back on the medication," he says. "For good, I think. To end this once and for all."

"I didn't see anything," says Dave. "Nothing at all, what do you want to give me a pill for?"

"For your own good, Dave," he says.

Dave hangs his head and looks sideways.

– What would Jimi Hendrix do? – he wonders. But he keeps it to himself and waits.

That night, he doesn't take his pill. He puts it under his tongue and pretends to swallow it, then spits it down the sink in his room.

She told him to come back that night, and he isn't going to disobey.

*

At the water's edge, the world is silent again. He is down on the dock, where the fishing boat *Acheron* once set out. This is where it used to tie up, all those years back. There's a little pleasure boat there, now – something fast and white and flimsy that on summer days a man in his 50s sits on with only his trunks, oblivious to the need for suncream. Red skin and the raised fur of chest hair, equally red in the light, like the bushy tail of a fox on his fat chest. Dave can see it all. He can see everything.

Along the sea wall, a man and a boy are fishing. A modern man and boy, from the now-time, with lights on their heads, that shine on him when they look at him, stealing the night and leaving little spots of black on his eyes.

He edges around the corner away from them, hears a siren in the distance as the police chase a joyrider through the morning streets. He sinks into a well of darkness as he clambers down on to a pontoon.

Wooden planks shift underfoot with the movement of the sea and the weight of his step. He becomes aware of how the sea means everything is moving. The continual shifting and changing of position of the boats, the whirring and the eddying of the water that makes the whole world seem unstable and unreal. How surface slides over surface, wave on wave, reflection on reflection. He hasn't been down here on the pontoon itself for years, and he realises how much at home he feels. The smell of the boats, that went out year after year, dragging nets, or pulling up pots from the seabed – little trapped creatures with massive clashing claws – hard on the outside, and pure sweetness in the middle, soft sea animals with hard shells, waiting to be opened and savoured.

He loses himself in a daydream that is a nightdream, and watches the eternal *bob-bob-bob* of the boats, and the light on the water.

That's when he sees eyes again, looking across at him. Except this time they are different eyes. The shape grows out of nothingness. At first, a photograph's face, a picture from the past. But as he stares, the face becomes clearer, and then the body, and the whole scenario – and this time he watches as a scene unfolds.

There is his brother getting on the boat: Jack moving among the other crew.

"What's up?" says a fellow fisherman to his brother, in that strong Pompey accent that squeezes vowels into tight packages of meaning.

"The Old Dear, mate," says Jack, and shrugs. "Don't want me comin' out tonight. Says I shouldn't let the little one get away with shirking." He shrugs.

"He's a slacker, alright, that brother."

"Nah. He's just not cut out for it. He's a dreamer. Should be on telly or summing. Not a fisherman. He's never gonna be a fisherman. They should ease up on him. I mean, he's a kid, and this isn't the 1920s or something. We got choices these days, and he's only been working the boat while he decides what to do. I told her, *I love this.* I'd go out on the fish, whatever the weather. I said to her: *the sea's my blood. Remember that. My blood.*"

Sitting on the pontoon just a few yards away, with the shadow of the seawall cast on him, Dave gives out a little yell of surprise.

The two look up from their work, where they are straightening baskets on the deck.

"Whassat?"

"Dunno, mate." They peer towards him, seeming to look him in the eyes.

In the wheelhouse, someone flicks on the diesel engines. The water growls and explodes.

Jack shouts: "Summing in the black there. A cat. I reckons it's a cat."

"Wants to catch a fish, eh?"

"Funny though, for a sec I thought it was someone watching – a person, like."

"Come on, let's go."

They cast off quickly, and the boat moves off from the dockside, into the night with the red and green lights on the water shattering into a million shards. After it has gone, with the steady sound of the engine dying slowly in the night, Dave is left looking down at a pair of eyes once more.

That face. The girl in the water. There she is again, like she said. She is close to him as he runs to the edge of the pontoon, leaning over the water, tears rolling down his cheeks.

His voice is broken as he speaks:

"Hello again."

Her cold hand comes out of the water, shimmering slightly in the moonlight, the air around it cold, as if it carries with it unimagined black depths – a climate of icy air. He shudders as she reaches up and wipes his tears with her hand, and then, her fingers glistening in the harbour lights, a tinge of red and a tinge of green, she moves the index finger to her mouth and tastes the tears.

Their eyes lock a moment, and he says nothing, but it seems that they speak, even though he doesn't open his mouth.

- I am told I am mad. -

Her tail surfaces for a second as she moves away from him, then swims in again.

- You can see me, can't you? You can hear me? -

- So I am mad... -

- No, you can see. You can see like we can see. -

- What? -

- Time is an ocean. We are in the ocean and can navigate it. You are a navigator, too. -

- No. I see the people who worked here. I hear voices from other times. It... drives me... mad. -

- It is only that you haven't learned to control where you look.... You will learn the freedom one day. A friend will show you how. -

- A friend? -

A tone of urgency enters her voice.

- Tell your mother what you know, before she runs out of time. -

- Tell her what? -

- What you have learned tonight. -

- But who are you? -

She raises her hand again and touches his face with a hand dripping little drops of seawater, placing fresh tears on his face.

- We live in the sea of time. And we live in your tears. Your people do not understand time. You do. -

He wants to reach out and hold her – to take hold of the proof of his sanity. But she senses his intention, and before he can move, she is gone, her muscular tail flexing in the moonlight for a moment before it vanishes.

- Go now! - the soundless voice says.

The taxi driver who picks Dave up at the side of St Thomas's Cathedral makes him his last fare of the night. The driver has tired eyes, Dave notices, as he pays him in coins, climbing out at St Mary's Hospital and wanders quietly on to the grounds.

At the door, there is a security guard standing inside the foyer. Dave waits a while, watching, wondering what to do next. All around him, reality is shifting backwards and forwards, year lying on year like the surface of the waters he has just looked at. Here the hospital is just being built, here it is about to be knocked down, here it is tonight, and here it is tomorrow. And in the centre of this shifting kaleidoscope of time, the security guard, bored, steps outside and lights a cigarette.

Dave moves in the shadow to one side, and passes behind him. The guard senses something in the night, like the passing of a cat on paving stones, and he hears the doors slide open. But when he turns to look, he can see nothing in the corridor, and shakes his tired head.

Dave heads through darkened corridors towards Catherington Ward, where he knows his mother lies, staring at the ceiling. She is alone, and she is dying, with no-one on the ward to keep her company.

Two nurses supposedly watching the ward are drinking coffee and chatting in a side room about boyfriends and families, and *Eastenders* and the latest scandal in the news. He goes past their little room, unnoticed, and finds his mother surrounded by machines, staring at the ceiling, gripping to life as tightly as her weak hands allow.

Her eyes are stretched wide open. It is this time of night she fears the most: when Night has folded its black wings around the building, seeming to have sunk down upon it to feed on the patients inside.

So, she won't close her eyes: to stop Night taking her. She can't bear the thought of it climbing over her, coming in through her mouth, following the route of her last breath, filling her with darkness...

She notices the figure at the end of the bed. It is unclear at first, just the idea that something is watching her – but then – in the hallucinatory whirl of morphine, the man becomes more real. Beyond the dulled pain in her smoker's lungs and the thickening lump in her throat – this figure shimmers into being.

– *A son, my son.* –

She knows that her dead child has come for her – sent by the night to gather her up.

"Mum," it says to her, and she shakes a little and smiles a resigned smile.

"My boy?" she whispers.

"I didn't know if you would know me?"

"Of course I know you. My son, I haven't seen you for so long!"

"Mum, remember the night of the accident?"

"I do, I do. I'll never forget it. Jack, oh, my dear Jack."

She reaches out a frail hand to him, as if it is a piece of paper that she is to hand over to someone else. She tries to touch this apparition, but her hand is pulled back and hurts where the Venflon is tubed into the vein, pumping in chemicals to take away the pain.

"Oh son, I need to touch you. Get this off me. Get this stuff, off me!

In a moment of frustration she starts to pull at her tubes. The one in her nose, that makes her want to swallow all the time, the one in the back of her hand – pulling off the tape that holds it in place.

"Mum, remember something for me. Remember what you were told. That last night?"

"What, what was I told?"

"Do you remember this: *The sea is my blood.*"

He studies her face in the half-light, here, in the beating heart of the hospital, the air-conditioning, the power surging through the cables, the breathing and snoring and gentle nightcries of the sick all around – the heartbeat of the hospital forever marking out time, in births and deaths and success and tragedy.

A smile comes across her face.

"It *is* you! I do remember... yes... Jack. I remember. Only you could know that!"

She smiles. Her son, her Jack, come from beyond the grave to take her with him to the world beyond.

"Couldn't keep young Jack away from the sea, could we?" she says to herself, and then looks to him again. "It's like you were part of it."

"It wasn't my fault, mum," Dave tells her, begging forgiveness.

"No. Not your fault, son. Never your fault." She sits bolt upright in bed, with a massive effort.

"Come here, son, come here."

With a final effort, she pulls out the last of the tubes, and takes him in her arms. She holds him like that, as she weeps, relaxes a little more.

"I'm ready," she says.

Then she says nothing more, as her body softens in his arms.

It is a full half hour later when the nurse finds them together. Dave holding her, standing by her bed. If she would only take the time to look, she would see a look of satisfaction, of peace on both their faces. But she does not take the time to look. She responds with an angry shout and challenges him. He looks up, startled, and she recognises the face of the madman she saw with the serious man on the early shift.

"You!"

Dave looks down to see his mother's blood on his clothes and hears the nurse raising her voice at him. Somewhere in the distance an alarm sounds. He can hear other feet coming nearer, their clatter echoing through the wards.

With a final goodbye, he places his mother gently back on the bed, and runs out through a fire exit, across the car park – running and running – out of the hospital grounds.

The voices he sometimes hears talking to him are loud now in his head. They all tell him one thing: *you must get away.* He runs as hard as he can across the flat island city, through the winter streets, past the football stadium – its expanse overlaid in his mind's eye with the fields that were there just over a century before. He runs past the KFC and the MacDonalds, and the retail park, and down further towards the wooded streets of Southsea.

A siren wails nearby. Instinctively he dodges down a side street. He wanders there, lost for he doesn't know how long – aimlessly circling, walking and thinking.

On one street he hides behind a plane tree as a patrol car rolls by, the tarmac seeming to make the sound of breathing as it goes. The night is brightening, a little patch of light in the Eastern sky eliminating the stars one by one. The air seems like water around him – dim and light at the same time – unstable and cold. It freezes his lungs.

– Home, I just want to get home. –

After wandering in this way for some time, he steps back into a familiar road and pushes open a door.

It is winter pre-dawn. In the hallway, Doctor Cassell is waiting for him, his face tired, concerned, watchful all at once.

"Where have you been, Dave?" he asks.

Dave shrugs. "Out," reticent, like a teenage child. He realises a redundant habit brought him here. He doesn't need it any more. He has the answers he wanted.

"I saw my brother," he says. "I saw him. And I told my mother about him, and she understood."

He notices the look on Doctor Cassell's face grow more grave. "Go to your room," he says. "I will talk with you later."

Filled with the habit of obedience, Dave drops his head and climbs the stairs. But as soon as he hears Doctor Cassell go into his office, he tiptoes back down again, listening in at the door. He can hear him on the telephone.

"Yes, he's here, Constable, as expected. You'd better pick him up."

– This is my chance. My one chance. To get away! –

Away from the drugs, away the mind-reading Doctor.

He jumps down the stairs and runs from the house, with no idea where to go.

Daylight is growing now, and the everyday nature of Southsea starts to stand out, bright all around him.

Saturday morning. The streets are busy, with people arriving to work in the shops, while a few morning-afterers, stumbling their ways home from others' beds and parties, from lovers or clients, mingle with those newly up to walk their dogs on the beaches.

As he runs through the streets he notices how all the cats stop in their tracks to look at him, following him with their green eyes, full of knowing and understanding. He is struck by their soft cruelty and their otherness, which has never shone through so strong as now.

He runs between the old Ellis Owen houses at the back of Kent Road, through Victorian elegance and birds singing in the trees, and still the cats watch him. Looking out from trees, from under parked cars, from the tops of walls.

On he goes, past Victorian Gothic buildings, then down the Kent Road past Georgian townhouses, narrow and upright, and squeezed. He hears a droning sound in the sky above, can see the wing lights of the police spotter plane.

- They think I killed my mother. -

He knows that's what they think. He hides under the leafy cover of trees by the side of the Common as the plane draws a slow droning figure of 8 and then moves off again. He runs – he has no plan where to go, so heads back to the Camber Docks – to the boats and the sea.

*

The police car catches up with him not far from his destination, pulling alongside him as he passes by a tiled Victorian building he experiences all at once in all its different incarnations – newly built, smoke darkened, cleaned up, repurposed – pub, tearoom, estate agent.

He is running, breathless, and the policeman winds down his window and tells him: "You've got nowhere to go, son." It's the same officer who called him a nutter in the van. He stops for a moment, seems to give in, bending over with hands on knees, panting out hot gasps in the icy air. But as the officer puts a leg out of the car, he throws his weight against it and pushes the door back, jamming bone against sill, drawing a shout and curse into being. The other officer is already out from the driver's side and Dave doubles back at a sprint towards the bulk of a round tower.

Atop the high wall that skirts the beach, throngs a crowd on the ramparts, cheering at something a way off. Tudor clothes: dull cloth of peasants, modest colours of the artisan classes and the bright velvets of the wealthy – all cheering a ship coming in from the Solent.

The vision fades.

Now he crosses a courtyard beneath the tower and runs through an arch, doubling back to the old streets of Old Portsmouth, where the cannon of old ships are used as bollards – past rotting wood fencing, through the smell of Victorian streets. Street urchins run here and there, in torn hand-me-downs of their brothers and sisters. He flashes past Camber Dock workers – fishermen stacking baskets in untidy piles, and the strong, strong smell of the sea, of rotting fish, and horse dung.

Behind him, he can hear the sound of running, can hear the police officer from the 21st Century one hundred yards behind.

Jumping a wooden fence he finds himself on shingle, with lapping water a little way off. A place where little wherries beach and fishing nets hang. He sits down, trying not to make any noise on the stones. Exhausted – his heart pounds in his chest and his blood rushes in his ears. He is panting, disoriented among lobster pots and bric-a-brac. A cat materialises as if from nowhere and jumps into his lap. It smells of coal fires and carbolic soaps and horses – and it lets out a loud mewling cry like a siren. He can see the policeman now, looking over the fence straight towards him. But the policeman's outline seems vague and unclear – his shape appears as if he is on the other side of a gel lens – a filter on a camera. Dave ducks.

The policeman begins to climb over the fence – getting a higher elevation to view the beach – catches sight of Dave, hiding by a boat.

"Stay right there!" he shouts.

Dave throws the cat off as he stands, and runs down the beach, towards the foreshore on the harbour mouth, while the policeman behind him shouts: "Still nowhere to go!"

The cat spits and hisses, facing the pursuer with violent eyes, its back arched, its tail jerking. At the shoreline, Dave carries on running, placing his feet in the water, pushing on and seeming to see, in the morning light, where the moon is still shining on the surface, a pathway across to Gosport.

If he can just get on to the path, he can get across.

Cold shock of water sinking in through his shoes. He jumps on to the moonlight. It holds him for a second, maybe two. Then he sinks, pulled down into the dark water, tugged down by the current as the whole of Portsmouth Harbour empties out through that narrow entrance.

Water closes over his head, as the policeman gets on his radio and starts to call the Coastguard and the harbour patrol – anyone – to get there on the hurry-up.

And the cat vanishes, in the way cats do.

*

Dave is moving in a dream in the icy water, sinking in darkness, with the grey, dirty current washing around him. He struggles to find the surface, lost, disoriented and goes deeper still. His hands reach out to grasp whatever he can find, but the water gives way between his fingers.

Panic. The sea rushes to fill his mouth and then his lungs. He feels the pain in his lungs, his body growing heavier.

Time, ever a jumble in his mind, stops making any sense at all. There is only blackness. A blackness, through which a white light appears in the distance, towards which he starts to float. Strong hands are guiding him now towards the light, taking him towards something kind and benign. He senses a presence – *her* – *yes* – *her* – the mermaid swimming with him, her hair like strands of seaweed streaming around his own head, her powerful arms guiding him towards the light.

He begins to dream a dream.

*

He is washed up on the shore just a few hundred yards along the beach, at the Hot Walls. The stones are hard beneath him, and he is icy cold. The morning is lighter, and the air feels warmer than it should be for this time of year. A seagull swoops overhead.

He lies there for a few moments, looking at the altered world around him. The street lights along the top of the Hot Walls have gone, the modern railings disappeared. Cannon jut at regular intervals. The pier to the east is a wide platform, with a steamboat moored alongside.

He is on the beach of a world he has glimpsed many times. There is seaweed around him, handmade lobster pots, the deep smoking churn of steamers heading out through the harbour mouth.

And there is the timeless sound of the gulls.

That same cat is on the beach, looking at him, seeming to know him, purring, reassuring.

– *I am like the cats* – he realises – *I am like the cats.* –

He stands, climbs up the beach, comes out through the Sally Port on to the street, where the Army barracks stand in line.

Later that day, he walks through the wooded streets of Southsea. Carriages spin by and the white bonnets of maids bob in chatter and gossip to Sunday school. Here, a policeman in a long coat and badged helmet takes hold of him.

"You're coming with me, son" he says, gripping him with iron hands. "We've been looking for you for some time," he adds, with a firmness in his voice Dave knows he can't resist.

The policeman marches him across the Common where he just ran a hundred or so years later. He notices the tents of massed troops on the grass, the sounds of the bugler calling the men to fall in. Sail ships in the Solent ply their ways between the shore of Southsea beach and the distant green of the Isle of Wight. A Navy Cruiser, black as coal, a full head of steam and coke smoke pluming behind, powers through the waves. The colours of the world are hard and solid, as if he finally sees reality with clean, fresh eyes.

They march up through the newly-built elegances of Kent Road, make their ways past Saint Jude's church, where a line of carriages delivers families in austere clothes to the arched porch. A vicar stands looking severe in the doorway. These families turn to watch Dave and his escort as they march by.

Then they are out, along recently-built townhouses, up and along, where lamplighters are out twisting out gas flames on lampposts.

He knows this route. He is being marched back to the hostel he knows so well, up the steps. The police constable yanks the bell-pull and somewhere inside a clattering ring sounds.

After a while, the Butler opens the door.

"Look who I found," the policeman says.

The Butler's eyes open wide. "It's you, it's you!" he cries, and puts his arms around Dave's neck.

"It's you Master Jonathan! We thought you was drownded! Oh, your mother has been dying away from grief! Come in, come in!"

And he runs indoors, as Jonathan is shown into the massive front room of the house, which will, in a hundred or so years become the dining room where his friends will sit.

"Jonathan! Oh, Jonathan, where have you been? " says a woman who walks hurriedly into the room. "What has happened to you? And what are these queer clothes?"

She embraces him in a desperate hug. A younger woman runs in breathlessly, and then an older patriarch with a moustache and an impressive set of mutton chops, who despatches the excited Butler to make tea. The mother gabbles on. "You said you wanted to go out on the sea to paint, and then the storm came up out of nowhere... When they found your boat all smashed up, we thought the sea had taken you. Where did you go to? Oh, dear Lord, you're never to go out on the sea alone again, young man! Where have you been these last six months? Where have you been!"

He looks at her.

"I... I can't remember," he says. "I can't remember."

*

The report in the evening *News* tells of the loss of a fugitive to the sea at Old Portsmouth early that morning. It makes the early editions in its bare form on the second page, but as more lurid details come out about the psychopath who appeared in the hospital and killed his dying mother, it soon ousts from the front page the story about a City Council wrangle over parking fines. The next day, national headlines ask whether we should allow these sorts of people to walk among us, and later that week there are questions in the House about the safeguards the Government will put in place to prevent this type of thing from happening again. "Lessons will be learned," a spokesman promises.

Doctor Cassell, keeping his head low during the excitement, waits for a call from the police to identify the body they all expect to be washed up in one of the creeks along the south coast any day now. But the body does not surface. Experts on the harbour waters make calculated guesses as to where it might be, though some suspect it may have got caught up in the rubbish that lies on the harbour floor.

After two weeks of searching, police divers give up looking for Dave's body, and the policeman who was the last to see him alive speculates with Doctor Cassell that it will surface in its own time, once decomposition takes its natural course, and the body fills with gases.

But months later, Dave's body is still missing.

Doctor Cassell thinks sadly of him sometimes, and wonders if he could have done anything differently. There will be an inquest, at which the truth will come out that Dave did not go out of his way to kill his mother, but that he may have inadvertently contributed to her death by interfering with her medical treatment. Doctor Cassell will testify that Dave was a paranoid schizophrenic who suffered from psychotic episodes, and whose mental health had been affected further by the use of cannabis, and that he was finally unbalanced by news of his mother's illness.

The story will cause another minor sensation in the local paper for a short while as it gets a second wind. Then, in due course, life will settle down and there will be a new guest staying at the house in a leafy street in Southsea, on whom Doctor Cassell can keep a concerned and kindly eye.

But Doctor Cassell won't be able to stop himself from thinking about Dave from time to time. At one point, about a year after his disappearance, urged on by an unexplained feeling of curiosity, Doctor Cassell will hunt around in the attic of the house, and find the painting that once hung in the room he now uses as his office. He will notice four people in that painting, showing some kind of family reunion.

In the picture, there is a young man with dark hair, whose face he cannot quite make out because time and damp have lifted the paint.

But sometimes, in a moment of uncustomary fancy, Doctor Cassell imagines that this young man has the same features as that face he knew during the years he was in his care.

His patient. His David. His troubled young client who somehow ran out of time.

THE SONG OF MISS TOLSTOY

1. An Unexpected Appointment

The moment Miss Tolstoy saw the note on her desk, she felt a pang of foreboding.

It read:

Dear Miss Tolstoy,
An appointment has been made for you to be Audited on 16th October at 5pm. Please attend at room 345.
Thank you,
M Hopkins
Co-ordinator, Audits.

She froze as she stood over her desk, then double-checked the date.

"But that's this afternoon!" she muttered, pursing her lips and glaring at the paper pointedly, as if she hoped it would take the hint and bother someone else.

The Guildhall clock across the square from the Civic Offices struck the hour. She looked up, her shoulders tensing. *9am. Only eight hours to go!*

"What am I being Audited for?" she spoke loudly to the open-plan office. No-one answered.

Discomfort surged through her and she looked around for reassurance, mentally cataloguing its familiar blue dividing screens, its rows of reliable filing cabinets, the stalwart heavy-duty office carpet. Then, in a moment of paranoia, she wondered if the letter's signatory was in the room, watching. She glanced around quickly to see if anyone ducked behind a filing cabinet.

Everyone was acting normally. A couple of colleagues were drinking tea and chatting in the kitchen area. Another, at the workstation opposite was diligently reading emails, in a detached iPod soundworld. It was all as it always had been.

Two weeks before, the government had announced they would be sending a team of Auditors to councils around the UK as part of an efficiency drive.

It was something of a shock to discover that after such a short time, Auditors were already in the building.

She took a breath and began a half-hearted attempt to bury herself in her work for the Department of Parking Regulation: assessing the island's roads for either the application or removal of double yellow lines.

Her morning was punctuated by bouts of deep unease. By lunchtime, she had worked herself into a near-frenzy of worry about the appointment. When she bumped into her departmental boss, Mick Solomon in the lift, she blurted out:

"Solly, I'm being Audited this afternoon…"

"Oh, are you?" he answered, not raising his tired eyes from a pre-meeting briefing.

"You mean you *didn't know?*"

He shrugged off-handedly and continued to read. Above his lined face he was balding, while below he was spreading out from the middle, *like a beachball*, she thought. The thick vertically-striped shirts he had taken to wearing to distract onlookers' eyes from his burgeoning horizontality served only to make him more… *beachballesque*, she decided, stumbling on the adjective in a rare moment of fancy.

"It's the new administration," he replied, still engrossed in his briefing. "They're bringing in so many directives – I'm getting buried," he waved the stapled sheets, then considered what she had told him. "This is the *Auditing thing* the government have been talking about?"

"Well, *I* was asking *you*," her voice cracked.

He looked at her kindly, this slight woman in her mid-twenties with her brown ponytail and downcast face. His eyes softened:

"Lynda, what's wrong?"

Such a timid creature, he thought. *They call her the office mouse, the way she blinks around at the world so defensively.*

"My job… it is safe?" she sobbed. "You're not thinking of… I mean, you know, letting me go?"

Solomon adopted a reassuring tone:

"Lynda, I have not been told anything about this, but I definitely will have a say. So, no, I'm not thinking of dropping you, or letting you go, saying goodbye, or whatever you want to call it. Relax, this is what all new administrations do: flex their muscles for a few months. They'll settle down soon enough. Besides, you're too good a team member to let go. You need fear nothing. Nothing at all."

Further conversation was curtailed by the entrance of another co-worker, leaving a relieved Lynda to turn away and discreetly dry her eyes – dabbing a tissue drawn from her sleeve.

Even so, despite Solomon's reassurances, Lynda couldn't relax. At excruciatingly short intervals she checked the clock on her PC. 1.17 pm. 1.22 pm. 1.31 pm... and so on, as if a bomb were ticking away on her monitor.

At 4.48 pm, she stood and wandered like a sleepwalker from her desk to the lift and pressed the button for the third floor. She felt as if she were being walked to the scaffold. She had decided to arrive at the meeting slightly early – but whether it was to leave a good impression or display half-hearted defiance that she could choose the time, if not the place, of her execution, she hadn't quite decided.

At 4.49 pm, she stepped from the lift and followed the corridor to the end, counting room numbers.

At 4.50 pm, she got to room 344.

Her heart thumped violently as she realised it was the final room in the corridor. She checked the note in her hand. It definitely said room 345. She shot accusatory eyes around her. No more rooms. The corridor just ended at a blank white wall.

After perhaps half a minute or so of formless panic, she pulled herself together and knocked on the door of 344. It opened just enough to allow a clerk with small round glasses and a bald head to peer out. His face showed no hint of emotion as he asked in a flat voice:

"How can I help you?"

"Hello, I'm looking for room 345," she said.

His eyes widened with surprise, then his face grew tight and impassive again.

"This is room 344."

"Yes, but I'm looking for 345."

"That's not here."

He closed the door and left her standing, mouth agape. *Well! How rude!* She reread the letter, then knocked again.

The man opened the door just a crack.

"You see, I'm being Audited," she explained, holding up her note. "It says to come to room 345, but this is room 344, and I can't find room 345." She blurted the second bit, afraid he would close the door in her face again.

He scrutinised her from behind his round glasses as if he were looking at noisy youths playing in the street. He took the note from her hands, looked at it dispassionately, and then at her even more so.

"Well," he exhaled, in a slightly patronising voice. "It does *say* room 345." He considered, then said decisively. "Wait here. I'm sure it will be along shortly."

He handed her the letter, and closed the door.

She stood in that silent white corridor with its blue carpet, not sure whether he was being sarcastic. Then she realised he clearly was, and with an acid taste at the back of her mouth read the note again.

No phone number, she realised, so she wasn't going to be able to get hold of anyone straight off. She'd have to go back to her desk and send an email or something. She knew in her heart of hearts that would be a terrible thing to do.

Miss Tolstoy was never, ever, late for anything. She thought back over that very morning to assure herself this was true.

7.00 am: woke to my flat in the suburbs. 7.02 am: shook the night's filing and sorting out of my head and stepped from bed. 7.03 am, made a cup of tea...

She recalled how, over the next 15 minutes, she ate breakfast in the tidy kitchen of her flat while listening to *Radio 2*. The BBC nearly always accompanied toast and apricot jam, although she did occasionally have honey on a croissant to *Breeze FM*.

Sameness, she thought with an internal sigh, *is safeness*.

After breakfast, she spent 12 minutes in the shower, etc, 10 minutes getting dressed... and by two minutes to eight after a brief walk, she was ready to make the short railway journey from the suburbs on to the Island itself, where, after 13 minutes, it ended at the city's railway station.

I am never late for anything, she told herself again as a statement of her creed, and began to fear something terrible was going to happen if she didn't make this appointment. A worm of panic wriggled in her tummy.

At 4.59 pm, she hurried back down to the end of the corridor, and traced the numbers again. 301, 302, 303... all the way through to the last door in the corridor, 344 – and once again came to that blank white wall ahead.

Close to tears, she turned to go. Then, to her surprise, a door opened behind her and a woman's voice called after her:

"Miss Tolstoy?"

It was exactly 5 pm. To her astonishment, the end wall *did* have a door in it. A woman in white, with deep chestnut hair in a neat, slightly mannish style, was looking at her through a pair of black-rimmed spectacles. A smile played on her lips.

"Miss Tolstoy, we are ready to Audit you now."

"I, I didn't see the door," she said, drawing nearer. "I didn't see it."

"I suppose it's the new decor," said the woman, whose pure white trouser suit seemed to radiate dazzling light. "Come into my office," she smiled.

As Miss Tolstoy entered, she noticed there actually was a white number painted on the door, just perceptible as a different texture on a white background.

"I am Miss Peters," the woman said, turning to hold out a firm hand. "I am your Auditor."

The room they stood in was equally white, without the slightest hint of dust, dirt or wear. At the centre of this featureless box stood a white desk. Miss Peters gestured Miss Tolstoy to take a seat, while she sat opposite. She pulled out a neat white tablet from a drawer and began to swipe pages, reading with a serious deliberateness.

Miss Tolstoy eyed the tablet with some concern, nerves jangling.

"I understand there is going to be some restructuring," she said. "With the new administration?"

Miss Peters said nothing at all, poring over the screen. After three excruciating minutes, she looked up at Miss Tolstoy, with a smile.

"Do you have a cat, Miss Tolstoy?" she asked, with a kind of detached interest.

"Er, yes... Yes, I do."

"I see," she said, and tapped the screen. "Any other pets?"

"No, but I hardly see what – "

"And what about parents?"

The question jolted her train of thought. Her shoulders slumped.

"They... well... when I was little, they... well, they were killed in a plane crash, I –"

"Aha!" Miss Peters held up her hand to silence Miss Tolstoy then scanned the notes before her. She tapped the screen again and repeated, with some satisfaction, "A plane crash..."

She levelled her eyes at the younger woman and continued:

"Do you have a lover, boyfriend, girlfriend? Or perhaps someone with whom you have occasional sexual encounters?"

"Well, I hardly see –"

"Please Miss Tolstoy, just answer the question –"

"No!"

"No, you do not?"

"No, I mean, it's private. I won't answer the question!"

"So I'll take that as a yes, then. What is his or her name?"

"Name? How can they have a name when they don't exi-?" She exhaled frustratedly through her nose. "Damn!"

Miss Peters smiled.

"Thank you," she said, obviously pleased with herself, and tapping another box. "Now, do you believe in God, spirits, an afterlife, creationism, reiki, homoeopathy, hypnosis, the power of prayer or dreamcatchers? A belief in any one of these will be sufficient to answer yes," she added when she saw the expression of overwhelm on the other side of the desk.

But Miss Tolstoy pulled herself together. She needed to make a good impression, after all.

"Well, to be honest, I haven't really thought about some of those things. But, I did think about God, once. You know, I was a little girl when my parents died, and for a while I thought that maybe, you know... it would be nice to think that..."

Miss Peters was leaning forwards, looking at her quite intensely.

"Yes?"

"...Well, that a belief that my parents were in heaven would be a comfort. But, to be honest, I am more of a down-to-earth sort of a person."

"Down-to-earth. Hmm. Yes. So, are you saying you don't believe in the afterlife?"

"Yes."

"Yes you do or yes you don't?"

"I mean no. I mean, no I don't believe in the afterlife."

"I see." She paused, continuing to look at Miss Tolstoy, expectantly.

"As for the other things on your list, no, not really."

"Not really. Or not at all?"

"Not at all, then," Miss Tolstoy answered, unable to suppress a caustic edge to her voice.

"Aha." She tapped the tablet. "What about astrology, tarot cards, rune reading or any other form of prediction of the future?"

"No… I can't say I've ever been interested in any of these things."

"Do you, or have you ever dreamed of flying?"

"– Look, what is this about?" Miss Tolstoy asked, uncomfortably.

"Just answer the question, please, Miss Tolstoy." Her voice was cold. "All will become clear."

"Yes, of course I have…" said Miss Tolstoy, at which Miss Peters's face suddenly looked rather disappointed.

"Oh, oh dear," she said.

Miss Tolstoy carried on, oblivious.

"…Except that I have the most awful fear of heights. So getting on a plane is not at all my idea of fun.

At this information, Miss Peters perked up. She tapped a note into the tablet. "A fear of heights…" she echoed as she wrote. "Excellent."

She looked up abruptly.

"Thank you Miss Tolstoy," she said.

She stood. Made her way to the door.

"What?"

"We'll be in touch."

"In touch, when?"

"In due course."

She opened the door and nodded her to leave. In a state of confusion, Miss Tolstoy left the room and stepped into the corridor.

"But when will that be?" she asked, with a slightly lost voice.

She turned to look at Miss Peters, but found that the door closed. It fitted absolutely seamlessly into the wall. It wasn't just that if you didn't know it was there, you would never spot it. Even if you did, you still wouldn't.

At that moment, the clerk from room 344 stepped out of his door, closed it and locked it behind him.

"Are you still here?" he said, with some surprise, then headed down the corridor on his way home.

Miss Tolstoy watched him leave and looked down at her wristwatch.

7pm.

The interview had taken a whole two hours!

2. The Doorway

That evening George Clooney was waiting for her, just inside the door when she got in. He rubbed her legs in the way he normally did, and demanded why she was late. She stroked his head with a gentle movement and said:

"Did you miss me?"

George said little, merely tipping his head and stretching luxuriously under her touch. She adored George Clooney, with his dark hair and his perfect looks, and gathered him up in her arms, burying her nose in the back of his neck, holding him like that for a few seconds of luxurious selfishness.

"Time to eat, eh, George?" she announced, and took him into the kitchen. He danced on the floor for her as she spooned pungent meat into a bowl and rattled some biscuits on top. How she loved him, with his dark fur! George Clooney. All purrs and stretches.

Her evening was the same evening she had enjoyed in privacy almost without exception, during her last 4 years working for the Council.

She got herself a healthy bite to eat from the fridge, and snuggled down in front of the telly, with George jumping up on the sofa beside her. Then he stepped on to her lap and dug his claws in for a few painful seconds as he turned around twice to find the best angle. Then he settled, resting his head on his paws and purred at the warmth of her body.

Someone from the new administration was on the tv talking about audits, she half noted as she prepared to watch something more interesting. She clocked the journalist's question: "Isn't this whole emphasis on efficiency avoiding the fact that you are planning to lay people off at an increasing rate?"

"Too right!" she said under her breath, before flicking the channel to watch her chosen night's viewing.

She didn't like new tv shows. Something old, from when she was young, hearing tv coming up the stairs as she hovered on the edge of sleep, while her parents watched below. She liked the reliability of a DVD. No distractions, and the comfortable nostalgia of old tech. She usually watched a romance, or it might be a comedy. Something light and witty and wholesome, *much like George Clooney*, she thought, *what he was like back then*. Or it might be something from the box set of all 10 seasons of *Friends*, or an episode of that old series *Sex And the City*, which she found hilarious and completely unlike anything her world had to offer. Then there was *ER*, which, of course, had George Clooney in it. When he was on the television, she would stroke her own George Clooney, and sometimes daydream that the real George Clooney had a hairy chest, just like this one, as she buried her fingers in its fur.

She liked American tv and American film. It was easy to digest, and nothing at all like her life. She regarded it as different, but safe, nevertheless.

Sometimes, she would imagine what it was like to live in America. She had no desire to go there. Other times she would tell herself that as Britain's only island city, Portsmouth was in fact the British Manhattan. Okay, it didn't have any skyscrapers, but it did have some high-rise flats, and the Spinnaker Tower, with views across the sea. *Not that I have been up any of them, with my fear of heights,* she would invariably remind herself, with a shudder.

No, what she liked about her life, about the town, and about her job dealing with yellow lines on the road were one and the same: they were flat. And that's the way she wanted it to stay.

*

After the Audit, life went on exactly as it had done before, and after a while of hearing nothing, its memory receded like a half-remembered dream.

That's why Miss Tolstoy was surprised to find, one afternoon, another note under a pile of paper on her desk.

"Why! – It's arrived out of nowhere!" she said to herself as she gawped at it, unable to believe that with her superb efficiency she hadn't noticed it earlier in the day.

This time the note said:

Dear Miss Tolstoy,

An appointment has been made for an Outplacement Interview on 18th November at 5pm. Please attend at room 345.

Thank you,

M Hopkins

Co-ordinator, Audit Department.

Her heart sank. *Outplacement* was a funny piece of management speak, she thought, but she knew exactly what it meant.

"They're going to make me redundant, after all," she told herself. "I can't believe it."

She looked at the clock on her PC monitor. It was 4.37pm. She had nearly missed the appointment, she realised with a shock. She stood up quickly to ask Solly about why, out of the whole department, she had been selected like this, but he was in a meeting with someone from the Ministry of Urban Regulatory Affairs.

She strode to his desk and left a note: "Urgent: We must talk – Lynda". She steeled herself, straightened her immaculate ponytail and wiped the palms of her hands down the front of her white blouse to ensure there were no wrinkles or creases. Then she headed for the lift.

*

The invisible office door shimmered for a moment as she approached, and when it opened noiselessly, Miss Peters stepped out with her powerful smiling face. Miss Tolstoy found her even more unnerving this time, because her expression appeared frozen in complete jollity.

"Hello! Ha ha! Yes, come in please,"

Miss Tolstoy, head bowed, sat at the desk.

Miss Peters looked at her for a moment, took a breath and then pulled out her tablet from the drawer. She proceeded as if working from a script.

"Miss Tolstoy... Lynda. May I call you Lynda?"

"If you like," said Lynda, feeling unexpected fear of this peculiar woman.

"Lynda, it is with some pleasure that I am now able to inform you that you have been selected to take part in a new training programme."

"Take part in..?" Miss Tolstoy was aghast. "I thought you were going to... outplace me."

"Yes! Ha!" said Miss Peters, then dismissing the thought, proceeded in a businesslike manner: "There is only one stipulation before your training begins." She reached in a drawer and pulled out a blank piece of paper. She drew a little cross on it at the base, and pushed it across the table to Miss Tolstoy. "Please sign where I have marked it."

"But this is blank."

"Is it?"

"Well, yes it is, actually."

The other woman smiled widely, showing off her teeth and pink gums.

"Well it won't be once you've signed it."

"But – but – why should I?"

Miss Peters smiled more widely.

"To state that you will not divulge the nature of the training to anyone."

"Not tell anyone? But why?" Miss Tolstoy blurted.

"It is part of the nature of the training that no-one you work with is aware of the training." She leaned forward and fixed Lynda with a serious look. "Unless, of course, you would prefer not to participate. Which would not be looked upon well by the Department, I have to tell you."

"Not looked on well?"

"Not well at all."

She continued to stare at Miss Tolstoy with sharp, glittering eyes, adding:

"Whereas taking part in the training most definitely will be."

She smiled broadly again and sat back.

Miss Tolstoy thought for a moment. Pushing the sheet across the table, she said:

"I just want to know a little bit more about the training."

"Yes, of course," said Miss Peters. "The training will commence soon. You have very particular qualities, and we believe that you are the best-suited for it."

"But what is it?"

"Just sign that you agree to do the training, and all will come clear," she slid the paper back in front of Miss Tolstoy and proffered the pen, or more accurately, waved it forcefully in front of her eyes.

"So, you're saying you can't tell me what the training is, until I agree to go on it. And once I agree, I can't tell anyone about it?"

"That's right," Miss Peters replied with a look that said that despite Miss Tolstoy's slowness in the thinking department, she had finally caught up.

"But that's stupid. How can I agree to something I know nothing about?" She slid the paper back again.

Miss Peters's face grew extremely fierce-looking. When she replied, she squeezed her words between very tight lips:

"You will have to trust us."

She stood, leaned over the table and glared down at Miss Tolstoy, seeming more muscular than ever. "We have gone to a lot of trouble on your behalf. We will not look on it kindly, now, if you throw this opportunity back at us."

Quite overwhelmed, Miss Tolstoy considered for a moment. Then she shrugged and pulled the paper towards her. She signed, with a sulky set to her face and a feeling of deep misgiving in her tummy. Miss Peters sat down, satisfied as she spirited the piece of paper away.

"Good."

"Well?"

"Well what?" Miss Peters looked up at her with some confusion.

"What's the training?"

"We'll let you know in due course."

"You said all will come clear," Miss Tolstoy protested, her indignation carrying her voice upwards to the featureless ceiling of this oppressive white box.

"Yes, it will. We will give you further information about it shortly. Thank you. Goodbye."

Miss Peters rose abruptly and walked quickly to the door, which she threw open with a violent jerk. She eyed Miss Tolstoy firmly.

"Goodbye, Lynda," she said, with an air of finality.

Miss Tolstoy got up and stared at this peculiar woman for a short while.

"But aren't you going to tell me more about it?"

"Thank you for coming," said Miss Peters impatiently, yet continuing to smile broadly. "Thank you."

"But, the training programme..."

"Goodbye!" She was suddenly standing uncomfortably close to Miss Tolstoy, her smile pushing into Lynda's personal space.

Her heart hammering, Lynda left the room. She hadn't gone half a step when she turned to ask one more time about the training.

Once again there was only a blank white wall behind her.

*

As soon as the metal box of the lift began its descent, her heart began to sink with it.

She ran over the interview, time and again, trying to recall whether there was anything she had missed that might provide a clue to its meaning.

Could she have said anything different? If she had just been more assertive? She had been on an assertiveness course just the year before, but it hadn't really been of much use and she never felt the need for it in her quiet job as a low-ranking Local Government Officer.

Sunk in these thoughts, it was some time before she realised the lift hadn't stopped at the ground floor. A big "B" came up in 1970s red lighting over the door, and still the lift continued down. It was peculiar. The doors stayed resolutely shut, while the occasional jolt implied she was dropping deeper and deeper down.

After few minutes like this, she began to feel uneasy, wondering if perhaps she wasn't descending at all.

Perhaps the doors had jammed? Yes, that was it!

She pressed the communication button and pushed her face close to the speaker grill. The ringing cut off.

"Hello?" the cold voice reminded her of the clerk from room 344.

"Hello, I'm in the lift. The doors seem to be stuck. I can't get out."

"Not long now," said the voice. "Soon be there."

The voice cut off.

"Hello? Hello?" She pressed the button again. The same voice. Impatient now.

"Yes?"

"I am trying to get out."

"Wait please." The voice cut off again.

After another two minutes, the doors opened.

She was peering down a dim corridor, with a door at the far end where a bright light shone through a keyhole. The corridor had more of the hardwearing blue carpet found throughout the building, and plain white walls. The lighting was out, leaving only the light from the far end. There were no other doors.

She pressed the lift button to take her back up, but the doors stayed resolutely open. After a minute or so of pressing unresponsive controls, she tutted and decided to find the stairs. *Really, it's just not good enough! The whole country is falling apart!* It had been like this since the former administration came in to power. And now it was worse. *This is ridiculous!*

She took two steps down the corridor. The doors shut smoothly with a gentle bump, and she whirled around to see an arrow pointing upward in red LED above the door.

Well, she wasn't going to get back in *that*, anyway. It was Friday evening, and she would probably get stuck. She had an image of a cleaner finding her body on Monday morning, dehydrated, with a swollen black tongue – or alive, but wild-eyed, delirious and dishevelled, spitting specks of foam. *Nope.* The stairs were the best option. She pushed along the corridor to find them.

What is this place? – she wondered as she sought a Fire Exit sign. *A basement store or something? Very strange!*

She approached the door. It was made of dense, heavy wood. It seemed to be extremely old, with metal studs set in it, and a wrought-iron handle twisted into a ring.

"Peculiar," she said to herself under her breath, feeling a sudden rush of adrenalin at the strangeness of things. "I had no idea this level existed."

She wondered whether she had found her way into an archive, like the British Library, with its massive storage rooms built under its courtyard. *Maybe this is the Portsmouth City Archive, right under the Guildhall Square.*

As she drew nearer to the door, such thoughts melted away. A smell was coming for the direction of that door, reminding her of something special. Something wonderful. As if she'd had a reminder of her earliest memories of her parents. A smell to do with playing in the open air on a sunny day. It struck right inside her, lighting up a sense of nostalgia, filling her body with deep longing and a sadness all at once.

Close up to the door, she realised the light coming through the keyhole was not white, but golden. More golden light leaked through cracks around the rough old frame. *It all looks quite mediæval*, she thought, remembering a visit she'd made to Arundel Castle, with its low, wide ancient doors set in massy stone walls. *What a lot of effort to go to, just to store some musty old records!*

She took hold of the cold metal handle and twisted.

The air that hit her body as it swung open was warm – pungent with the smell of wildflowers and summer. As her eyes adjusted to the scene before her, she gasped – half from surprise, and half from delight.

In front of her a meadow swept away to a valley floor, beneath a bright blue sky where birds flitted and whirled, filling the air with chirrups and twitters, and the flutter of feathers. Insects, large and soft-bodied moved with focussed purpose among wildflowers, while a mixture of hedges and taller trees stretched down the hill on her left-hand-side.

Not a cloud in the sky. Nor a sun, in fact, but the bright, golden light seemed to emanate from the land itself, imbuing everything with the feeling of one of those romantic movies she loved. The air was so clear she could count the speckles on the feathers of the starlings above and see the red tongue of the blackbird perched on a tree far down the vale, singing – singing its golden, happy heart out.

Immediately, she was overcome with a sense of joy and utter peace, and she wandered through the meadow, down the hill, past brakes filled with the chirrup of insects and the scents of lost memories, in which she luxuriated. She smiled – finding a long-buried childlike wonder in herself. And at that moment, and thereafter, if you had asked her to find her way back to the door, she would not have been able to tell you where it was, nor even what it looked like.

3. Songtime

Soon, she found a track winding through the trees. She followed it down the hill, the wildness of the woodland steadily becoming more tended and ordered, until she was walking through a grove of fruit trees, neatly planted in rows.

All was rich abundance. Intertwined with sturdy branches and luxuriant foliage were vines laden with soft purple grapes ready to burst. Crimson apples – great swollen orbs – were accompanied by pears, peaches, apricots, and yet more exotica – star fruit, kumquat, mango – a profusion of bright colours and scents filling the air, leaving a thick, rich, almost sickly taste at the back of her throat.

"It's better than the best fruit stall I've ever seen," she thought to herself in wonder, then considered the local superstore along the road from her flat. "It's even better than Sainsbury's!"

She reached up and plucked an apple, rubbed it on her blouse, eyed her own reflection blinking back from its waxy red skin. The look she saw on her face was disbelief.

"What is this place?" she spoke to the air. "How did the Council get planning permission for it? What will ratepayers say when they find out? They made such a stink about the Spinnaker Tower! And how do they squeeze it all in, under Guildhall Square?"

She bit into the apple, feeling in super-reality her teeth breaking the skin, the sweetness spraying a tiny cloud of mist on her lips, her mouth and tongue coated in the shock of juice.

It was phenomenal. She savoured the satisfying crunch with joy – a perfect mix of bitter-sweetness spreading across her palate, making the muscles of her jaws ache with an acid burn: utter pleasure.

"Mmmmm…"

As she bit again, she became aware of a pair of eyes watching her from the leaves of a blackcurrant. They started wide when their owner realised they had been spotted, and a diminutive figure ran off through the bushes.

"Hey!" she called, and dropping the apple to the ground, followed on. "Hey! Come back."

Behind her, where the apple fell, it decayed immediately, and began to sprout, so that within thirty seconds of its touching this sacred soil, a sapling was winding its way up to the sky.

*

The movement of the bushes, swaying with the rush of a passing body, grew still. The light slapping thumps of feet on flat earth grew distant, until she could hear them no more.

Alone again in another part of the grove, Miss Tolstoy walked aimlessly on. Then her foot alighted on a patch of flattened earth – another rough path through the trees. She followed it in a daydream, basking in the warmth, walking in a near-trance induced by the heady drone of bees circling under light filtered through leaves. Or *from* the leaves – she still could see no sun.

She felt the air change: a cool breath of fresher wind caressed her face, and she heard the lonely cry of a seagull backed by a low, gentle roar. Her heart leapt. *The sea!* Salty tang in her nose. Breasting a low rise, her body pulsed in response to the wide blue ocean opening before her, the full harsh noise of shingle raking shore. *Kashush, kashush, kashush,* over and over.

In the distance, the tiny figure of a child ran from her. With a sense of urgency, Miss Tolstoy lengthened her stride.

The shingle crunched beneath her feet, the shifting stones throwing her off balance. Ahead, something appeared in the distance, slowly growing more discernible as she approached. A huddle of upright strips, backed by other shapes, wide and square, bright with colours, deep with shadows. A small settlement, in front of which stood a group of people apparently waiting for something. She picked them out more clearly as she drew closer – fit young men and women, children, the curved outlines of bodies bent with age. The child who had run from her joined them and turned to look back at her, clinging to the skirts of a fine-looking woman dressed in a simple, brightly-coloured cotton dress. A semi-circle of thirty or so people, smiles on their faces awaited. Wonder played inside her soul: light on a pool that had lain long dark.

They had assembled to greet her!

A dark-skinned and lean young man to whom Miss Tolstoy took an immediate liking stepped forward with open hands.

"Welcome," he said. "Welcome home."

"Home?" she echoed, as if she had been waiting for this moment all her life.

*

The village where the community lived was a basic affair.

Gathered on a tip of land pointing into the sea on three sides, with a small, boatless natural harbour to the West, the place they called "the village" itself was not really a village at all, but a collection of low-fenced enclosures filled with cushions, where villagers gathered to eat and sleep. The enclosures were roofed with light fabrics that somehow cast shade beneath, though they provided refuge from a sunless sky.

Fruits and cooked vegetables were served in wooden bowls three times a day, brought by a villager from the direction of the trees. Often it was Lensher, the girl Miss Tolstoy had followed, who brought succulent and tasty food on a wooden tray.

The food was varied and simple – wholesome and richly nourishing. Miss Tolstoy found herself smacking her lips at the rich juice dripping lushly from exotic fruits, or guzzling the bitter-sweet milk of coconut with a satisfied *aaah*.

Life in the village was more than pleasing. The days developed a sleepy rhythm: lounging by the sea, swimming, or taking part in silly games both amusing and utterly pointless.

Something struck her in her very earliest days there. Before her arrival she had never really experienced gratitude. Yes, she had thanked the bus driver who waited for her because she was late, and wrote a letter to an aunt for a Christmas present. But the villagers expressed gratitude on a grand scale.

She sat with them as they discussed the pleasure in their lives – they noticed the tiniest things: a beetle glistening on a leaf, a fish jumping in the waters, the wind singing songs in shells held to their ears. These observations made her realise how she had never really paid attention.

Every evening, the villagers performed a ritual. They sat under the yellow stars, and one of them began to talk in a sing-song voice that transformed to a simple tune that after a few basic notes grew in complexity until it became an extended melody.

Each song turned into a celebration of the land. Rich, dazzling words cast images in her mind of eternal golden light, of smiles, laughter. The villagers around her would then join in, weaving in their own melody lines and harmonies to enrich it further. Each day the song was different, though it was similar in content: praising the flora of the island, naming each fruit tree and bush. It named the birds and the mammals, the fishes of the sea, the porpoise in the waters, the stars above.

The villagers created each song on the fly, interweaving patterns of joy and happiness, possibility and delight, until it reached a crescendo naming the kindnesses and friendships between all, the loves, the remembrances of those passed, the gratitude for the foods that arrived each day. At this, Miss Tolstoy, always a foodie, found herself joining in, in a strange half-ecstasy weaving her own tune into the melody.

This ritual the islanders called *Songtime*. It happened every night, sending up songs to the fat, glowing stars, which twinkled all the more brightly. After Songtime, Miss Tolstoy fell asleep, nestled among the villagers, experiencing a calm she had never known elsewhere.

In the days that followed her first participation in Songtime, different foods arrived. Miss Tolstoy was surprised to see proffered to her the things she loved most, which she had thought she could not possibly taste here.

Was she actually *ordering* this food at Songtime? She decided to experiment. Sure enough, over the following days, Lensher brought her Earl Grey tea, a latte, a mochaccino, along with croissants, apricot jam and honey.

This got her thinking.

One day, after a particularly perfect cup of cappuccino with vanilla syrup, the puzzle of the food became too much to bear. She was on the beach with that handsome, dark-skinned man who had first welcomed her, a fisherman whose name was Paris. Fixing him with an inquisitive eye, she said: "Paris, where does the food come from?"

He smiled and shot her a puzzled expression. "You mean you don't know?" he answered. "Isn't it obvious? You sang about it last night!"

"Yes, but where does it come from? It must come from somewhere?"

But he could give no further explanation than *you sang about it.*

"Okay – I get that I order it, but I mean who made it?"

"You did."

"No, really, who – "

"When you sang. You made it."

A preposterous thought, but after he had given the same answer at least twenty times, she gave up. What was he keeping from her?

That night, she sang of a curry – the one she had eaten on a rare social occasion when she had joined a departmental celebration of a workmate's birthday.

As she sang, the memory of that curry rose up in her from nowhere – a lovely lamb balti cooked in an earthen pot, rich with exotic smells, with a garlic naan, piping hot. But she felt self-conscious, troubled by what she was doing.

The next morning, sure enough, a lamb balti arrived, as piping hot as she sang. It looked *exactly* how she remembered it, but somehow its taste was sour. She glanced around her, suspicious.

"What's the trick?" she said out loud. The villagers stared puzzlement at her.

Paris's father was Old Lemu, the village elder. He considered her a few moments, then looked away to pat the head of a boy who buried his face in the old man's chest.

The novelty of the place was wearing off. Signs of hidden industry and evidence of unseen agency pointed to something beyond. The mostly forgotten logic of her former life came back to her, and she cornered Paris:

"Who is in charge? Who arranges the food? Where is it prepared?"

"What does this mean? This *prepared?*"

Miss Tolstoy took a breath. She could see he did not know what she meant.

How to explain?

"Fruits come from trees. You pick them and they are ready. The trees have made them, yes?"

"Yes, I see," he answered hesitantly.

"So, who makes the coffee? Coffee has to be ground and boiled."

"Does coffee come from trees?" he asked.

"Yes, yes." she agreed impatiently. "Then it is ground and mixed with hot water. Who does that? And the milk, it comes from cows. There must be a kitchen, somewhere."

She was expecting another of his vague, evasive answers. Instead, he stood up and replied with a shrug:

"Not a kitchen. You must mean The Farm."

He gestured her to follow him.

Is this the answer, then? Miss Tolstoy thought, as she trudged along behind him, shooting peevish glances at the back of his head. *All this evasiveness just a matter of the using the right jargon?*

He took her along the beach, and back up the rise she had walked over on her first day there, the sound of the sea and the gulls in the air growing quiet behind them. Then they descended a shallow slope and were soon walking on coarse grass. After a while, they were stepping through the lush green groves she had seen when she arrived, with their buzzing bees and fat shiny fruits that were always ripe. Next, they headed in a new direction, picking their ways through the regimented fruit trees until eventually they came to a patchwork of fields filled with all kinds of low trees, bushes and plants, stretching on as far as she could see.

"This is it: The Farm," he said, making a wide sweep with his arm. "The fields here produce everything."

She looked around her with surprise. Not a kitchen stove, a chef nor a farmworker to be seen.

Corn grew in one field, rice in a paddy field, cows chewed in a paddock. But –

"How do you *make* the food?"

Paris looked at her blankly. "Make it? What do you mean?"

"Who cooks it? Who prepares it? And where are the farmers?"

"We are all the farmers," he said. "We gather the harvest."

"But who plants it? And how do you water it? I mean, there has to be some watering going on or something..."

"Why?" he asked.

"Why? Why! Because otherwise it would all die. And you can't just have food out of nowhere."

A joyous, raucous stream of giggles issued from him at her words, which he clearly thought were complete nonsense. "It's not from nowhere," he said making that sweeping gesture again, which this time Miss Tolstoy found infuriating. "It's from here."

He turned to go back, and she followed him, firing more questions, her voice growing increasingly strident.

In reply, he shrugged and said:

"We gather the food in the morning. It grows here. When you sing of something you want, that grows, too."

That night, as the villagers prepared to go to sleep for the night after their daily song together, she wandered back to the fields and looked at the Farm more closely. Not all the crops and plants were familiar. Strange-looking succulents gave off a rich, wholesome smell. A flower the size of her hand with broad leaves and bright purple bell-shaped flowers had a more acrid scent.

She decided the best way to get her answers was to stay up all night, to see exactly who produced the food and how.

The night deepened further, with its imperceptible creep, blacking out the fields until only a residual glow from the fat, golden stars remained. It was a quiet night, disturbed only by the steady *guzzle guzzle* of the plants pulling up nutrients from the soil – a rhythmic sound making soft music in her ears. She propped herself up against a tree trunk and kept her eyes fixed intently on the shadow-bound fields.

At several points she found her eyes growing heavy and her head nodding. Each time, she stood, made a circuit under the starlight of the shadow-wrapped plants, suckling from the earth with a vegetable sound that somehow seemed contented. From time to time, too, another sound broke in the darkness, as of a gourd expanding, or a vessel filling with sap. It was a reassuring sound, and try as she might, the darkness took her, and she drifted off into sleep.

*

She was woken the following morning by the sound of footsteps in the undergrowth, then a snapping sound and the rustle of leaves as a bush somewhere sprang upright after being tugged. She sat up, cursing herself for dozing off and blinked around to find food all around her. The wholesome-smelling bread plants had actually grown small, fresh loaves of bread! Lensher was snapping a croissant from a bush where it hung from a stalk.

Miss Tolstoy pulled herself to her feet with a slightly angry movement, then stepped to one of the purple-flowered plants. As she neared it, she recognised the familiar smell she'd noted the day before. She tipped one of its bells to look more closely, and inadvertently dispensed hot coffee on to the rich earth at her feet.

"I don't believe it," Miss Tolstoy said, a deep sense of misgiving settling in the pit of her stomach.

"I just don't believe it."

*

"What is this place? What is it called? Tell me!"

Paris shrugged. He was fishing at the water's edge, a simple rod and line in his hand.

"This place is called *here*."

"Here? No. It isn't *Here*."

"Well, where is it, if not here?" he asked.

"It isn't *called* Here," she insisted.

He thought a moment and pointed a little way off. "Although that is There."

"No, Paris, listen. What is the name of this place?"

Finally, after a long pause he said: "I have heard it called *The Island*. Someone called it *Paradise* once, I remember."

"Paradise? Paradise?" Miss Tolstoy echoed, aware of a possibility she had been avoiding.

She took a breath and held it to give her comfort as she approached the thought.

Am I dead, then? Is that it?

She lay down and stared at the sky, hopelessly. She thought back over her life – tried to make sense of it. What things in her life had actually meant something?

She remembered a little figure in Cosham. *If I am dead, who will look after George Clooney?*

She sat up. It didn't matter if she were dead. She had to get back.

More of her former self came back. In Portsmouth, she was a cog in a bigger machine. If this were Paradise, it had to be organised, right? It had to have an organiser...

"Who's in charge?" she demanded, remembering her assertiveness training – specifically the roleplay about complaining to the hotel manager. "I want to speak to them, now!"

"In charge?" he repeated, trying to make sense of the words.

She had been undoubtedly enamoured of this extraordinarily-good-looking-if-a-little-dim man, but she now found something in his uncomprehending shrug and his unquestioning contentment with life difficult to accept.

"Clearly, that's not you," she bit. "There has to be someone whose purpose it is to –"

"Purpose?"

"Yes, purpose. Meaning."

His silence made her more angry.

"What's your purpose in life?" she stamped. "You must do something!"

"I do," he said, unsure what she was driving at. "I sit on the beach. I play with the children. I catch fish and throw them back. That is my purpose. Why? What is your purpose?"

She thought hard about her old life and the world she had left behind.

More fragments came back to her. She drew herself up, tilting her head proudly as she told him about double yellow lines on roads, how people couldn't stop on them, and if they did they were punished. Somehow the ideas didn't quite hang together as she expressed them. When she finished he laughed and said:

"The way you speak – it definitely *sounds* like it's important." A grin spread across his face. "I think this is important," he gestured his heart and his body. "Health, happiness, the way I feel." The rod he held began to twitch, and in short order he pulled a scintillating fish from the water. After he unhooked the line he took some time to admire its pulsing, iridescent scales glistening in the golden light, considered the slow swish of its tail, how its gills worked as it panted for air, its gasping mouth. Then he threw the wriggling creature back into the waves with a muted plash.

*

A few days after her attempt to find the source of the food, Miss Tolstoy joined the villagers for Songtime as usual, though with the same feeling of puzzlement that had, for the last few days, kept her so quiet and withdrawn. As she nestled on a big soft cushion, the villagers looked to Paris with a knowing smile, and he walked across the little fenced-off area towards her, his eyes flickering with excitement and reflected starlight.

"Lynda," he said. "It is the natural order of things that everybody starts the Songtime at some point. We have agreed that tonight is the right time for you."

An electric tension rose through her body.

"Me? Start off a song!"

The villagers' encouraging smiles had the opposite effect. She had never done such a thing in her life!

She grew rigid. Her mind blank.

– Blank – but for all the expectant smiles of these people with their eyes upon her. Or nearly all of them. Old Lemu was watching her with guarded eyes.

Miss Tolstoy smiled through her embarrassment. "No, I – really – I can't!" she turned her head to block out the sight of these people. Paris stepped closer. She arched backwards defensively.

"But we insist!" said Paris, laughing at her resistance.

"Yes, start the song!" shouted Lensher from the far side of the enclosure. Others joined in. Excited voices laughingly demanded a melody.

Paris stepped back and began to sway rhythmically in front of her.

"Song," he said, marking the syllable with a handclap. "Song..." and soon the whole settlement was clapping along, and laughing.

She felt as if a giant hand were trying to squeeze the life from her. The pressure in her head became unbearable. She jumped up, panic tumbling through her.

"No! No! I won't sing. It's impossible. All this food, from singing? It can't happen like this. I'm telling you, it's absolutely impossible!"

She was shouting, the realised.

The villagers fell silent. Only the sound of the sea could be heard. They were clearly wondering what this passionate song from the newest member of their community could mean, as the yellow starlight shone on her neat ponytail.

Having started, she couldn't stop herself:

"You have to do some kind of work for this. Some kind of *sacrifice*," she explained, walking the length of the enclosure. "Don't you see it? There's some massive trick being played – I don't know why – to keep you here. I don't know how it's done, but it stops you taking responsibility. Things aren't just given. You can't just see out your days in a dream! It's impossible!"

No-one spoke. Everyone was looking up at her as she paced in front of them. They looked amazed.

Why couldn't they see that there was something wrong..? Unless... unless they were in on it!

She stopped pacing, her shoulders drooped. With frustration rising, she implored them:

"Tell me how it's done... What's the secret? Where are the kitchens? The workers? Your slaves? Show me! Because those plants at The Farm – I'm telling you now, they're gimmicks – they can't be real!"

The silence stretched on longer. Did the villagers understand what she was telling them? Perhaps they did. Something undefined in the night had changed. She definitely sensed something, an alteration.

The moment stretched on for a whole minute, then another, and another still.

And then...

Nothing happened.

Nothing at all.

She'd only imagined there was a change, clearly.

At last, overwhelmed at the thought of performing before this crowd, she rushed from the gathering and headed to the woods, burning with her own stupidity. The old fear and stress that had been with her all the time in her previous life, now it was invoked, had taken hold.

*

After she had gone, a murmur of disquiet rose up from the villagers. They looked around at each other.

A quick exchange of views resulted in Paris being sent after her. He went willingly, feeling responsible for her outburst.

He caught up with her in the woods.

"Wait," he took her soft hand in his.

It comforted her in a way she didn't expect – an act of physical kindness she was so unused to. As a child she had never been shown affection – by the distant aunt she had grown up with, by the kids at school who somehow seemed to fear the contagion of orphanhood. A lonely life.

"Come," he said. "I'll show you the island. It's here in one place, and you'll see there are no *kitchens* as you call them, or *slaves*. You'll see it all laid out beneath you under starlight."

Unsure what he meant, Lynda let him lead her. After a short walk they arrived at three trees that reached high into the sky. Through a strange freak of nature, (as if those *were* strange, here) high up the trunks converged to form one continuity, where a natural platform hung at a dizzying height.

"*What the bloody hell is this?*" she said with growing apprehension, noticing how shapes in the bark formed natural steps that spiralled into the sky.

"This is the Looking Tree. From the top you can see far more than I have shown you. Not just The Farm, everything..." he made a wide gesture with both hands and pointed upwards into the dark night, where she could just see in the heights more of those natural steps. "From there you can see the whole world. Come!"

He jumped onto the steps, but Miss Tolstoy's feet remained resolutely planted on the ground.

"I can't," she said, in a faint voice. "I can't go up there."

Paris jumped down to look at her. Once again it was as if he didn't understand the language she spoke.

"Can't?" he asked. "Yes, you just put your foot here..." He reached down to guide her.

"No! No! No!" she cried, shrinking with fear. "Keep away!" Her chest was tight, a giddy whirl shook her body. She raised her arms to protect herself, as she had done years before in the playground: children gathered round, taunting her, unprotected prey. Back then, loneliness and fear had welded together in her soul, on asphalt painted with yellow hopscotch lines.

Paris and Lynda stared at each other as if seeing each other clearly for the first time beneath the starry sky, and in that moment of shocked stillness, both heard something soft and leathery whistle as it sliced the air. Both sensed a shadow, something terrible blacking out the stars in slow-moving sequence. It was a presence Miss Tolstoy knew to be deeply evil. Malicious, baleful. A creature from her nightmares.

She scanned the night sky, her heart contracted to cold stone. Then with a gasp she ran, before that shadow tracked her down.

4. "What Is Fear?"

The next morning, the sunshine child Lensher skipped to The Farm to gather the morning food as usual. She came back 20 minutes later, nothing in her hands, puzzlement on her face.

The villagers gathered around, waiting expectantly to hear the explanation for this novel event.

"There is no food," Lensher announced. "Nothing to eat at all!" She shook her head vigorously, spread her upturned palms wide and shrugged theatrically, enjoying being the centre of attention.

Old Lemu's face grew stern and he grunted to himself.

He despatched the tribe's tallest man Nalsshar to investigate, reasoning that since Lensher was the shortest, their two reports together would cover all of it. After a while, Nalsshar returned, rested a palm on his cheek, and blurted –

"Lensher is right! It is as if the food plants have changed. Or died – which is the same thing."

Old Lemu called the oldest village members together, reasoning that their memories combined would cover nearly all of history, while the remaining villagers looked on in reverence. All declared nothing in this vein had happened before. Shallgam, a small dark woman in bright dyed robes with a fish design on them spoke of the strange behaviour of Lynda Tolstoy the previous night. All agreed her actions were the root of it.

The whole village decided to consult her, though Old Lemu was not optimistic, and said so.

"But she must be able to help us!" Nalsshar countered from his great height, while the villagers clapped their hands. "Was it not her who sang of this?"

"And do we wash our faces in the mud that made us dirty?" Old Lemu replied.

But the other villagers, sure she could put it right, set out to find her.

They searched around the village, then scattered along the shoreline without success. Then Old Lemu spoke with Paris, who climbed the Looking Tree to gaze over the whole island, but he reported to those at its foot that she could not be seen.

Old Lemu called Paris down. He quizzed him closely over the previous night, asking precise questions about what was said and done. He was interested in her refusal to climb the tree. But most of all, he was shaken by news of the shadow in the sky. He thought long and hard, and pronounced:

"She will be near to the ground, out of sight of eyes above."

To the villagers' pleas for guidance, he said: "Search beneath the trees."

Nobody was surprised when he was proven right.

They found Miss Tolstoy seated and asleep in the fruit groves, propped beneath a bush, hugging her legs with her arms, resting her ear on her knees. She was woken by the sound of people approaching, and remained completely quiet as they came nearer, though they gently called her name. She continued to be still, but this was not the best strategy, since she then found herself in the embarrassing position of looking at all the villagers' feet and ankles as they assembled around the bush, in a polite circle, knowing full well she was there.

"Lynda," they called, bending down and peering at her under the leaves. "Lynda?"

She climbed out, dusting herself down and feeling distinctly foolish about this unscheduled visit. Her feelings changed quickly, when, without any hint of anger or accusation, they asked her what they should do now there was no food.

"Why ask me?" She was mystified.

Shallgam stepped forward, her bright fish-patterned robe seeming less vibrant than before:

"Because you told us the food we ate was impossible. Now, it is impossible – whatever that means. So, we would like you to unimpossible, please." Her voice was simple and matter-of-fact.

"What?!?!" Miss Tolstoy shot back angrily. "It's not my fault your stupid harvest failed – or your slaves have gone on strike. How can it be my fault? I haven't done anything! All I did was speak!" And with that, she climbed back in under the bush and sulked.

The villagers were at a loss that she should ask them this, since the answer was self-evident. They muttered and shook their heads, then shrugged their shoulders. Some wondered if Miss Tolstoy were actually mad.

Somebody had to take charge of the situation, or it would have gone on like that all day, and eventually Old Lemu stepped forward from the group, bent down under the bush so he could get a good look at her, and said:

"The villagers say they will wait for you to fix it. Come and see me, Lynda, if you need advice."

Then the group turned away and headed to the sea, where they spent the day on the beach, playing with the children, or frittering away their time in simple games.

After a while, Miss Tolstoy started to feel hungry, and so followed them. When she saw them on the beach, she watched from a distance, indignant that they were somehow blaming her for their problems, and walked away.

*

That evening the villagers began to grow more seriously hungry. A group of adults explored the grove in the hope of plucking some fruits, or finding something to sustain them. After an hour or so, they came back to the village and reported there was nothing – not even a single gooseberry. Paris, meanwhile, reported how the fish in the sea were suddenly refusing to be caught. There was not a scrap of food to be had anywhere.

Still Miss Tolstoy stewed on the accusation that this was somehow her fault, even though she had by now wandered back to the village again, drawn by hunger.

She flatly refused to start Songtime, even though it was her turn. There was a trick here, and she knew it. Instead, she went to sleep on the beach, under the yellow stars, with an emptiness in her stomach that woke her in the night in the same way loneliness does.

*

The next morning, the story was the same. The villagers sat around fanning themselves weakly or rested their heads in their hands disconsolately in the golden light of the day. Water ran in a fresh stream down to the sea, and they dipped their cupped hands in it, gulping greedily, or lowered their faces to it as if they were kissing something so precious that it made them cry – which is how it looked when they raised their heads again. Without food, the water acted to steal away the discomfort for a few minutes, only to be redoubled soon after.

By the afternoon, Old Lemu was listless, rolling his eyes upwards, and speaking with his son in a hoarse voice. Paris nodded at his words, then the old man let go of him, and looked up with pained eyes at the cloth roof to the enclosure.

A pale and drawn Paris walked over to where Miss Tolstoy sat sulking on the beach.

"Lynda," he said, speaking her name with deep respect. "Please help me to help Old Lemu."

"I can't help him!" she shot back angrily, her ears reddening and sending a patch of crimson spreading across her cheeks. "None of this is my fault!"

Paris took a breath, suppressing an emotion. His tone, nevertheless, beneath his dignity, was desperate.

"Lynda... He is my father. Please help him. He is ill..."

"But it has nothing to do with me!" she said. "How could it? It's just insane!"

Paris squatted on the shingle in front of her. Looking steadily into her eyes, he simply said:

"Come and speak with him. He will explain..."

Reluctantly, she followed him to the enclosure where Old Lemu lay. She was shocked when she saw him lying there – his pale face turned up to her, his movements weak and slow. Only when she saw him did she realise how bad she felt, too. Her stomach was empty and she was all pinched and giddy. *We live in a desert,* she thought. *A green, lush desert.*

Other villagers were lying in the same enclosure, so that in her mind it took on the semblance of a hospital ward.

They gazed at her helplessly as she looked down at Old Lemu. She realised they were all suffering silently, just like the old man, accepting their hardship with the same calmness they had shown when the food was plentiful. The thought of their simple, stoical suffering made her feel sad to the soles of her feet.

Old Lemu beckoned her to sit next to him, patting the back of his hand on the cushions, and she threw herself down with a sense of helplessness that made her eyes ache and her throat sore. He leaned towards her, beckoning her closer still. His voice was weak when he spoke:

"Now, Lynda," he said with deep, calm dignity as his sickly eyes rested on her. "You have to help us. You must help us get our food back."

"But how can I –" she began in a pleading tone. He reached out his hand and laid it on hers, and she fell silent.

"What are these words?" he asked her. "Really, what are they? *How can I?* Is that what you really mean, or do you really mean *I can not?* That is how they sound Lynda, and they are a discord here. They are not part of our song."

Lynda took a breath, and looked at her hand under his. She spoke again, resignation in her voice.

"How can I change it?"

He paused for a few seconds.

"That is a better melody for those words – a question and not an answer. It is not perfect, but it is better. That is the start of a melody. Whereas the other way of saying them is an ending."

He pulled himself up to rest on his elbow and looked her in the eyes.

"How can you..? Answer this question. How can you do *anything?*"

"What?"

"How can you see the world when you open your eyes every morning except that you bring it into existence?" he asked.

"I don't underst–" she began, but he went on before she could finish.

"You must begin to think differently," he said. "You are new here, which is why you don't know. You must understand: when you sing a thought here, it becomes true. That is how it is. Your singing on the night you started the Songtime was discordant and harsh – "

"But I wasn't singing!" she replied. "I was talking!"

Old Lemu ignored her, and pushed on. "The problem is, that melody now is working its course. It is in the minds of the people, and they cannot change it. Only you can change it. Unless you begin to sing a new song, then none of us – you included – will survive for long."

This last piece of advice took the strength from him, and he put his head back on the cushions. "There is a harmony here," he said huskily, his eyes focussing on infinity. "Keep singing the wrong note for the chord, and nothing works any more."

*

That night Lynda sat by the sea, looking out over the waters reflecting the yellow lights of the lamp-hanging stars. She had heard Old Lemu's words, but she did not understand them – did not feel them in her body with the resounding note of truth. Was it possible that the village was starving because of one thought she had uttered? The villagers believed it. They really believed it. But – and she said it out loud: "It is ridiculous!"

Above the unending voice of the sea, she heard the *kush kush kush* of footsteps behind her. Paris was standing over her. He squatted to face her and said:

"Lynda, I have something I need to ask you. What was the feeling you had at the Looking Tree those days ago?"

He studied her with an intense gaze in the warm night air.

A tear poked its way to the front of her eye and tumbled down her face. He saw the movement in the starlight and instinctively put his thumb to it, wiping it sideways from her face.

"What?" he said, more puzzled than ever.

"It was fear," she said, her body feeling smaller even as she said it.

"What is fear?" he asked, genuine curiosity on his face.

Miss Tolstoy shrugged.

"I don't know," she said. "It is a terrible thing. A beast that lives inside."

"What is the beast like?"

"Horrible and cruel," she said, without really knowing what she was saying.

"And does the beast make you not want to climb trees?"

"Well, yes, sort of."

"What would happen if you did climb the tree?"

"I might fall."

"And then what?"

"Well... then... I might fall." She replied, nonplussed by the question.

"And is that such a terrible thing?"

She saw the panicked tumble and felt the pain of smashed bones she always experienced when she thought of heights. She told him of a dream she had – of falling from a tower, surrounded by lightning. It was different from the way she thought about flying, she realised, which was to imagine a burning wreck plummeting from the sky, her parents on board. But both were the same because they were about a fall from height, and they induced pure terror.

"What is a tower?" Paris asked.

She explained, but just thinking of these things, she imagined something dark in the skies above, a shadow moving at terrible speeds intent on her destruction, just as she had seen at the Looking Tree.

"Fear is really terrible," she added. "My dream says all that need be said about it!"

"And if I show you that it isn't so terrible to fall, what then?" he asked.

"What then?" she echoed and put the palms of her hands upwards as she shrugged. "I mean, it *is* terrible to fall. That's all there is to it."

She looked down into her lap as she spoke, only raising her eyes at the close of the sentence. But by that time the night air was empty in front of her, and all she could hear was the *kush kush kush* of his walking away, and the sea's incessant movement.

*

Later that night, Miss Tolstoy woke from a dream to the sound of singing. She listened attentively to a melody. Strong and sturdy, regular and repetitive, with a simple tune that contained a kind of power and dignity. As it went on, she sensed something massy and powerful in its lines – something deep and haunting that reached down into the ground.

It is unrelenting and timeless, she thought, before its steady rhythm rocked her back to sleep.

*

She awoke on the beach to see a wide circular stone tower beside the sea. The villagers were moving around listlessly underneath it, tiny dots against its white hugeness. She walked to it, mouth agape, a tingle of trepidation in her blood.

Four figures stood in a group. Paris, beside his father, who was weaker then ever. The old man was supported under the arms by two other villagers.

As she approached, they greeted her, all with the same serious intent in their eyes. She forced a smile, then looked beyond them to marvel at the sheer vertical walls of the tower. She took in the ramparts, noticed how the dark little openings in its walls seemed to make the structure stare sightlessly at the world.

"Paris, what is this?" Miss Tolstoy asked.

"It's called a *tower*, Lynda!" he answered excitedly, as if the concept were new to him. "Is it not what you described?"

"But where did it come from?" she asked.

Paris babbled on like a child amazed at his own cleverness. "We had a meeting last night and we sang! We, all of us believed, and the Island listened to our belief..." With these last words, he looked at her with sudden gravitas. "That is how it is, here."

Lynda shook her head and tried a different question.

"But what are you doing wi – ?"

"Lynda, listen to me." – Old Lemu cut across her. "We need food..." he said it meaningfully, as if explaining something complex to a child. "We need food, and we need you to *change your mind...*"

More villagers appeared from a doorway in the foot of the tower and advanced on them. They gathered around Old Lemu and laid their hands on him. All the while, he directed his wise old eyes at her.

He went limp and the villagers lifted him off the ground, holding him like a roll of carpet above their heads.

"What!?

Filling the air with a slow chant, they moved to the tower while Miss Tolstoy stared bewilderment.

They began to climb stone steps on its side, up and up. Paris stood beside her, watching the dots ascending. Their outlines stood clear against the sky when they reached the top. The chanting continued.

"Paris, what are they doing?"

He took her hands gently, locking her pale fingers between his dark sinuous ones in a hold that rooted her to the spot. He held her gaze.

"Lynda, you started Songtime but did not finish it. Because none could join in, no-one can continue the song. Now the food depends on your song and only yours. You sang how we need to sacrifice for food. I don't know how many sacrifices you need, but we are doing as your song bid us..."

"What?!?! No – wait – that's – that's not what I meant!" Her body jolted as the words registered more fully and she turned her head to the tower's top again. "No! You can't be serious..."

She disentangled her hands from his and ran to the steps. "Stop! No! Stop!"

But as soon as her foot touched that hard edge of stone, her legs buckled. She threw herself to the ground, desperately clutching at the ground spinning below her.

She pressed her lips into the shingle, reassured herself by resting her cheek against a patch of coarse sand, till the panic unwound. She stood, craning her neck, watching impotently the action unfolding above.

Old Lemu was placed on his feet by his carriers. A larger crowd had assembled. Young children hugged Old Lemu, adults wished him well, kissed his hands. She could see him smiling and joking with them. She could feel anticipation building in them all. How calm they all seemed! How dignified! She sobbed at what she feared would happen next, but was unable to look away.

It was over in a moment.

The group moved as one. Without ceremony, they hoisted him above their heads and ran to the edge of the tower. There, they slung him from the edge with a synchronised heft.

As the old man span into the empty air she let out a howl of rage. It drew the villagers' attention from looking over the tower's far side where the old man disappeared.

They turned as if animated by one soul and stared at her.

A dark shadow moved across the sky – distant, menacing, cruel. The villagers pointed, gave shouts of amazement. It hovered a moment, wheeled on dark wings, then cut a line across the sky as it flew away.

It all happened in *no-time:* that change in consciousness that squeezes centuries into thimbles, stretches milliseconds into great oceans of eternity.

The scene burned into her brain – the throw, the figure spinning in the air, her electric shock of fear, the villagers staring, the dark creature above – all super-intense, super-real.

She sobbed loudly, uncontrollably.

When Paris stepped towards her to comfort her, a wave of revulsion and recrimination rose through her.

"How could you do this to your own father?!"

Her face was a mask of rage. She recoiled instinctively, sobbing, and ran from the tower.

Blinded by fear, she rushed to the fruitless groves, her feet snagged by the weeds that had begun to grow and huddled into a ball.

She lay there a while, deep in shock.

Emotions rose up in her. She wept from the depths of her soul, seeing over and over again in her mind Old Lemu, a silhouette spinning against the sky before he dropped out of sight.

Staring through the leaves, she shouted at the blue above: "What is this insane place? Oh God, what the hell is going on?"

Slowly the sobbing subsided and she found herself in the emotional limbo that happens when a storm blows itself out.

After a while, she noticed tiny sounds around her. Even the noise of the bees moving lazily in the air seemed listless and starving, she thought. How alone she felt! How confused! How helpless!

It was then she saw Paris standing by a tree, watching her. Her heart missed a beat. She leapt up stepped backwards, shouted: "Keep away! Keep away from me!"

To one side was a tree with a great split in its trunk. She put it between them, afraid that he might catch hold of her and do something terrible.

Paris remained unmoved. In fact, now she looked at him more closely, she could see a smile playing on his lips beneath eyes that twinkled.

"My father has asked to speak with you," he said.

"What?!"

"He says you are not to cry. He wants to speak with you."

She furrowed her brow and swiped the back of her hand across her eyes, seeming to be deliberately making room for a far more effective frown. His words slowly formed into a meaning in her mind.

"What? How?"

"Come," he said. "I will take you to him."

He held out his hand, which she took in a whirl of dazed confusion. Thus he led her like a child back to the village.

*

Old Lemu was sitting on the beach, looking weak under the sky, but most definitely alive.

As she drew nearer she felt foolish – then suspicious – then angry. A few yards from him, she blurted: "How did this happen? I saw you! I saw you fall!"

Old Lemu said nothing, but pointed to the top of the tower. As she watched, mouth agape, the figure of Lensher hurtled over the stone edge. Miss Tolstoy watched in horror as the little girl plummeted towards the beach. Then, as she neared the ground the fall slowed. She touched down with a soft *kush* on the stones, and skipped off up the beach, laughing and shouting with joy.

"But that's impos – " she stopped herself half way through saying it, even as Old Lemu raised his hand to silence her.

"One wrong note," he said to her, "And you could change all of this. You could break this precious belief like a spider's web!" He paused for a moment before he went on. "You talked about a sacrifice," he said. "Now we are asking you to sacrifice something. Your belief in everything you believed before. Sing for us Lynda. Learn how to make your world. You will see."

She stood a moment, considering the impossibilities that had happened in the last few weeks. She saw a ghost of her previous life – a dim image of a woman, who looked much like herself, sitting at a desk. A room with electric lighting, computer before her, commuting on cold days that never quite stopped being night. All in a flash, it came and went. She put her feet on the ground, and imagined double yellow lines spreading out from under her feet, and found comfort in them.

"I will try," she said. "Tell me what I need to do."

*

When word spread that Miss Tolstoy was going to sing their food back, a satisfied murmur began to circulate among the villagers. They came to the enclosure, took their seats, attentively looked up at Miss Tolstoy.

She watched their arrival, her heart thumping. *How tired they all look,* she thought, *how lost. How much they need me!*

It was a strange thought – one she had never experienced before. She felt important. This in turn made her feel stronger, because it wasn't only about her. She grew a little braver. She gave the villagers a nod to reassure them. She would not let them down.

When they had settled, Paris stood and smiled to the assembled group. Speaking with a kind of modest self-importance, he placed his hands on the front of his green shirt, like a barrister holding his robe, or a farmer with his thumbs hooked under his braces.

"Friends, friends," he said. "We know why we are here. A few nights ago, our friend Lynda struggled with Songtime. She did not believe food could come from her words!" He shot a playful look at the good-humoured crowd, and a ripple of laughter moved in the air. "But now, now she is ready to lead Songtime," he said, holding his hands up. "Soon, the Island will be renewed!"

To a burst of applause, Paris beckoned, and Lynda walked to the centre of the group.

She took a breath. She would sing of the flowers and the trees, as those who had sung before her had done. She hoped to make her song more wonderful than all the others, to make this world she lived in so much better than it had been the day before – to breathe life into it again.

She stood there, images fluttering in her mind: the flight of gazelle over the plains (she had always like gazelles, so thought they would make a picturesque addition to the island), the wind blowing in the rushes, the sound of the sea, the blue, blue water, the trees that suckle and grow on the breast of the Earth, the bees that buzz, the creature that flits in the sky above...

Her mouth opened. She was ready to sing. The villagers leaned forward, hoping soon to add their voices to hers as soon as they could gain a sense of the rhythm and direction of the melody.

The creature that flits in the sky above!

The phrase came to her again. She was unable to take her thoughts from it. That dark creature, blocking out the stars! She remembered the fear she felt at the Looking Tree. This, out of all things, was the thing most real to her.

She looked to the tower to counter her thought. It seemed as nothing in comparison to that creature. The villagers were inconsequential things that would wither like the grass in contrast to the awful, massy solidity of... *Fear.*

She was afraid. She felt it in her. Afraid of everything. Afraid of the heights, afraid of the new world her singing would bring. Afraid of a world without yellow lines on the ground, of a world not completely flat. What comfort lay in a flat earth if that flat earth could sprout impossible food and impossible people? There was a trick here. Something wrong.

There was a disturbance in the air once again, a flapping as of canvas in the wind. The leather-winged creature appeared, circling high above the village, beating the air with terrible, slow strokes. The villagers scattered from beneath the canopy to get a clear look at it and point, and she was swept along with the others out under the blue sky.

In daylight, she could see its body more clearly now. A reptile, with great dark wings and cruel teeth in its jaws. It glared down at her – and her specifically. She crumpled beneath its shadow, only to be caught by Paris, before she hit her beloved ground.

"Don't let it take me," she said, weakly. "Please. I can't do this. Is there something else I can do?"

Paris hugged her close, a little exasperated, but mostly with kindness in his heart.

"Lynda, beautiful Lynda. You have to learn about this thing you call *fear*. That is all."

He held her close and covered her head with a protective hand.

*

Later that day, she was seated on the beach with Old Lemu. The old man had been considering the question she had asked of Paris. After a while, he turned his tired, kindly eyes to her and said:

"I will give you a task to perform. It is a simple one. There is a plant on the other side of the island," he raised his arm and pointed north. "If you can find the *Flower of Golden Flame*, cut it and bring it back to us here, then there is a chance for us to survive. When you find it, it will mean you have sacrificed your fear."

"A flower? That's more like it!" Miss Tolstoy said it before she could stop herself. A relieved smile lifted the corner of her mouth. She felt like a child who'd got away without doing her homework.

"So, where is it?" she asked.

"Follow the island round. You will know when you find it," Old Lemu said. "But hurry," he added, looking far older than earlier that day.

5. Miss Tolstoy Steps Out

The villagers waved goodbye to Miss Tolstoy as she set out to follow the line of the shore north. What she was doing was completely alien to her, she reflected. Never before had she struck out in a foreign land, alone. To think! She had been afraid to go to New York!

Old Lemu's instructions were vague to say the least. A flower of golden flame that she would know when she saw it, that she must cut and bring home. Yet even so, she set out with a smile on her face, picking her way through familiar surroundings near the settlement, the fields and trees, the dormant Farm that seemed to hold its breath as she went by its edge, then moving into unknown terrain as she followed the shoreline, keeping the sea to her left.

She walked for some time, enjoying the heat of the day and the elegant sweep of the land by the sea. At one place the shore receded creating a vast inlet of salt water that flooded the fields, creating a great lake that sprouted boggy patches of grasses in low islands. She skirted its edge, from time to time crossing expanses of marsh where her feet sank deep into the weed. Everything was fresh and clean as if seen for the first time, and she exulted in the light sparkling around her – icy droplets splashing her legs, pulling up goosebumps – while gulls cried and wheeled above.

Further from the village, the land was filled with brightly coloured flowers – deep reds and bright oranges – *but no Flower of Golden Flame* – Miss Tolstoy reflected. Old Lemu had assured her she would know it when she saw it – and none of these plants were close.

Later, she found herself moving through a wooded area, and became aware of the bustle of animals in the brush and song of birds in the trees – a burgeoning richness that made her marvel at the fatness of this land

– even though, as she looked, she could find nothing to eat. At other moments, large, multicoloured butterflies floated like little paper things in the air or drowsed lazily in the sunlight – they flamed with fluttering colour, or supped in a stupor against the deep red of a flower, their soft bodies silently pulsing with the nectar they tasted.

On she pushed. As she headed north she saw in the distance to her left the remains of an old castle standing over mudflats far across the sea. *A civilization flourished here,* she thought, *and now it is gone.*

The woodland grew thicker. She pushed through dense brakes of fern and thorn, treading with care in her bare feet, clambering over earthworks that blocked her way. She explored them, to find buildings, walkways and rooms, buried in the strangling undergrowth – as if the place were an ancient temple in a tropical forest, or a line of fortifications, long forgotten

As she walked upwards along a gentle slope, the scene began to open out ahead of her. At the top, an ancient wall dropped away steeply on its far side. She looked down, and with a giddy shock lost her footing. Ferns and brambles, a spin of vegetation, stalks and leaves, bitter green at the back of her throat, woody sharpness, then a rotten stink.

She finished face down in wet mud.

She pulled herself up, wiped her eyes with muddied hands and blinked across a 100 metre expanse of water. From the far side, a thickly wooded shore rose up to great heights.

She laughed at herself. It was new to her, this sense of freedom spinning inside her. *Excitement.* She stepped into the water and washed the mud from her arms and face, cleaned her cuts and grazes, eyeing them with pride. Despite the strangeness of the situation, despite the *terra incognita* ahead, perhaps because of it, she felt – what was it –

– *Important?*

People she cared for were relying on her. She had never experienced it – this sense of connectedness.

She wondered if she would find the Flower of Golden Flame on the far side of the water. Perhaps she should head into that dark forest. It beckoned her: the world beyond the creek. But doubts arose, hovering in her mind, clouding her thoughts. Could she swim it, she wondered. Perhaps she could, but what if there were currents that pulled her under? Were there any creatures in the water? And what of people on the other side? Who might they be? Would they be as welcoming as the villagers... or unfriendly... *dangerous,* even?

She waded a little deeper. Now, with her body lower in the water, the trees seemed to rear up from a dark land: shadowy, monstrous, silent.

Oh. Now it's terror incognita, she told herself, but felt the attempted joke die inside her.

She took a breath, felt the water grow colder, saw darkness ahead. An electric tinge of fear grew inside. She stopped, at a loss what to do.

At that moment, a heart-rending shriek pierced through the trees, echoing around the branches and turning the air to ice.

It was a desperate sound. Helpless. Agonised. But when it cut off, the silence hanging in the air was worse

A wave of terror rose in her. She shook in time with her crashing heart. In wide-eyed panic she turned, half running as she pushed against the resisting water – and breathlessly half-waded, half-swam back. *What was that cry?* She skittered unsteadily on the mudbound shore, peering intently through the trees, crouched low, ears primed for sound, eyes wide. The urge to run and hide, shrink to a nothing, to disappear in the trees and never come back rose in her.

But something stopped her. *What was she running from?* Surely it would be worse if she didn't find out? She couldn't leave without knowing who or what had made that terrible wailing cry... and why...

Reluctantly she pushed through bushes and ferns along the shoreline toward the source of the sound. *Slowly, slowly.* The mud was heavy around her feet, and she laboured not only against its sucking grip and the thorned undergrowth that snatched at her clothes, but also with her deep, life-sucking fear.

Her terror grew inside her, clamping her arms and her legs in a paralysing grip she had to shake off with each move she made. The feeling became too much, and she was about to stop completely, turn away and hide when she scented a wood fire – and with it the rich smell of cooked meat. Her hunger overrode everything else. Though she felt weak and sick, surely, with some food in her she would have a chance to recuperate – gather her thoughts..? And so she crept on.

At the point where the narrow stretch of water began to open out into wider sea, a long, low ship lay on the strand. It was carved with a dragon's-head prow. From a single mast, jutting amidships, hung a square, blood-red sail.

Men were moving on the beach nearby. Fearsome men, in warriors' iron helmets and leather leggings. She watched as two of them broke from the ship and walked to where the fire burned on the shore. She craned through the undergrowth to follow their path with her eyes.

Then she saw it. Instantly, a wave of nausea made her dry retch, while her body flopped flat on the ground – as if the muscles had lost all their strength. She gasped, closed her eyes. *Had she really seen – ?*

She shook her head, took a breath and raised herself on weak arms to look again.

Where the fire burned, a man with his back to her was turning a spit suspended across two wooden forks.

On that spit was...

She froze in horror.

A man! A full-grown man, impaled, his flesh roasting steadily.

Her legs gave way and she collapsed to the earth, a wave of terror and disgust rising through her body. She suppressed a moan of terror. The world span.

Weak with fear, she crawled into the brush, shaking, weeping, retching once more as the greasy smoke filled her nose.

*

When she reached open ground, she broke into a desperate run. Nerves shattered, thoughts scattered, in a nightmare she hurtled on, numb, unaware of the direction she took. She crossed soft grassland, passed glistening leaves of bushes on slightly higher ground, heard the flutter and drone of the insects. All these things now wore a terrifying aspect, perhaps more sinister because their beauty existed in the same world as... *that!* She shook her head slowly from side to side and cried out loud, beating back the stark image she kept seeing again and again: *Flames. Spit. Its gruesome load.*

Tears streamed. Her nose bubbled. An ache opened at the back of her throat.

Overcome with weakness, she dropped into a hollow in the tall grass.

She lay there, hugging her arms around her, staring up vacantly at the blue sky, noticing in the corner of her eyes the gently-dipping seed-filled grass heads, the glittering buzz of a fly. Only after a period of unmarked time did she become aware of herself again, huddled, blinking as the overwhelming sense of horror began to drain from her limbs.

The smell of more smoke brought her sharply back to the present. Perhaps it had been in the air and she hadn't noticed, perhaps the wind had changed. But this smoke was different from the beach. *Dry, dusty.* She coughed, poked her head from the hollow and surveyed the land around her. A dark cloud rose ominously in the distance.

Alert to danger, desperate to make sense of what was going on, she was once more overcome with an urgent need to know its source. She rose, and approached warily, stepping with leaden feet, stooping low and watchful as she came over a grassy dune to see before her charred wooden posts throwing up clouds of cinders through heat-shimmered air. The remains of a village. Low square huts, burned out, reduced in places to piles of glowing charcoal.

She wavered, wondering whether to continue. But the need to know drove her on again, and she crept down among the ash and burning posts: blackened teeth on sandy soil.

No-one was to be seen. The wind lifted ash that circled in front of her. A humming came to her ears, from the village centre. She followed its direction. It intensified. An insistent, hectic sound, low, shifting, buzzing.

Ahead something lay on the ground. A black, iridescent mass, moving, shifting. *Flies.* She approached fearfully, drenched with sweat, dread in her stomach, palms filled with electric fear. The flies lifted in a single buzzing cloud. She gazed in blinking incomprehension on the body of a man, a spear through his heart, transfixed to the ground, a wide stain of blood soaking the earth.

A fresh wave of nausea and fear rose through her. As her heart turned crazed somersaults in her chest, her thoughts broke apart, became disjointed impressions, as numbness reached through her, till the world was only images and feelings with no meaning.

A wail brought her out of her shock: *Human voices, sobbing and crying!* She felt the need in their voices and responded instinctively. Dropping into a crouch, she crawled on her stomach toward them.

The wailing grew louder. She could hear voices of women and children in fear and distress. She inched a few yards more toward a small stone building – perhaps a grain store.

There were captives inside. Some voices spoke in despair, others spoke comfort, though they themselves despaired.

"Oh, my Shalmach, where is my dear Shalmach?" a woman's voice rose over the others.

"Lost... dead. Taken by these men," another said.

"What will happen to us?"

"Calm, calm," a stronger voice, with a hard music to it that spoke of authority, of a will unbroken. "We are alive, yet."

Another, the voice of a boy, said:

"Ma, will we die?"

Miss Tolstoy reached the building and pressed herself flat against it. She edged sideways and peered around a corner.

At the front of the stone hut a warrior from the dragon-boat lay on his back, asleep on the grass. From his open mouth a rumble issued. A bottle lay by his side. She took a moment to take him in. He wore a hide tunic and rough cloth leggings that ended... *oh!* They weren't feet, but cleft fleshy protruberances with two delicate splayed toes: bestial, fleshy. His pink skin and short hair, his wide nose... she had the feeling he was not a human at all, but the twisted outcome of animal experiments...

- *A pig* - she thought - *he looks like a pig!* - and felt disgust mix once more with her terror.

She saw herself, then, in clear outline: standing at the junction of two futures. Each stretched out before her in her mind. In one, she slunk away, ran back to Paris and Old Lemu. *After all, I will need to warn the villagers,* she reasoned, seduced by the option.

But in the other future, she saw terrible things awaiting those inside the stone prison. And... in that future she saw herself do something to save them.

She wavered, one foot in each world. Which would it be?

She took a breath to steady her nerves and slipped back around the side of the building, where she found an opening in the stones, three palm-widths wide, just enough for light and air.

She pressed her face to the opening. Inside, frightened eyes in darkness looked toward her. She whispered low, her voice urgent: "Listen. Shush-sh-sh. Listen, I'm going to get you out."

A dark-haired woman in her twenties appeared. Pale skin, a straight, sharp nose, intelligent eyes – the owner of the voice of authority.

"You'll free us? – How?"

"I'll think of something. But please... Don't make a noise. The guard he's asleep by the door..."

The words were lost as soon as spoken.

"Who's that, Karelia? Who you speaking to?"

"There's someone here!" another shouted. A cry of relief went up. Karelia grasped their danger, turned on them.

"Shhhh! Quiet!"

"Someone's come to save us!" – another voice shouted shrilly, and started the hubbub again.

Miss Tolstoy begged Karelia:

"Shut them up! *Please!*"

Karelia nodded, turned to the women and children with an urgent whisper. "Silence! Now!"

This time they obeyed.

Miss Tolstoy again sidled to the front of the building, peered around the corner, the whirl of fear in her body making her every movement seem massive to herself, every sound thunderous. But no, the pig-guard lay in his stupor at the building's other corner. Between her and him was the door.

Miss Tolstoy took one more calming breath, then stepped forward. An iron bolt was all that held the prisoners captive. She would slide it back and spring the door before he even knew she was there.

She reached for it with shaking hands, closed her fingers around the stub-handle on the rusted iron bolt and pulled. It shifted. Slid a little way. Then with a loud squeak, it jammed. The guard's eyes opened. She froze for a second, then redoubled her efforts, putting her full weight against the bolt. It wouldn't move. Panic welled.

The guard sat up, wiped his eyes.

She pulled more frantically.

He turned his head, saw her, weighed her in his eyes, snorted, rose on knuckled toes. *Swagger. Menace. Short, ugly blade pulled from belt.*

A realisation flashed to Miss Tolstoy: – *The women are pushing against the door, jamming the bolt in the eye!* –

She slammed her weight desperately against it, shouting *"Step back. Step back!"* The guard came toward her. From inside, Karelia's voice echoed the command – and –

The bolt slid free! She staggered away as the guard slashed at her. The door crashed open, throwing him sideways with a deep grunt. Women and children pushed past.

Wits muddled by drink, he snatched at the escapees – caught a boy's arm –

"Help, Ma, help!"

Karelia, regal, poised, in long white dress, turned back at the cry. So did others. An older boy, not yet out from the hut looked to them with meaning, slipped down on the floor on all fours behind him. Karelia saw her chance ran at him, ducked his slashing blade, crashed into him. He tumbled, flying backwards, a bag of meat and bone clutching the air.

Karelia, a whirl of long black hair and rage, followed and closed with him before he could rise. Two woman and the older boy joined her, pinning him on the ground while Karelia prised the knife from his hand. There was a shout and struggle. Steel glittered briefly. A gurgling grunted cry.

Miss Tolstoy looked away, sickened.

When she looked back Karelia had climbed off the corpse and was wiping her bloodied hands on its tunic. She straightened, walked to Lynda, in red-stained white dress, composed, certain.

"I am Karelia," she said, with no further explanation. "And who are you? Where are you from?"

Miss Tolstoy immediately felt her force of personality. Her question couldn't be denied or deflected even if she'd wanted to.

Forty villagers, women and children gathered behind Karelia, looking gratitude and suspicion at Miss Tolstoy at once. Miss Tolstoy raised open palms.

"I am from the far side of the island," she said.

Karelia looked at her. "The far side? There are other people on the island?"

"Yes, yes," she said urgently, feeling how exposed they were. "Look, there are more of these creatures on the beach with their dragon ship – there could be others, nearby. We need to get to safety."

Karelia raised her hand to silence Miss Tolstoy. "How many people do you have?"

"How many – ?"

"Yes, how many people on the far side of the island?" Karelia turned an impatient look to Miss Tolstoy. "Our men are gone. The invaders cut their throats in front of us." She looked down at the ground and exhaled as she relived the memory, then shook it from her mind. "But two-score of us remain. How many do you have?"

"There must be about the same."

"Men and women?"

"Yes – we just need to hide a while – "

"Hide?" Karelia looked at her with contempt, clearly about to say more, when another woman's voice asked:

"What do we do, Karelia?"

A chaos of voices broke out. Karelia made a decision, raised a silencing hand.

"How do we get to your village?"

Miss Tolstoy told them of the path she had taken around the island, across the edge of a lake, and pointed in the direction she guessed she had come from.

"Beyond the Great Morass?" said an older woman with long, wavy hair. "No one lives there."

Miss Tolstoy assured her that was where she had set out from that very day.

Karelia considered Miss Tolstoy's slight form, her wide-eyed honesty and her obvious fear, then looked back to her women. She considered a while longer.

"Take us there. We cannot stay here."

*

It took Miss Tolstoy a while to re-orient herself, but eventually she found her way back to the shoreline overlooking the creek and the rising land beyond. They followed the way she had come, clambering in blind haste over the bramble-grown buildings in a landscape that had grown silent and oppressive – so different from how it felt to Miss Tolstoy that morning. Night was drawing in when they arrived at the edge of the salt lake where seabirds circled, voicing thin cries like fear.

"We can't cross it now," Miss Tolstoy advised. "The marshland has a kind of path through it, but there are deep pools, too."

They rested in the cover of a thicket by the sea.

Here one of Karelia's women, a tall figure called Darga, lit a fire from her sparkstone. Others had gathered shellfish from the shoreline as they had gone on, and carried cockles and mussels in their skirts. Now they placed them near the fire on raised wood and cooked them. Others had gathered fungi, herbs and leaves from the wilds. A boy found a stream and followed it until it was no longer brackish. And so it was they managed to find food of sorts and water between them.

Sitting that evening under the cover of the trees, Karelia and Darga told Miss Tolstoy a little of what had befallen them.

"A blight came on the land, a few days ago," she said. "The men would go to the sea to fish, and no fish came. I sent women out to hunt. But somehow the birds and animals evaded our arrows. It was as if the land ceased to know how to be."

"What does that mean, 'how to be'?" Miss Tolstoy asked.

Darga spoke up. "Before, there was an order. The order was disrupted. Then there was no food," she said tersely. "When the land doubts itself, the creatures do not know how to be."

Miss Tolstoy looked to her, quizzical, almost laughing. "The land has beliefs?"

"How else would animals know to be eaten?"

Miss Tolstoy had no answer.

Karelia spoke:

"Then the dragon-ship came. The pigs came to us in our sleep. Otherwise things would have been different. And they came, too, because the land doubts itself."

*

The next morning at first light, they rose and set out. They hugged the edge of the water, constantly wary, checking behind them for signs of the blood red sail or movement of the pig-men, but none was to be seen. Then, Miss Tolstoy led them across the marsh, stepping from hillock to island, wading at times.

Finally they were pushing through bracken and bushes, and found themselves among the lush groves of the south, where the Looking Tree stood and where The Farm lay in silent neglect.

Paris had climbed up to search for signs of her return, and ran back to the village to let them know. Duly, the villagers were lined up by the sea, hopeful, waiting for the salvation they expected Miss Tolstoy to deliver.

They were surprised at what they saw: Miss Tolstoy dirty, tired pony-tailed, at the head of a straggle of women and children, some tired, some staring silently, some angry. A blood-spattered, straight-backed woman with blazing eyes walked beside her.

The villagers gathered around them.

Miss Tolstoy began to tell her story of all that had happened, while the villagers from the South by the Sea stood and listened, amazed at what they heard. Old Lemu listened intently, his face tipped to one side, his dark eyes watching closely. He was evaluating her, it seemed, nodding approval from time to time, considering and weighing every word she spoke. When she had finished, she looked at him and said:

"I am sorry, Lemu – as you can see, I didn't find the Flower of Golden Flame as you asked."

Old Lemu shook his head and sat weakly on a rock, saying quietly: "Maybe you have brought it with you, after all."

But a new thought occurred to Lynda.

"This explains why the food stopped, doesn't it? These are the farmers and cooks who prepare it every morning..." She turned and glared at Paris. "They were on the north of the island. You must have seen them from the top of the tree. Why didn't you say?"

Paris's denials were curtailed when Karelia could not contain herself any longer, bursting into a loud string of curses before adding in her proud voice:

"How *dare* you? – We hunt and we fish, we gather shellfish on the shore. We wouldn't farm for you people in the south, even if we knew about you!"

"We aren't slaves," Darga added, her height adding authority to her words. Others indignantly voiced their agreement, while the southern villagers looked surprised and embarrassed at their rage.

Karelia went on: "Where are your tools? Where is your hunting gear? Your knives?"

When the Southern villagers made it clear they did not know of such things but for Paris's fishing rod which he used solely for fun, Karelia turned on Miss Tolstoy:

"You brought us here for what?"

"To be safe..." Miss Tolstoy answered in a voice that felt very small.

"There is no safety here. The pigs could come at any time, and you people, what would you do? Play games and pick flowers!?!"

Old Lemu stepped forward now, and spoke in his calm way to Karelia.

"These things you say, they have wisdom, Karelia, chieftain of the People of the Northern End of the island. Perhaps we can help you. We have ways here you do not know. We will share them with you. But as the saying goes, *the song of hunger is a growling beast.* Let us send it to sleep. Show us how to find the food we need, so we can talk with kinder words and clearer heads."

Karelia heard him and nodded. She could see the value in his words – how could they plan when they were still hungry?

She addressed the women and children of her settlement in the North.

"The old man speaks right," she said. "Show them how to gather food and what grasses can be eaten. The fungi that grows around them, the roots that sustain. There may not be animals to catch, but there are things to eat, even so."

Thus, with infinite practicality she began to divide her people. One group would show the South Sea villagers how to find the hidden foods of the sea, identify edible leaves, the roots with sweetness at their core, the flowers that offered flavours and taste. Others she told to find cooking utensils. When these returned empty-handed, she cursed again.

Her mood changed when Old Lemu took her to a low dip in the ground, filled with pots and pans, plates and cutlery. She looked down at it, puzzled.

"Where is this from?" she said.

"When the food comes to us, it comes in cups and pans, sometimes," he said, and shrugged. "When we have eaten we throw it, here."

Karelia climbed down and picked out a metal bowl in which one of Miss Tolstoy's curries had arrived. She sniffed it curiously, then looked up: "What is the trick, here, Lemu?"

"No trick," he said, and smiled. "But we can show you how it is done, later."

*

So the South Sea villagers learned that food could be foraged and gathered. They spent the morning under the guidance of those from the North End. Others showed how to bring fire to life, and others how to cook in the pots drawn from the hole. The South Sea villagers were fast learners, and threw themselves into the task, Lensher laughing with Darga as they stirred the pot, while tall Nalsshar looked on at the Northerner's tall form, and felt a happiness at meeting another as tall as he.

So, the two tribes gathered together in a feast, as night fell and the South Sea villagers ate with greed. A hot shellfish soup, with mushrooms and scented flower, seasoned with seawater, made a flavour that danced on the tongue. Discussion broke out between the two groups, and laughter followed. Now, Karelia spoke to the whole group and to Miss Tolstoy who sat at her side. She said:

"For some reason the villagers sent you on a mission, and that mission, though I do not understand it, brought us fortune. For that I am grateful to you," she bowed to Miss Tolstoy. "In return, we have shown you how to gather food, and that is to your advantage. So, we have aided each other. Now we need something different for the dangers ahead, for all of us."

"What, then?" asked Old Lemu, eyeing the figure of Karelia with quiet respect.

"We need hunting weapons, tools for murder – we will need to fight."

A silence fell over the village. Those from the South Sea tribe looked at her as if she spoke another language.

Paris's brow creased in puzzlement. "But what is this? What is *fighting?*"

Karelia turned towards him in real surprise. *Didn't every man know about fighting? It was part of human life, surely?*

After the surprise, anger rose in her:

"Did you not listen to the story she told you?" she shouted, pointing at Miss Tolstoy. "Do you understand nothing?!?"

The South Sea villagers fell silent. Miss Tolstoy stood, trying to find the words to explain to Paris, and eventually said:

"Fighting is a way of struggling with others to make them do your will," she explained, not sure if she understood what she had said, herself.

Nalsshar stepped forward, tall and determined.

"How do we fight?" he said.

Karelia looked to Old Lemu. "You have a hole in the ground with metal pots, cups and plates. I do not believe what you said before that you have no tools to hunt. Tell me, honestly, where is the hole with the weapons?"

He and the other villagers from the South Sea registered blank expressions.

"Weapons?" Old Lemu replied. "What are they..?"

Karelia's eyes blazed with disbelief: "You people really have no weapons? You don't know how to fight?! And you had no food before we came here?!?" She glared at Miss Tolstoy. "Did you free us only to bury us?"

Miss Tolstoy found her voice, speaking timidly:

"Karelia, you know how to fight. I saw you – "

"What can we do with bear hands against sword and spear!"

The group exploded into a cacophony of fears and argument. It cut through to Miss Tolstoy's core, overwhelming her, and to her surprise she found herself shouting at the top of her lungs:

"Stop! I need to think! I need to think. I'll think of something!"

All fell silent as she stepped away, walking to the beach to clear her head.

As she went, she felt her doubts and fears swirling around her, picking at her skin like seabirds.

It was deep night by now, a night that was beginning to reach toward the next day.

The wind was fresh on her face here, as she drew nearer to the sea. She felt helpless and alone, blaming herself for everything that had happened. From the very start she had made things go awry here. She had brought something to this land it seemed never to have known: doubt, fear, lack of belief. She had poisoned everyone's lives, driving her influence into the people, the animals, the soil itself. She felt useless. Worse than useless, a bringer of a curse upon this land. And it went back to *that* songtime which she got so badly wrong. If only she could believe...

Miss Tolstoy was struck by the real lives of all these villagers again. People who only a few weeks before she had thought impossible, that there was some trick to. Yet here they were, suffering, genuinely afraid, from north and south. She felt close to them, in a way she had never felt before.

She looked up at the great circular tower by the water. Its shape evoked a memory from a distant time, a distant land. She remembered the fortifications she grew up with in Portsmouth. Images sprang before her eyes, and she walked further from the group, who had resumed arguing heatedly among themselves.

The sound of the sea in her ears and her feet on the shingle blocked out other sounds as she scrunched across the beach to the impenetrable reality of the tower. She hit the flat of her palm against it, then clenched her fingers and beat it with the edge of her first, feeling its massy solidity, its undeniability – and wondered about it again. *Had it really appeared from nowhere?*

She was so wrapped in her thoughts she didn't hear that Paris had followed her. He stood behind her, watching her at the tower's base as she looked up in wonder and bafflement at its presence.

He reached out a reassuring hand, rested it on her shoulder. She felt it, put her own on his. Something was happening to her, she realised. As if after weeks of stumbling blindly, she understood herself better, saw herself with a new perspective. She turned to him, eyes alight, and threw her arms around him, in need of support, of closeness with another. In return he closed his own arms around her. She felt his heart beating hard.

"Paris, if the dragon-boat comes, this may be where this all ends." Tears pushed their ways from the back of her eyes. "I feel *I* have never really started."

She looked up at him, kissed him on his cheek. She had never *really* kissed anyone in her life, starved as she was of confidence, love, affection.

She held him a while, grateful for his warm, solid reality, feeling close to him in a way completely new to her. A word spoke in her mind. Love. Was this the birth of some sort of Love? Love that makes all things, love that weaves and binds together, the wellspring of creation, from the beginning to the end of time?

She felt light, dizzy, laughed unexpectedly. Then, to his amazement, she gave out an ecstatic stream of whoops.

"I get it! I finally get it!" With new light breaking in upon her, she urged him:

"Paris! Go up the Looking Tree. Look out for the dragon-boat. We need to know when it comes. I know what to do."

She embraced him again, kissed him on the lips – a hot, passionate moment taken from the eternity that is Love, and borrowed for a while, as it always is.

*

A few minutes later she walked back to the villagers, a new purpose in her stride. Lemu and Karelia, now in discussion, fell silent as she approached.

She nodded to Karelia and turned to the Old Man.

"Lemu, tell me again: how did you make this tower appear from nowhere? What did you do? What exactly?"

He smiled, a look of joy in his eyes, while Karelia looked on baffled.

"We sang it. It is simple. We sang in harmony together in the way that we once sang in harmony about our food."

"Then I know what to do." She said. "I want everyone together by the tower. Everyone."

They assembled in one mass on its landward side, where there was a little area of flat land. To the North Enders, with their strong faces and sceptical looks, and to the South Sea villagers with their childlike eyes and soft ways, she explained she would teach them a song and that they must join in.

There was uproar from the Northerners.

"What is the point of this?!?" Karelia shouted, and the Northern children began to cry. The Northerners were practical types. The singing of a song – this was clearly a joke!

Miss Tolstoy knew there was no point explaining. She started the song, hoping her melody and idea would somehow transmit to them.

It must work, she told herself.

In the first lines of her song she sang of warfare, of fortifications, of steady piles of stone that are hard and that keep you safe. She sang of unforgiving toughness, and the nature of strength, of determination, the gutsiness of an island. She remembered war films from her earliest memories, the ones her father had watched on Saturday evenings before he and her mother had been taken from her by fire in the sky. She sang of heroes, and the power in a people united. She sang about the act of building, of walking on ramparts overlooking the seas, of platforms where defenders might be placed, and of armour.

Then, one North Ender who had fallen under the song's spell brought her own melody to twist it with Miss Tolstoy's. An insistent rhythm with the sound of marching and fighting men echoing inside it. It spoke of the hunt in the fields where she grew up, of sharp blades, of the stealth one needs to overcome, the battening of the doors of North Islander homes when winter storms came. She sang of resistance, and of strength.

One by one, each of the North Islanders fell into the song, adding their own motifs and experiences. – What it was like to lie in wait for your quarry, how the women worked with their husbands or their wives or lovers, stalking, and capturing, laying a trap. The song rose louder and stronger, as the strong island sang its strength, and the people rose up inside themselves. Proud, defiant, always alone, always separate from the rest of the world and always together. The drumbeat and clapping, the steady rhythm of feet stamping in the dust grew louder still, weaving new patterns, new fortifications, and a mighty chain of iron that lay across the sea.

And still the singing grew louder, as the South Sea villagers added their own strands – of patience in the wait before the battle, of the knowledge that all support the tribe, in the love that binds a people together and makes them stronger and more defiant. Together with Miss Tolstoy, the islanders imagined battles they had survived before, little glimpses from Miss Tolstoy's mind of history lessons, and the maps she had seen of her home town that had once been bombed and yet stood proud. Louder the song grew, and louder.

Then it stopped. The song had been in the weaving for so long that it was morning.

When they began to become aware of the village again, they saw that Paris was among them, standing beside Miss Tolstoy, and shouting:

"They are here! The dragon-boat is coming!"

6. Battle

The Islanders awoke from the Song of Miss Tolstoy in the way people wake from a deep, vivid dream: blinking, disoriented, now remembering where and who they are – looking around them at the new world that is morning.

In the new day's light, they saw their way to the shore blocked by a massive structure. It stretched all the way round this corner of the island. On the landward side pointed bastions thrust up from a deep moat, pushing into forest and green fields. On the seaward side, a long curtain wall loomed forbiddingly. The South Sea villagers marvelled at the design of this new thing, while the North Islanders were startled it had happened at all.

As Miss Tolstoy's song cleared from their heads, an echo of its words prompted them to climb the ramparts. So they filed up its stone steps. Here men, women and children found light, impenetrable shields and perfect-fitting armour. They examined them in the light, the Southern villagers with wonder, the Northerners with grim satisfaction that they now had the tools for war. Within a few minutes, a detachment of armoured bow-women took up position along the ramparts, Karelia showing those from the south how to notch an arrow, draw a bow, take aim.

Others were sent by Karelia to join the fight below. They clambered back down, the sound of their equipment echoing against white stone.

Miss Tolstoy watched them come. Her armour was on the ground, for her song had never included her having to climb. Instead, she waited in gleaming golden cuirass near the base of the circular tower, standing beside a newly-made many-armed capstan.

Here her soldiers gathered, alert, watchful, the sparkling sea reflecting on their faces in the bright light of day. As they waited, her fellow villagers took time to learn from the Northerners how to hold their shields, slash and stab, defend and attack. Miss Tolstoy watched their at times comical efforts, hoping these peaceful men, women and children would be enough to turn the fight.

After an hour, Lensher arrived, panting and gleeful, with word that lookouts hidden in the orchard reported a blood-red sail, square against the sky.

A silence descended on the infantry, and Miss Tolstoy felt a knot in her stomach harden. Thus they waited, aware of every breath they drew.

Finally, a shout from the walls above told them the ship had rounded the headland and was ploughing toward them.

At the capstan, Miss Tolstoy directed eight men to put their weight against its jutting poles. The wooden cylinder began to turn, grinding and clanking, an ominous rhythm, pulling a length of rope as thick as a man's leg. It was attached to the first link of an iron chain stretching across the harbour mouth. Each link was a metre long, immensely heavy. Miss Tolstoy directed coolly, looking out to ensure it was tensioned just below the surface. She locked the capstan in place with a wooden beam.

High on the walls, the villagers held their breaths and looked down on the pig-men in the dragon-boat glaring up at them, hearing the ship's bows cut the water, the slap of the sail. These hard-faced creatures were silent except for an occasional order barked in an unknown language. Thus the ship drew in under the walls, headed toward the circular tower, probing for a less defended landing place.

When they saw the harbour beyond the tower, they seized their chance. So the ship drew on toward the harbour mouth, a shout going up from the pig-men, intended to curdle the blood of those they hoped soon to overrun...

...And, with a crashing creak of timbers, the ship ran into the chain. It lurched and shuddered to a juddering halt.

The raiders fell flat on the deck, some losing their helmets overboard. They scrambled to correct the boat while the blood-red sail spilled its belly, cloth flying loose against blue sky.

Wind and tide held the boat on the chain: a sitting target. Now the women archers looked to their comrades. Each had wound cloth around their arrows and dipped them in oil. On Karelia's command, they lit them from braziers and rained fire from the stone walls.

Chaos broke out on board. Mail-clad warriors dived into the water and sank beneath. Some surfaced, struck for shore. Stones pelted, arrows pierced. The water grew red with blood, while the dragon-boat caught light and provided an increasingly hellish backdrop of flame to the slaughter, fire-reflections coating the water's surface with gold.

The invaders who made it ashore were penned into a killing zone by the high walls. Figure after figure collapsed, stuck with arrows. Their blood sinking into the shingle ran down the beach and out to sea, creating a deep crimson shadow in the water.

Under the shelter of those walls, Miss Tolstoy (yes, she who was formerly a lower ranking local government officer in the Department for Parking Regulation), led her infantry to a pair of heavy wooden gates. She paused, her heart banging in her ears beating the music of war, her stomach a stone-hard ball weighing in her abdomen.

She took a breath, nodded to her warriors and signalled the bar to be lifted. Then, with a shout of rage she ran with her troops out on to the beach...

...And slowed to a halt, her eyes agog at the scene ahead.

The beach was strewn with bodies, the gasps and grunts of dying invaders growing quieter and fading to nothing. No raider was left standing.

It took a few seconds for the scene to make sense in the minds of her and her infantry. The archers on the walls had done their work. There was no fight to be joined on the beach. As the realisation hit home, a shout went up. A shout that contained so many emotions. Joy and relief were two. Pride was another, along with its stablemate, hatred for those who lay dead. And then, at the sight of their lifeless bodies, shame. And, as a defence against shame, superiority. Finally, came the overall sensation that wiped everything else away: victory.

Miss Tolstoy felt these emotions burn through her in succession and joined her shout with the others. A crazy frenzy broke out among her soldiers. In their relief they hugged each other, kissed, joined hands, began to jump in a crazy dance on the shingle – shouting and singing, crying and laughing.

As the intensity of that first moment passed, Miss Tolstoy picked her way down to the sea, walking with sadness and horror among the bodies, and stared thoughtfully at the dragon-boat that lay blazing on the water. Paris joined her at the waterline. She turned to him, weak, suddenly afraid of what she had done, and was relieved when he clasped her close to his chest. Tears ran down her face.

"It worked!" he half-shouted to her above the swell of the villagers' revels. "You did it! Your song!" He turned to the villagers, raised his fist, shouted, "Victory!"

The shout was taken up rhythmically by those on the beach and those on the walls till the word echoed to the sky, blending with the constant crying of the gulls, who circled for the feeding time to come. She looked at the blazing boat a while longer, and felt a new sensation growing inside her.

Those sounds of shouting, together with the sea and the cracking of the boat by the flames created a harsh, cruel ringing in Miss Tolstoy's ears. A song of its own, it stiffened her back, placed a bar of iron in her body, an implacable will in her soul. She exhaled, with a new realisation, looked at Paris imperiously and said:

"I can do anything!"

A dizzy spin of exultation. She felt immense, as if she had grown to vast proportions, her arms able to stretch around the whole world.

"Look what I can do with *my* knowledge of the world. *My* knowledge – not yours, or anyone else's! *Mine!*"

Paris's eyes clouded. He stepped back from her, not recognising this wild, dangerous creature before him.

"Lynda? Lynda? Are you – sick?"

"Sick?" she laughed. "I am really very well indeed!"

She stepped toward him, not noticing the doubt in his expression until he instinctively stepped back again.

She didn't care. Who was Paris to her? She was a giant here, among these pygmies. She could make and create, kill and destroy, all in equal measure, through the power of her song.

The boat crackled on the water, the hissing of burning beams in water filling her ears. Something inside her responded to that noise. Something dark that grew inside her, taking an ever-tighter hold

The world appeared to her in a new way. All was stained red, as if the crimsoned sea before her had spread all over the world.

She saw herself in a new way, too: cruel, hard, domineering. Her lip curled into disdain and superiority. *She could be anything she wished!*

"I am a goddess," she said to her increasingly alarmed friend. "A goddess, Paris! I can see the future of this world – what I will make it. I will be the queen to rule here, setting the law, enforcing the rules. I will bring order. And there *will* be order," she warned.

She felt the righteousness of her words as she spoke of her plans. These childlike people from the southern village would come under her leadership easily. They were crying out for guidance. For a purpose. To be put to work, made productive…

Paris listened with increasing alarm. A deep sense of foreboding rose inside him, welling like a tide.

"What is this? Where is the Lynda I know?" he asked. "Where is the kind young woman puzzled by the world?"

"Where is she?" she replied. "Haha! Gone!"

Paris felt his wits twisting on themselves, confusion and horror whirling inside. "Lynda. This is not you. Come back to us." He moved forward with outstretched arms, his instinct to protect her.

"Get away from me!" she said. "How dare you..!"

When he saw her blazing eyes, the emotionless set to her face, he turned and ran.

"Let him go," she thought, and shrugged dismissively.

She thought back over her previous life, her work at the civic offices. She remembered time and motion studies and efficiency drives. Some of that organisation could be used to bring better lives to the people here. Art galleries, municipal projects, government, targets… *yes!* And she could introduce business, too, create a world below as was above. Then, when there were cars, she could add… *parking restrictions!* Yes, yellow lines on the roads. And fines. Fines for parking there, wherever she decided they weren't allowed to stop.

She inhaled deeply, sucking in the air that would sing this new world into being. It would be familiar to her and so she would feel safe – because though it would be largely the same as the one above, there would be one massive difference. *She* would be in charge of it! In charge of every tiny detail.

She saw her future: an uncompromising queen, exerting full control over her subjects. She would ban singing, in case anyone sought to usurp her power. She would sing a song to rob them of their voices so only hers could be heard. And if by some chance anyone were caught trying to make a new song, then their throats must be cut – not to kill them, but to break their voices.

This decided, she wondered – *what of other rivals?* The woman Karelia, she would need to be controlled – *even got rid of –*

Her reverie was broken by a sharp splitting sound and a deafening crash from the water.

The blazing wreck convulsed and shuddered as it settled further on the sea. Its spars shifted and dropped low. Miss Tolstoy watched in wonder as the flaming sail floated down from its crossbeam, falling towards the contorting deck.

Then something uncanny happened that made her catch her breath. As the ship settled further in the water, it veered toward her in what looked like deliberate, conscious movement. The villagers both on the shore and walls grew silent, gathering to watch, as disquiet grew among them. The wreck moved steadily, inexorably, appearing to pull itself along the chain.

When it reached the foot of the tower, it ground to a halt with a deep rumbling, scraping sound against the pebbles. There, it wallowed for a few minutes. The fallen sail lifted on the wind again, creating a sheet of flame on either side of the hull, rising in the air. *Strange*, Miss Tolstoy thought. *That sail – like a pair of wings...*

In a few more seconds, the transformation was complete. From the burning wreck of the ship, something new emerged. A living, writhing, terrible thing. Its scales made of flame, its body made of living fire – a dragon born from the wreckage, vast and cruel, blazing bright and hot.

With a roar, it leapt into the sky.

The villagers near the shore threw down their shields and ran up the gently shelving beach, some panicked and screaming, others silenced by their fear. The creature soared above, then glided down, surveying the retreating shapes, cunning eyes seeking the weak.

A withering blast seared the spot where Paris had just been standing, missing him by a hair's breadth, blackening the stones behind him. Men, women and children rushed through the beach gateway, racing along the inner side of the wall, casting frightened eyes skyward.

The dragon circled, cut the sky steadily, sniffed, then swooped.

Miss Tolstoy watched with deep fascination. Separated from the villagers, she had made her way to an archway. Here, she studied the creature closely. And while she tried to make sense of it, a part of her noted its actions with a growing sense of satisfaction.

The dragon was moving with a purpose, she realised. It swooped, blasted balls of flame, first in one direction, then another. While the archers on the walls shot ineffective arrows, the villagers below ran to avoid its fiery breath. They scattered at first, but with a deftness and agility – a blast ahead, another behind – the firedrake herded them together. Steadily, it forced them to the steps of the circular tower. Then, with growing confidence, the whirl of winged destruction forced them upward. The villagers climbed breathlessly, ran out on to its heights. Miss

Tolstoy watched Old Lemu helped by Paris reach the top, little Lensher, her mother Jarla, tall Nalsshar, Shallgam in her bright robes, along with elegant and long-bodied Darga. All were greeted and helped by Karelia, bow in hand, strong-willed, retaining her poise even in the face of this new development.

The dragon circled again, this time pushing them along until they were lined up against a wall with the tower behind them – eighty Islanders, young, old, boys, girls, men, women. – *My friends* – Miss Tolstoy realised with sudden disquiet as she wondered what this firedrake would do next.

It landed on the ramparts, directed a blast of flame into the sky. Then, inexplicably, it looked down to where Miss Tolstoy stood beneath her archway. They exchanged a look that startled her. Was that... was it an invitation..?

She stepped out under the dragon's intense gaze, her own face impassive, her body numb. She understood. She was to join it. Join *with* it. It was there to help her. They would rule this land together.

She made her way to the tower, feeling as if she were floating above her body, somehow watching herself, detached, devoid of feeling.

At the tower's base, she placed her foot on the first step, readying herself to climb. Immediately, her legs grew weak, while the world span and the ground came up to meet her.

Above, the creature convulsed in a rhythmic contraction, made a cruel sound like the rush of a jet engine.

It was laughing. Mocking her, belittling her.

She clutched at the floor, whimpering with fear, sobbing at herself, desperate to be strong and yet, here she was – weak, pathetic, afraid. She buried her face in the charred ground, her head spinning with fear.

The dragon turned its attention again to the group assembled before it. It exhaled, opened its mouth, this time not to breathe fire, but to speak. Its voice held a song of its own that was cruel, timeless, like a thousand forests burning.

"So I am freed, by your leader's weakness," it said. "Making me sole sovereign and ruler of this land."

It considered a moment as it gazed with baleful eyes upon the villagers, the soldiers-in-arms, the archers, the children, all its subjects now assembled.

Another brief burst of flame made them cry out as one. It spoke with cruelty in its voice.

"Kneel before me. I am your king, now."

One by one the villagers did as they were told. Paris helped Old Lemu to the ground before joining him there, Lensher clasping tight to Jarla, who dropped to her knees. The others followed their example.

Only tall strong Darga and Karelia remained standing. Both stared defiance. Then, Karelia turned to to Darga, nodded and signalled with her hand, and Darga, too, went down on her knees. Now Karelia stood alone, jaw jutting, head upraised, proud in armour and helmet, bow still in hand.

"Do you not fear me?" the creature asked her.

Karelia laughed.

"Yes," she spoke grimly. "Yes, of course I fear you. Ha! Who would not?"

"And yet, you do not obey me? Why?"

"Why do you think?" she shot back, a mocking smile on her lips.

"Because you do not value your life."

"Oh, no, that would be wrong. That is not why."

"Because you are too proud?"

"Perhaps I am, but that too is not the reason I will not bow to you."

"Then why?" It asked, its eyes glowing with deep, deep red, as it turned its rage and bafflement on her.

"Because I will never give in to my fear," she said. Then she raised her bow and fired an arrow straight at the dragon. In the heat radiating from that creature, the shaft vaporised mid-flight. Karelia nodded to herself, suspecting this would be the outcome. She threw her bow to the floor. "Do what you will," she said. "I will not kneel to you!"

The dragon laughed scornfully.

"So, now I know," it said. "You do not kneel because you are a fool!"

It opened its jaws – and in an instant Karelia's tall figure disappeared in flame.

A wail of desperation broke from Miss Tolstoy's lips. She was overcome with remembrances. The night her parents died, the aunt who came to see her, stern-faced, afraid even to speak with the little girl for fear of her emotions. She remembered how as a girl she took her aunt's lead, and so fear grew inside her. Fear of feelings, fear of others, fear of the world. She saw how her need for safety, a need that drew her ever inwards, had made her unable to connect. She saw it all, how lack of connection had always been with her because of her fear. She looked up again.

The dragon was sniffing the air, and... yes... it looked to her briefly, snorted dismissively, then turned its head away.

Miss Tolstoy let out a yell of rage.

"You will not disrespect me!" she shouted up to it. "You will not hurt my friends."

Above her, the dragon's laughter came loud and fast in reply.

"Will I not?" it jeered. Another rush of flame. A shriek. The dragon was shifting its head from side to side, shooting bursts of fire ever closer to the Islanders, toying with them, enjoying their fear. Growing stronger with each wail of terror. Miss Tolstoy, in that moment felt deeply alone. Separated from her friends, helpless - and deeply ashamed at her powerlessness.

– Why me? –

The thought came unbidden. Why had it picked on her, separated her from all these other people? Why was she the only one here, alone?

She did not know the answer, but she realised she must be the one to fight this creature. It had been hunting her ever since she had failed to climb the Looking Tree – had tracked her since she failed to sing at Songtime. This beast, the dragon-boat men – somehow they were one and the same. They had come for her and intended to destroy her world.

– Well – she thought, with new resolve. *– The pig-men died, and so will this creature. –*

She picked herself up from the floor, cast around for a weapon and a shield, and hefted them.

At the foot of the tower, she checked her gold armour, put her hand to her helmet and breastplate, took a deep breath, readied herself. She raised her right foot, placed it on that first step, then the next. She thought of her people, her friends in danger above, raised another foot. This time, the earth did not spin up to meet her. She clenched her jaw with brutal determination, stepped again, growing in confidence as she went.

She gained speed as she climbed, feeling the fear draining from her, replaced by a new ferocity burning inside. At the top of the stairs, she ran along the battlements, advancing towards the dragon's rearing shape. Its red eyes glinted. It turned to meet her, the cowering villagers trapped behind its flaming form bulk. It weighed her in its eyes, considered her, gave a roar of delight and recognition. Perhaps she even saw pride in those terrible eyes.

"So, Mistress, once again you join with me. Are you not pleased with my work? Are you not pleased you summoned me?"

The words rang through her mind seeking meaning.

Mistress?!?! What could this mean?

"I? Summon you? I never summoned you!"

"Do you still not know who I am, then?"

"What? Wh-who you are?" she repeated in confusion.

"I come when there is danger. I come to destroy. I am he who comes to do your bidding."

The shock of its words scattered her thoughts further. She fought to find their meaning. Finally she said:

"You do not act for me!"

Seeing Miss Tolstoy's astonishment, the dragon began to growl.

"Do I not?" it asked, hurt and angry at this rejection.

"I do not want you to act for me. I am here to kill you."

The firedrake heard the tone in her voice – strong, determined, deadly and appraised her with fresh eyes, its body tensing for battle.

She advanced again.

As she did so, it let out a single, prolonged blast of flame.

She raised her shield high and pushed on beneath the weight of that blast, her skin singeing, her hair burning.

Still Miss Tolstoy drew nearer. Fifty paces away, forty, thirty, a small woman in golden armour resisting its onslaught. But then her legs buckled. She kneeled, her head reeling, straining against the pain. Just ten steps away

The creature concentrated its breath. Her metal shield began to buckle, her body shook in agony. Her hair burned to nothing. She could feel her skin beneath the armour cooking, bubbling, as if she were that poor North Islander cooked on the spit...

The flames stopped. The dragon spoke again. Its voice was almost pleading.

"Always I come when you call me. Am I not yours? Do you not recognise your own?"

"Recognise my own..?" She repeated the words through teeth gritted against pain.

"Yes! I am yours. I always was. Do you not know I am your fear... Mother?"

Its final word resounded in her ears. *How dare this creature mock her, she who had lost her own parents to flame –*

A pleading, begging tone entered its voice.

"Recognise your child! Join with me! Mother..."

Now, finally, she understood! The creature spoke truth:

Her fear was speaking to her.

She understood, now. She had created it. If she wished, it would do as she bid.

She saw the future it offered. They would rule this world together – she an indomitable Queen, while the dragon, her son – her soldier – he would enforce her law. The days ahead would be dark, hard and cruel, but she would be safe. Unassailable. The mistress of this world.

It was a glorious future. She would control everyone and everything around her. Her words would forever be feared. She would be unstoppable!

She imagined her friends in that future world. She saw the hatred in the eyes of Old Lemu and Paris. The people's terror at her presence. Nights of watchfulness in which her son would intercept the shadowbound attacker, deflect the assassin's arrow, the duplicitous spear-thrust. She saw day after day how she had to test her food for poison, saw the quaking fear of her subjects. At the centre of it all: herself, dominating – controlling them with a nodded command to her faithful child. She would be powerful beyond compare...

Miss Tolstoy pulled herself unsteadily to her feet. She looked the firedrake in its eyes. She felt sick. Sick and tired of this creature that had so long lived inside her and so exhausted her... this *parasite*.

Beyond her fatigue, she felt something else. Pity. Pity for herself in her own future. Tears for the people she loved. Compassion for those her fear craved to dominate.

Instead of that awful future, she saw another that might exist in its place. A future filled with kindness. Filled with love. She wept for these people who might one day be her subjects, but who were already her friends.

She lifted her disfigured head beneath its buckled helm and said in a quiet voice, full of resolve, "I disown you."

The dragon saw her anew then. It saw Miss Tolstoy's anguished face reflected in its eyes. It saw her tears, and trembled.

"That you cannot do!" the dragon answered with rage, though unsure of its words.

Its mother was transformed in the dragon's eyes: a creature of a light brighter than fire. The sight of this new Miss Tolstoy, caused an unfamiliar sensation in its body. A worm in the breast, winding around its heart ever tighter, stifling, freezing it to the core.

Fear. It felt fear!

In panic, the dragon blasted her with flame once more. But as it began to pour out its rage, Miss Tolstoy stumbled forward – and with a final shout, fell upon the creature, thrusting her sword deep into its cruel heart.

Where she cut, it released a jet of fire.

It looked like a flower.

A flower of golden flame.

*

Miss Tolstoy woke to find she was lying on cushions. She was back at the village under the awnings. Lensher was running from the direction of The Farm, a bottle of champagne in her hand, swinging it wildly above her head.

"The Farm – it's growing again! We have food!"

The spell was broken.

Miss Tolstoy dragged herself up, felt the pain in her body, the stiffness in her arms. She did not know how long she had slept, but her burns were healing, her hair returning. There was magic here, and so her scars were fading, even now.

She stood, gingerly, wandered among the villagers, feeling somehow different. A new woman, with new powers, new capabilities. The villagers came to her, embraced her, caressed her face, shouted and cheered.

They sent gatherers out to bring more food, and a wild, impromptu party took place on the battlements, overlooking the sea. Up there, in those heights, she gazed out over the water with wonder at the world around her. She felt a bigness inside her chest, a swelling inside. It was her heart. A heart filled with love that once had been shrunk by fear. A love that flooded out from her and encompassed everything and everyone around her.

So, while all were gathered there, she sang a song. A song to bravery and remembrance. A song to Karelia and her people, to the North Enders and their knowledge of hunting and fighting that had saved them. She sang of healing, and a tree that would grow where Karelia had fallen, and whoever walked beneath it and plucked a leaf to carry with them would always know bravery and strength. And she sang of her gratitude for her life, and how she would always embrace it, and do new things each day. The villagers listened repsectfully, and after she was finished they came to her and hugged her, told her of their love for her. Jarla, Shallgam, Nalsshar, Old Lemu and little Lensher, with her brilliant smile and happy grin, who told her of the love of all the world, and the joy of all at her return.

After Miss Tolstoy finished hugging the girl, another figure came to her, put his arm around her and held her tight. She looked into Paris's face, at his smile in his dark face. Then she imagined a kiss, and sang to him of a brush of the lips with a smile radiating across her face – and as it always was on the Island, when you sang of a thing, it came true.

They embraced for what seemed an age, Paris with tears in his eyes, feverish and loving and sad all at the same time, as if this would be the last time he saw her. Then they walked off, hand in hand, to the Looking Tree. They climbed it, and looked out over the peaceful island. And later, back on the ground, under its dark shadow they became lovers.

It was then, after that wild embrace, as the sound of celebratory drums beat on in the distance, it seemed to Miss Tolstoy that everything she had ever known in her previous life had gone from her forever. She was a new woman, with her old impurities burned out.

Later that night, as Paris huddled asleep beside her on the grass, she lay wide awake, deep in thought, propped up on her elbows, staring at the patterns of stars in the sky.

She had the sensation of noticing the sky properly for the first time. *There's something about those stars,* she thought, *something strange.*

She thought back and remembered the sky above Portsmouth, her home town, on a clear night, and looked up at the golden, yellow light of these different stars. They were like nothing she had seen back home... except... there was *something...*

She felt her heart miss a beat as she traced the regular lines of lights above, the more curvy shapes in one sector – and the absence of stars all around – as if a vast sea of darkness were waiting to close in on the island of light above.

She knew those patterns. A memory of her previous life came back to her. In her job in the Department of Parking Regulation, she had many times pored over the maps of the city, identifying where a yellow line could go in, where a yellow line could come out.

Surely... surely... those lines above were the outlines of the streets of Portsmouth? Yes! The whole outline of the island's roads was hanging there above her, although the patterns were reversed, as if looking at it in a mirror! Wasn't that how it was?

But no... surely not.

She rose from the springy grass and looked more closely, straining her eyes at the lights.

Was it? Could it be?

She peered harder – longing to see the stars a little closer. And as she thought this, it seemed suddenly that space had no meaning at all, and that weight and mass and all the earthly concerns of life were nothings. They were tiny ideas that crawled in her mind and which she could cast out at any moment, and change for grander, more wonderful things.

She reached her hand toward the lights. After a few minutes she realised the ground was far below her. She had detached from the world and was floating up to see them.

As she drew nearer, she could hear the stars hum, making a song of their own – a low steady noise like the sound of electricity. Closer still, she could see that each light was covered in glass. She reached out and the light reflecting from her hand revealed the star she was reaching towards was fixed in place by a metal tube stretching up, and away. All the stars were the same. *Lampposts!* Black lampposts hung upside down from the sky! Like old Victorian gas lamps, but converted to modern day use.

Further down their length the lampposts thickened out into a wider cylinder. She examined them more closely. On each of these wider parts was a rectangular cover on which was cast the crescent moon and star of Portsmouth. Underneath, in inverted letters were the words: "Heaven's Light Our Guide".

She took a breath and imagined that on the other side of the sky, beyond the roots of the lampposts was a layer of tarmac. She imagined the tarmac was at the base of other lampposts. She imagined traffic moving there, yellow lines painted on roads she had once overseen and logged, and mapped and made decisions about. A whole city and a whole world above her on the far side of the sky... Her Portsmouth.

She gasped a moment at this revelation, putting her hand to her mouth in wonder.

"It's time to go back," a familiar voice said.

Miss Peters was standing next to her on the empty air.

Before she opened her mouth to reply, she looked down at the tiny world below and saw it was gone.

7. Room 344

When Mick Solomons reported Miss Linda Tolstoy missing from work at Portsmouth City Council, the police called in at her little suburban home to find a house completely empty. There was no sign where she had gone.

Appeals went out in the way that appeals do. People were questioned. A search was made of Miss Tolstoy's desk by two police officers seeking clues.

In that search, they turned up a letter dated to the very day she disappeared – a note from the Department of Audits requesting an outplacement interview in room 345.

The two police officers, one heavy-jowled and the other, pale and long as a noodle walked the same long white corridor Miss Tolstoy walked. They were accompanied by Miss Karwell from HR, a nice older woman with a baggy pink jumper and a pleated grey skirt.

Just as Lynda had done before, all three of them found a bare white wall facing them once they passed door 344.

Even Miss Karwell, who prided herself for always having her finger on the Council's pulse, was privately flummoxed. Though she didn't want to admit it, (because, after all, she was HR), she knew nothing of any audits. None had been arranged.

When Heavy Jowls and the Noodle knocked on door 344, a curt bespectacled man peered from a crack in the door and tried to send them away. After some insistence from both HR and the two officers he let them into his little office.

He introduced himself as Kaufman. He was an accountant, he explained in his efficient manner, as if he were assessing every word for maximum value.

Yes, he had seen Lynda in the corridor. Yes, it could very easily have been on the day she disappeared.

"And are you also an auditor?" One of the policemen asked, resting a suspicious eye on this inscrutable man with his neat round glasses and his tight spare frame.

"An auditor? No. An accountant. I prepare the accounts. Auditors come in – to check my work. But I do not audit. No."

"And when did you last have an auditor in?" asked the heavy-jowled policeman.

The clerk pulled an old paper diary from his desk and looked at it. He turned the pages precisely.

"Nine months ago," he said.

The two officers surveyed the room for a few minutes, then looked to Miss Karwell. She shrugged, not knowing what they wanted from her.

Finally, they said, "Well, thank you. Please make yourself available for further questioning," and left.

"Something strange about that Kaufman," the Noodle said to Heavy Jowls. He turned to Miss Karwell. "Can we see your records on him?"

Miss Karwell nodded, but felt a little weak. She had an uneasy feeling which became more pronounced when a search of the system revealed no-one working in Accounts by the name of Kaufman. In fact, no-one of that name worked for the entire council.

The officers hurried back to room 344, and found the door locked. With a push and a shove, they broke it down, to a clatter of brushes and cleaning fluids.

Room 344 was a cupboard filled with janitor's equipment.

They looked at each other and at Miss Karwell. How could they write this up in their reports?

They agreed that none of them ever would.

And thus the disappearance of Miss Linda Tolstoy continues to go unexplained.

*

Two years after the kerfuffle died down, Mick Solomons, more beachballesque than ever in his thick vertical-striped shirts, was sitting at home on his PC gazing idly at some holiday snaps from his nephew Chris Solomons, who was taking a gap year doing charity work in Guatemala.

In the background, he thought he saw a figure he knew. The hair, no longer pulled back into a neat ponytail, was flowing over her shoulders and her body shape was leaner and fitter – but there was something about her he recognised...

He stretched the image on his screen, peering more closely.

Though he couldn't be sure, the impression stayed with him. Months later, when nephew Chris returned, he went out of his way to have a chat with him at a family Christmas party.

"Chris, there was a young woman in the background, in one of those pictures of your trip," he said.

Chris, a vacant young man with a scrub of ginger hair, looked at him with a grin.

"A young woman? What's this, Unk, a midlife crisis?"

"No," his uncle shot back, with impatience. "Listen, there was a young woman. In Guatemala. With her hair down over her shoulders. Slim looking."

Chris frowned.

"Uncle Mick, you're being a bit creepy."

"No, no, no!"

In frustration he pulled out his smart phone. "Look. This picture, this one here."

Chris stared at the screen and the penny dropped at last.

"Ah! You mean *Gisela?* Oh, yeah, she's cool," he answered, reliving a memory of her. "She's done all sorts. I mean, totally amazing. Told me she helped out flying meds into remote parts of West Africa, travelled up the Amazon meeting natives, climbed K2. She's a helicopter pilot. Amazing. Hot, too."

"Gisela?" Mick asked, with disappointment in his voice. "Not Lynda, then?"

"No, Uncle Mick. Not Lynda."

Mick sipped on the punch his sister always made so strong and asked, "Gisela... Is she German?"

His nephew blew his lips together with a half laugh.

"German? No, British I'd say. Totally cool."

"Did she say where from?"

"Nope. Never did," his nephew shrugged. He looked awkward. "Unk, you're getting a bit–"

"What?"

"Stalky..."

Mick Solomons ignored him.

"Well, did she say how she got into flying helicopters?"

"Nope. Didn't say nothing about that, neither. Look, what's this about?"

Mick Solomons pressed on.

"Chris, did she say when she left the UK?"

He felt as if he were staring at the bottom of a well that hid a mystery in its depths. If he just threw a few stones down it, something might get stirred up...

"Nope."

Mick let out a hiss. "Jesus!"

Chris thought a moment.

"She was fun, though. She had this thing she did."

"What thing?"

"She sang. She would just sing about anything. Sort of making the words up as she went along. About the day, and what she wanted to happen. It was weird, really, but no-one minded." He pulled out his own phone. "So, now you mention it, look, I got another shot of her here. When she was about to go flying. *She was so cool,*" he said again.

He scrolled through some images, proffered the screen to his uncle.

Mick Solomons gasped.

There she was! The dead spit of Lynda Tolstoy, in pilot's gear, with a rucksack on her back, and something – something small and alive poking from the top.

"What's that?" Solomons asked his nephew. "In the bag?"

"Ah, that's her cat," he said. "She takes him everywhere."

It was her. Surely it was her.

"And she didn't say anything about her life before?"

Chris looked at his uncle, mystified.

"No." He paused for a moment and a new thought came to him. "But – oh, wait! You know, you're right – she *did* say something happened that made her leave home."

Mick eyed his nephew expectantly.

"And?!?" he asked. "What? What happened. What did she say?"

"Yes, I remember now," the young man answered. "She said – what was it? Oh yeah... that was it." He looked his uncle in the face. "She said: *something wonderful.*"

Then he added:

"But she never explained."

A NOTE FROM THE AUTHOR

Thanks for choosing to read my book. I do hope you liked it. Working as an independent author can be tough, so if you enjoyed Weird Tales From The Island City, please tell people about them. Writing a review or giving a rating on Amazon.co.uk and/or Goodreads.com would really help. You might also mention Miss Tolstoy and her companions on your blog (if you have one), on social media or recommend her story to friends.

Finally, thank you again. It's not true to say that without you, I wouldn't write, but my goodness, you make it easier.

Fiction

Portsmouth Fairy Tales for Grown-Ups - anthology
By Celia's Arbour, A Tale of Portsmouth Town - Walter Besant and James Rice
Dark City - anthology
The True Picture – Alison Habens
Southsea Stories and Beyond – The Uncollected Stories of Arthur Conan Doyle
Charlotte Temple – Susannah Haswell Rowson
20 x 12, Writers To Watch – anthology
A Study In Scarlet – Beeton's Christmas Annual 1887, facsimile edition – Arthur Conan Doyle

Non-Fiction

Mysteries of Portsmouth – Matt Wingett
Portsmouth, A Literary and Pictorial Tour – Matt Wingett
Ten Years In A Portsmouth Slum – Robert Dolling
The History of Portsmouth – Lake Allen
Recollections of John Pounds – Henry Hawkes
Conan Doyle and the Mysterious World of Light – Matt Wingett

Humour / Novelty

A Pompey Person's Guide to Everything Great About Southampton
Southampton Person's Guide to Everything Great About Portsmouth